THE DIRTY MARTINI CLUB

TESS KINCAID NOVEL

Jude Randazzo

The Dirty Martini Club
Jude Randazzo

ISBN: 978-1-7325147-2-0 (print)
ISBN: 978-1-7325147-0-6 (e-book)
Library of Congress Control Number: 2022909419

Published by Haberdashery Press, Castle Pines, CO 80108
www.haberdasherypress.com

EDITED by Susan Hindman
BOOK DESIGN by Robert Schram, Bookends Design

This is a work of fiction. Names, characters, places and incidents either
are products of the author's imagination or are used fictitiously. Any
resemblance to actual events or locales or persons, living or dead,
is entirely coincidental. JoAnne Carner actually won the 1976
women's LPGA U.S. Open.

First Edition
Manufactured in the United States of America

To Al

1

The Dirty Martini Club, November 1978

THE SMOKE OF cigarettes and cigars filled the room, dense, acrid, and reminiscent of a battlefield, barely being pulled upward, slowly, swirling, and snakelike, to a fan that hung from the ceiling. The Dirty Martini Club was filled with several hundred patrons on this Friday night, and Tess watched waiters—all men and mostly older, with white aprons tightly wrapped around the front of their bodies from the waist and starched white shirts and black bow ties—maneuver around tables, balancing trays above their shoulders as they efficiently served martinis. The club's martinis were legendary, and tonight bartenders were furiously cranking out concoctions the color of lime green, pink, and gray, some with sugar rimming the glasses. This was a place frozen in time from the earlier era of speakeasies and Prohibition.

Tess watched patrons consume drinks at a pace that would have had her sliding under the table in fifteen minutes. At two bucks a martini, the bartenders couldn't shake them fast enough to satisfy the demand. Her table was near the entrance and looked down over dozens of other tables that sloped away from her and toward a stage at least a hundred feet away and perhaps ten feet below. Walkways along the outside walls had steps leading down to the stage; another walkway down the center was a ramp that cut the room in two.

The Dirty Martini Club was tucked away in one of the dingier parts of Albany and had survived since the days of Prohibition. The freestanding building was flanked by a pool hall on one side called Eight Ball, and on the other side by an unnamed pawn shop with a sign that asked "Need Cash?" Neon signs, some only partially functioning and looking sometimes comical, sometimes sad, adorned the fronts of many of the drab buildings nearby, drawing attention at night. The club had always attracted the kind of crowd you wouldn't see at church on Sundays or at a government office at 8:00 a.m. during the week. And Albany, capital of the great state of New York, was bulging at the seams with government buildings, built in the forties and fifties and looking a little grimy themselves.

No, this was a place and a part of town controlled by two mob families, the Cuchinelli and Spinozza clans. They'd owned this town since the 1920s, and people living here were abundantly aware of that fact. The crime rate in this locale was basically zero as almost everyone knew that justice was served quickly and with brutal force by the families. There was no vandalism, no corner drug trade, and if there was an occasional robbery, the perpetrators had little chance of escaping the informant network that caught just about every meaningful piece of intel. But the club was a no-fly zone, a place of neutrality for the Spinozza and Cuchinelli families to meet, drink, and party without turf battles.

The place pulsated with energy, and people talked in loud voices to overcome the cacophony that built on itself.

The buzz of chatter sounded like dozens of old window fans to Tess, who watched a few of the social bees bounce from table to table gesticulating and erupting in spontaneous laughter. It seemed like a high school dance to her, where the self-appointed in-crowd circulated among as many people as possible for the sole purpose of making their presence known.

Tess sipped her Manhattan slowly, glancing at the lone maraschino cherry at the bottom of the glass. She knew her limits, which were to make her way to the bottom of this drink and finish by eating the solitary cherry. Martinis packed too much of a punch for someone like Tess, whose drinking habits consisted of a glass of wine at dinner and maybe a beer while watching a football game on a Sunday afternoon.

She leaned back in her chair and perused the setting as if she were watching the St. Louis Cardinals play baseball on a warm summer night back home in Illinois. Her presence as an outsider gave her that liberty. Although she now lived in Florida, Champaign, Illinois was where she'd grown up and where her family still resided and her home base. She viewed the scene in front of her from a distanced, detached, and intellectualized viewpoint, what one does when the surroundings are strange and unknown. She was so far from her normal element that she was reminded of a similar feeling she'd had in her first college class, Psychology 101 at Colorado State. She sat there with 150 other freshmen, not knowing anyone or precisely why she was there; it was uncomfortable and awkward at best, unnerving and disconcerting at worst. The club was loud, bustling, and felt like the set of a gangster flick; but here she was. She willed herself to stay positive and friendly.

Her attention was drawn to the stage, where workers were moving off equipment from the last band that had performed. The stage was three feet off the floor of the pit area and surrounded by a black curtain. It appeared large enough to hold a good-size band or even a small orchestra. The workers began arranging different instruments into place for the next performers, Eddie and the Martinis. *Lots of logistics in the live entertainment business,* she thought, *a little like a golf tournament, only not nearly as much.* The xylophone was removed and the microphone was placed in a different position. The setup was altered to accommodate a different drum set, a bass, a trumpet, and a violin for what Eddie called a hybrid sound of a big band and miniature orchestra, part retro, part imitation. She'd never heard them perform, but the Martinis play songs mostly by Dean Martin and a few by Elvis and Frank Sinatra. Four years before, in 1974, Dean Martin had left his highly popular variety show, but he was still famously part of the "Rat Pack," the essence of cool. *What were those guys' names? Frank, Dean, Sammy, and those other two guys who weren't nearly as famous ... Never can remember their names.*

Eddie Spinozza was the reason she was here, and she considered him to be cool too. Eddie was her boyfriend, even though it seemed a little strange to think in those terms. It was new, raw, and so unlikely. A blond-haired, blue-eyed, straight-laced Protestant, conservative, midwestern girl who played professional golf for a living and a dark-haired Italian, Catholic pilot from New York. Oil and water. A round peg and square hole. But here she was because he was irresistible, annoying, good-looking, and crazy about her. It was about as likely as a snowstorm in summer.

Spotlights streamed from the ceiling to the stage and reflected off the smoke that continued curling upward. My *clothes and my hair are going to stink from the smoke. I hate that, but nothing a shower and laundry can't fix. Stop being such a stick-in-the-mud. Relax and have some fun.* She sneezed. The Dirty Martini Club was excessively heated on this chilly November night, and the crowd only made it warmer. She could feel a trickle of sweat on her lower back and wondered if that was their strategy to sell more liquor. She wiped her watery eyes and noticed that even though the place was packed, there were two tables on opposite sides of the club that were empty, a white cardboard "Reserved" sign prominently marking them for two groups apparently important enough to have space held for them.

Tess noticed that almost as many women as men were smoking and thought how different this was than any place back home in Champaign where, even though it was 1978, far fewer women were lighting up. *Maybe, I'm just being judgmental, but I can't imagine any woman in my family smoking, not like this anyway.* She saw cigarettes dangling from women's lips like loose appendages, with ashes a half inch long still affixed to the end. *I know my relatives wouldn't be pounding vodka or gin martinis like iced tea, either. The last time I sat at a table with my mother, grandmother, and aunt, we ate pot roast and drank Coca-Cola. Different world, different place and people. So, so different. I'm like a fish out of water. I can make this work. I know I can. Everyone here has been nothing but courteous and generous to me. Try harder.*

ㆁㆁ

Tess snapped out of her solitary musings. She sat at a four-top across from Eddie's mother, Connie Spinozza, Eddie's only sister, Teresa Spinozza, and Eddie's sister-in-law Tiziana Spinozza. Tiziana was married to Frankie, one of four boys in the Spinozza family. Tess stole fleeting glances of Connie, trying to avoid what felt like a stare from her that penetrated like Superman's x-ray vision. Connie was fifty-something, impeccably and conservatively dressed in a dark blue suit, and stoic. Her face seemed to have been carved from marble or maybe paraffin like the celebrities at a wax museum. Connie or Mrs. Spinozza—Tess didn't know what to call her—hadn't said two words since she had taken her seat at the table. Tess had tried to initiate conversation several times with casual questions about the club, Eddie's band, and the martinis, only to receive one-word answers. *Okay*, Tess thought, *maybe she's very reserved and doesn't engage in light conversation. I'll respect that.*

Connie sat there as erect as a preacher at Sunday school, smoking a cigarette and taking inventory of the crowd. Her Lucky Strikes and sleek silver lighter sat next to her martini glass, which was almost empty. Tess thought she was about as approachable as the Grim Reaper. *Maybe*, Tess wondered, *she was expecting, maybe hoping, that Eddie would choose a girl who lived closer to home, was Italian, wasn't blond, wasn't me? It's very possible that she was expecting Eddie to be with someone else, someone who fit in better. I'll try harder. I've only met this woman, and she's just brimming with distaste. She looks like she's been sucking on a lemon when she looks at me.* Connie finished her drink and raised her hand, snapping her fingers for a waiter's attention. Moments later she ordered another martini without so much as making eye contact or uttering a perfunctory thank-you to the man. Tess was beginning to feel pressed about keeping an open mind about Connie, who seemed hell-bent on being disagreeable.

Teresa was twenty-eight, maybe five foot two, although her hair made her look nearly half a foot taller, and looked every bit the stereotypical Italian woman with an olive complexion, dark eyes, and a coif that looked wind-blown and held in place by what must have been sprayed-on lacquer. She wore heavy makeup, red lipstick, high heels, and a skirt that couldn't have covered more than twelve inches of her legs. She carried the conversation for everyone at the table, intermittently gulping half a martini at a time.

From the day Tess and Teresa were introduced, their friendship had grown. They'd met two years earlier at Eddie's apartment, a month after he and Tess had survived the crash of a plane he was piloting. They'd gotten tangled in trees thirty feet above the forest floor, and Tess had managed to get Eddie out of the plane and safely down to the ground. A month later, Eddie was home in Chicago recovering from his injuries, with an ankle-to-hip cast on his left leg and confined to a wheelchair. Teresa had flown in from New York to be his nurse and personal assistant, titles he had given to her. Eddie had promised to cook dinner for Tess, and now extended the invitation, though it was Teresa who cooked the meal, being the one who knew all the family's centuries-old recipes. Tess found her funny, irreverent, viciously loyal, and brutally honest. They had become friends as her relationship with Eddie developed over the next two years, and they communicated regularly.

Tiziana, Eddie's sister-in-law, was also diminutive and appeared reserved and uncomfortable. She seemed overwhelmed by her surroundings, or maybe it was the company, her in-laws. Her posture, facial expressions, and reticence all screamed "I want to go home!" Was this real-life imitating art or a movie scene, or vice versa? The martinis, the smoke ... Tess shook head her head and blinked several times. It was one of those "Where am I, and why am I here?" moments.

Tess had chosen to wear her signature attire tonight: white silk blouse, jeans with a big silver buffalo belt buckle, and cowboy boots, old and broken in but shined to a gleam. She'd fallen in love with the look eight years earlier, when she'd spent a year at a college in Colorado. The western look was so out of the mainstream that she always felt a little bold and rebellious when she showed up at social events looking like a cowgirl even though that was the farthest thing from reality. For accessory purposes, she had a purple scarf wrapped around her neck. It seemed right. She wore almost no makeup, but had curled her blonde hair in long spiraling rolls and wore a silver necklace that matched her silver looped earrings. She noticed there were only a couple of blondes in the crowd of over two hundred people, not exactly a true representation of the American population.

Teresa smiled at Tess. "So how do you like it?"

"You mean the martini?" Tess asked in a raised voice over the din.

"No, the club? You know this is my Uncle Joey's place, and everybody who is anybody in Albany comes here when Eddie sings. He only comes back home once or twice a year, and it's a big deal to the family."

"I can tell, but this can't be all family. There are so many people here."

"No. No. About a third family, a third friends and business associates, and the other half, I don't know."

Tess did the math in her head and decided that martinis could play havoc with fractions.

Connie sipped her gray-tinted martini and pulled a long drag on her cigarette. It seemed an interminably long time before the smoke reappeared, snaking out of her nostrils. She inhaled again and blew smoke from the side of her mouth, and slightly nodded her head toward Tess. "So, back in Iowa, do you have places like this?" It seemed to Tess that her tone wreaked of judgment, negative, and decidedly critical. Snarky.

Take the high road, she thought. "Illinois. I'm from Illinois. Oh, I'm sure we do. I just don't have many opportunities to go to clubs. You know, traveling all the time. I actually live in Florida now, and there's a lot of nightclubs in Miami."

Connie made a full head nod and pursed her lips. "Have you heard Eddie and the Martinis sing?"

"No, and I'm really excited about tonight. I've only heard Eddie sing, and he is such a wonderful singer."

"He's sung for you?" It sounded like cross-examination.

"Oh, only a couple of times, but he was great. He has a wonderful voice."

Connie nodded and finished her martini in one gulp. She signaled with her index finger to a waiter standing nearby. He approached the table and was about to speak when Connie said, "Another martini, and I want the good stuff, not that shit you gave me before." The waiter was about to speak when she cut him off with a slicing motion of her hand. He turned and left. Tess flushed and realized that she may have inadvertently irritated Connie with her attempts at polite conversation.

Tess turned her attention to the adjoining table on her right and recognized several of Eddie's cousins, but did not see his uncles, father, or grandfather anywhere. She looked closer at the vacant table on her left and saw "Spinozza" written in black magic marker on an oversize reservation card. *Oh, I guess they'll be sitting there. Why would they be late if this is really a once-a-year performance? Did they have a business meeting at this hour on the Wednesday night before Thanksgiving? Unusual. Maybe they're just late. Maybe they're just waiting to make a big entrance, make their presence known. What do I know?*

The table directly in front of her was occupied by four women she hadn't seen before. They were dressed similarly to Teresa and talked among themselves, smoking continuously. Tess noticed red lipstick smudged on all the cigarettes scattered in the ashtray.

Her thoughts were interrupted by the emcee, who had made his way to the center of the stage. He pulled the microphone in front of him down to his face, adjusted the stand, and tapped on it several times. He was a short, balding, paunchy middle-aged man with a flat, broad nose and wearing an oversize disco-style suit replete with enormous bell-bottom pants. "Good evening again, ladies and gentlemen. I'm Benny Silva, your host and center of attention tonight." Some of the patrons laughed, but it seemed that most of the patrons knew Benny's routine. "Happy Thanksgiving to all of you, and welcome to the Dirty Martini Club. I'm very happy to announce that Eddie and the Martinis are doing their annual show tonight!" There was a loud round of applause. "Just a reminder that all martinis are two dollars all night. So, without further adieu, here's Eddie and the Martinis."

As the crowd clapped enthusiastically, the four Spinozza brothers and several musicians sprang from the side of the stage. Frankie, the eldest brother, grabbed the bass from its stand. Joey, the next oldest, perched on a seat at the drums. Tony, the third son, and five years older than Eddie, pulled a trumpet from its case and wiggled his fingers in preparation to play. The other musicians picked up their instruments as Eddie tapped on the mike and adjusted its height.

"Hey everybody, I'm Eddie Spinozza, and these are my brothers." He waved his arm in an expansive arc across the stage. "We form the undeniably killer combination of good looks and great music all in one … Eddie and the Martinis!" He laughed, and the crowd hooted and howled its approval.

"What a ham," Teresa said.

"No kidding," Tess acknowledged.

"Tonight, in addition to welcoming all my family and friends, I'd like to extend a special welcome to my very special guest, Tess Kincaid."

Tess covered her face with her hands and took a deep breath. "I may have to kill him," she said under her breath. She thought about sliding down her chair and under the table.

"Yes, folks, the famous professional golfer and television personality is here in the house!" Mild applause as the crowd craned heads to find Tess. "Stand up, Tess, and wave!"

Tess smiled faintly and said, "Teresa, I can't be held responsible for my actions tonight. I *am* going to kill him." She sat still and looked down at the table, hoping the attention would go away.

"Come on, Tess, where are you?" Eddie put his hand up to his forehead, mimicking a visor, and looked out into the room.

"Go ahead, Tess. He won't stop until he shows you off," Teresa advised.

Tess pushed back her chair and stood up. She weakly waved in several directions before doing a finger wave back at Eddie. A long round of applause and whistling followed along with catcalls. "Easy boys, she's with me." More applause.

Tess sat back down and shook her head as she bit her lip. Connie looked quizzically at Tess. "What does he mean by 'personality'?"

"Nothing. I've done a couple of commercials. I really *am* nobody." Her tone was apologetic.

"Nobody! Nobody who won the US Open two years ago! And has her own line of clothes, perfume, and sunglasses. And is in about every golf and woman's magazine," Teresa announced loud enough for several tables to hear.

"Hmm," Connie said, tilting her head and snuffing out her cigarette.

A woman at the table in front of Tess turned and stared at her for an extraordinary length of time. *Do I know her?* Tess wondered. The woman's intense focus was a little un-nerving and broke off only when Eddie's voice boomed through the mike again. If it really existed, *that* was the evil eye Eddie had talked about. What did he call it? Malocchio. The look one person gives another if they are jealous or en-vious. A curse. *But I don't even know her.*

Eddie introduced his brothers, then continued. "As you know, folks, we sing the songs of one of the world's great crooners, Mr. Dean Martin. He's a movie star, television star, and a bona fide member of the Rat Pack with his buddies Frank Sinatra and ..." He was stopped by thunderous ap-plause for Sinatra. When the applause died down, Eddie did-n't bother to introduce the other legendary members.

"Our first number tonight is a family favorite." He backed away from the mike and looked at the band members, who each acknowledged they were ready. The band played several notes, and Eddie sang "Volare."

At the conclusion, Eddie waited for the applause to stop. "His real name was Dino Paul Crocetti. Is that Italian or what?" Again he had to wait for the applause to stop. He snapped his fingers three times, and the band began playing the track for "Everybody Loves Somebody."

Tess glanced over at Connie and thought she was beaming with pride or at least smiling. When that number ended,
Eddie grinned broadly but remained silent for several seconds. "Do you know that song knocked the Beatles out of
the top spot in 1964?" The crowd murmured. "Next, we're
going outside our normal boundaries tonight, and I'm going
to honor my special guest with a Roy Orbison song."

He pointed at Tess's table. Tess felt herself melting with
embarrassment again. "But first, by special request we'd like
to treat you to something exceptionally rare. My brothers
and I are not the only musicians in the family. We are truly
blessed by the unheralded talent of our sister, Teresa, who
plays a mean harmonica. Put your hands together for her,
folks." Applause rippled through the audience.

Teresa looked at her mother for help. "Mom! No! Tell
him no!"

"What are you, five years old? You tell him," she said
sternly.

Eddie's voice boomed over the crowd noise. "Come on
up here, Teresa."

Teresa shook her head back and forth in protest but slowly
stood up from her seat. She waved her arms like an umpire indicating safe at home plate and mouthed the words "No I'm
not coming onto the stage." She pushed her chair back hesitantly, and the crowd noise grew. In exaggerated fashion, she
pretended to stomp toward the stage and, after climbing the
three steps, met Eddie with a punch to his arm. He opened his
arms to the crowd, appealing for support. Tess surmised that it
was a rehearsed act they'd done many times in the past.

Teresa continued the stunt by pulling a conveniently
stashed harmonica out of her jacket pocket and began playing. A minute later, she was marching back and forth across

the stage, kicking a leg up with each elongated note and drawing round after round of applause from the audience. She had obviously played harmonica for some time, Tess realized that Teresa was very proficient. And so was her routine, which included wild gyrations and a brief crowd-pleasing dance number.

"And who's the real ham in this family?" Connie asked.

"That's a tough one to answer," Tiziana responded.

Then Eddie launched into Orbison's "Pretty Woman." The crowd showed its appreciation by clapping well after the song began. With the last line of the lyrics, Eddie pointed at Tess, and she felt color rise in her cheeks. It was the same feeling she'd had when she'd been asked to her first prom. She controlled her breathing and covered her mouth with her hand.

The Martinis finished and then huddled together onstage. Tess watched Teresa make her way back to the table, stopping to hug people Tess assumed were friends or relatives. When Teresa finally sat down, she asked, "Well, what did you think? Do I still have it?" She was breathing hard.

"Absolutely! You were amazing," Tess said.

Eddie announced they were going to do an Elvis song, "You're the Devil in Disguise." The crowd applauded, and the guitar player strummed with intensity as Eddie began singing. "You look like an angel, walk like an angel, talk like an angel. But I got wise. You're the devil in disguise. Oh yes, you are, devil in disguise. You fooled me with your kisses. You cheated and you schemed. Heaven knows how you lied to me. You're not the way you seemed."

Tess watched the woman who had stared at her earlier stand up and gyrate as she sang the lyrics in sync with Eddie. She was as short as Teresa and cute as a button, brown hair, big brown eyes, and cheeks glowing red with rouge and excitement.

Tess thought she looked like Annette Funicello from *The Mickey Mouse Club*. As Eddie finished the last verse, the woman pointed at the stage, put two fingers in her mouth, and fired off an ear-piercing whistle. She turned to Tess's table and puffed up like a prizefighter. "We used to sing that song together," she announced with pride.

"Oh sit down and shut up!" Teresa said as she waved dismissively.

"Tu piezza di merda!" the woman seethed.

"Mimi Fashoni, you're calling me a piece of shit? Give it up. Oh wait, you already have a thousand times!"

Mimi Fashoni is real? Tess remembered Eddie telling her about a girl he'd known in grade school who he had adored, but Tess had assumed she was fictional. He had called her the human grenade … or was it the human trampoline?

"Putana" the woman said, as she gestured with her hand.

Teresa pushed her chair out and stood up to face Mimi. Eyes from around the room were drawn to an impending catfight that appeared like it might get vicious quickly. *Must be a lot of history.* They stared at each other for several seconds.

"Siedi!" Connie commanded with a voice that would make a drill sergeant cringe.

Teresa didn't move.

"Tu siedi! Ora!" Connie said. "Sit down, now."

Teresa took her chair.

"Su, comportatevi, bene," Connie said.

Tess assumed that Teresa's mother had told her to sit down and behave herself. The room grew quiet for a few seconds, and Tess saw heads turn toward the entrance, where Eddie's father, Vincent Spinozza, "Vinnie," had arrived. Teresa leaned over and whispered in Tess's ear, "That's my father, my uncles, and my grandfather."

CHAPTER

2

THE OLD MAN AND THE TWO UNCLES stood behind Vinnie, looking like bodyguards surrounding a celebrity. All four men were dressed in dark suits covered by black topcoats. Eddie's grandfather was diminutive, slightly stooped, with wispy gray hair on the sides of his head; his eyeglasses had slid down his nose. He wore a sweater and a soft cap with a short brim. Vinnie hesitated after taking a couple of steps inside the door, holding up the procession before making their way to their reserved table. As they passed Tess's table, Vinnie did not acknowledge his wife, Connie, but instead seemed to be surveying the room. One of the uncles pulled a chair out for the old man. He sat down and fumbled with his hat before whispering something to Eddie's father. Vinnie raised his index finger for a split second in the general direction of the attending staff.

A waiter arrived at the table moments later, and Tess watched as the men removed their coats and ordered. Vinnie and his brothers sat down and seemed to close in, leaning toward the center of the table conversing in hushed voices.

Eddie's father glanced at Tess for a split second, catching her staring. A wave of fear and anxiety made her feel slightly queasy.

Tess noticed that Teresa and others had suddenly turned their attention back to the club's front doors. She followed their eyes and watched as another group of four men made a similar grand entrance. *What is this, some kind of arrival ritual by the oldest men in the family? Seems overly theatrical.* The noise level lowered several decibels, and a number of people returned to their tables. Tess watched Eddie crouch down to talk to someone below stage level, probably about a sound or lighting adjustment.

Tess leaned to her right and looked across the room at the table of men who she concluded must be the Spinozzas' business competition. Why else would they sit across the room as if on opposing football teams? The oldest man at that table wore a sport coat and a tie that was too thin to be fashionable. He puffed on a short, stubby cigar and stared at the Spinozza men's table. Tess glanced back at Eddie's grand-father, who puffed on a similar cigar and stared back at the man. She wanted to laugh at what she thought looked like a Kabuki theater routine. *These guys watch too many movies.* She returned her gaze to the older man across the room as she heard Eddie talking into the microphone. "Now for our next number…" She stopped listening when she saw the man extend his open hand toward Eddie's grandfather.

As if watching a tennis match, she snapped her head back toward Eddie's grandfather, who, without changing his expression, blew cigar smoke in the other man's direction, apparently signaling something to him. Tess turned back to the other table and saw the old man throw his hand up in the air, in a gesture of frustration and disgust. She watched his eyes move toward the stage and then stop just before it, where a man in a black overcoat nodded to him and turned around.

She quickly looked at Eddie, who had an incredulous look on his face as he stared at the man just below him in the black coat. Eddie raised his hands and took a step backward. Tess heard two shots that sounded like muffled pops from an air gun. Several band members dropped to the floor, and Frankie, who had been next to Eddie, fell hard as well. Tess saw the shooter bolt away and exit out a side door.

Instantly, pandemonium broke out. Connie screeched in a voice that sounded like a fire alarm and stood up with such a jolt that she knocked the table over. Vinnie briskly walked to her and grabbed her from behind as she wailed. Tess heard him say, "Connie, we have to leave."

"Frankie! Frankie! They shot my Frankie!"

He moved her by force to a side door that seemed to be overlooked by the stampeding crowd. *We have to leave? Why? Why would they have to leave now?* She heard Connie fighting tooth and nail as they disappeared out the exit.

The screaming and panic that followed drowned out a call for calm by someone at the club's front entrance. Tess was so stunned by the sound of the gunfire and the frenzy that followed that she froze in her seat next to the upturned table, paralyzed by what was going on around her. She'd actually only heard gunfire a few times in her life, and now this. She saw Eddie move toward the back of the stage and noticed that his grandfather hadn't moved. He blew out another puff of cigar smoke before his other sons engulfed him and ushered him out of the same side exit.

Teresa screamed as two men appeared and attempted to grab her to move her to the exit. "Get your freaking hands off of me!" They tried again to restrain her, but she kicked at them with her high heels and broke free, plowing into the crowd moving in the opposite direction of the exit. Tess watched her battle her way through, as if in a rugby scrum.

Tess realized that trying to reach the stage through the crowd would be a battle, but almost all of the frightened patrons had moved to the center of the room and fought each other to get to the doors in the front. Tess stood and stepped back and looked at Tiziana who seemed paralyzed from shock. Tess grabbed her arm, and the two of them slid along the wall leading to the stage as tables and chairs were knocked over and people screamed in horror; the panic, like a forest fire, was fueling itself.

They made it to the edge of the stage and climbed the steps. Eddie, Tony, and Joey were bent over next to the drum set. Tess could hear Teresa screaming, but she was only halfway to the stage. She stepped over the microphone stand that had been knocked down and around the bass, which was lying askew. She laid her hand on Eddie's shoulder, and he turned around and glanced up at her. That's when she saw Frankie on his back, the front of his shirt covered in crimson red.

"Oh my God!" Tess cried.

Eddie was holding his hand over Frankie's chest as a compress. Tiziana knelt down next to her husband and cupped his face in her hands. Tess pulled off her scarf and handed it to Eddie. "Use this."

Tiziana took the fabric from Eddie and held it to the wound as Teresa reached the stage. "Tess, keep her away!" Eddie said in a commanding voice. Tess turned and only with the help of Tony were they able to pick Teresa up off the floor and move her away from Frankie. As the sound of sirens grew closer, Tess also noticed Frankie's blood had begun to pool on the floor.

CHAPTER

3

Six Months Earlier: May

TESS HAD BEEN HOME in Florida for several weeks before normalcy began to set in again. A three-day trip to Arizona and Colorado in late spring had turned into a wildly out-of-control, thousand-mile escapade involving drug dealers, drugs, and a near fatal moment or two, and none of it had been predictable, or within her control. Tess had been called to rescue a friend from what sounded like a romance issue, but the resolution turned into a life-and-death situation. It was over now but not forgotten. It had disrupted her everyday life in a profound, if short-lived way, and only now was she beginning to return to her daily activities and sleeping again. It took Tess playing in two tournaments before she was able to regain her rhythm and reestablish her long-held routines.

Now it was the end of May, and she was in the middle of the LPGA season, ranked as the number one player in the world and number one on the prize money list, as well. Winning on the LPGA tour didn't necessarily equate to huge earnings as the tournaments weren't televised and the purses were miniscule compared to the men's PGA tour. Tess's winnings were substantial compared to other female golfers, but only made her a well-paid professional on a level with successful doctors or lawyers, not entertainers or famous sports figures.

Being ranked number one didn't mean a whole lot to Tess. It didn't change what she had to do every week. In her mind, she still had to go out and beat a hundred of the best female golfers on the planet if she wanted to make a living. That had become somewhat less financially burdensome now that she had leveraged her growing celebrity status in business endeavors. While it seemed insane to her that people would buy products unrelated to golf because her name was on them, she also knew that people bought cars, nylons, and even deodorant because anyone from Joe Namath to Liz Taylor promoted them.

Tess had developed several brands, marketed under different branches of her company, Kincaid Incorporated. Kincaid-Wear sunglasses, which were manufactured by a major eyewear company, were selling in high-end retail stores in the US and Canada. Kincaid-Wear casual clothing including, but not limited to, golf wear was marketed in mid- to high-end stores. Kincaid Inc., using a French manufacturer, had begun production of a fragrance called Tess!, which had started off with a bang.

She also continued to do magazine photo shoots for a watch company, a luxury car company, and a chain of high-profile steakhouses. Her mother had told her recently that she saw her more in magazines than she did in person. Tess had told her she needed the income to fulfill what had become commitments to a number of causes that had taken on a life of their own. And she had expansive aspirations and goals that would require even more income. There were days, to paraphrase Thomas Jefferson, when it felt like she was holding the ears of a wolf and couldn't let go yet felt it was impossible to hang on.

All these business enterprises were important to her, but none outweighed what she considered to be her most important and significant contribution to the welfare of humanity: her foundation, Kincaid House. It was the home in Champaign, Illinois, that she'd grown up in until she left for college in 1970. A year later, she had made it to the LPGA tour. Six years later, in 1976, her parents had temporarily separated and sold the house. Unbeknownst to them at the time, Tess's newly formed foundation had purchased the property. Now in its third year of service, Kincaid House was a home and refuge for abused and homeless women. Originally it only provided shelter on a short-term basis for a small number of women in extreme straits, but now, with Tess's mother, Betsy, the CEO and a driving force of the foundation, it aided the women with medical services, counseling, and outreach programs for housing and job training. One of the most important additions was child care. Many of the women had escaped terrible situations and brought with them children and little else. Kincaid House was able to provide temporary shelter for nine women and up to eighteen children at one time. It was almost always at capacity, so Tess considered it a top priority to expand, considering the number of women who had to be diverted to other missions. All of this required funding from an outside source, and it wasn't wealthy donors or the government; it was Tess Kincaid.

Tess was a very busy woman. She would turn twenty-seven in June, and on top of tournaments, business meetings, and public appearances, she continued her rigorous regimen of exercise and training. No one on the tour did the level of physical fitness training that came close to hers. Every day, six days a week, she ran four to five miles, ran stairs, lifted weights, and stretched. At five foot six, blonde, tan, and exceptionally toned, Tess was very attractive and photogenic.

Yet her self-confidence on and off the golf course was newly developed and had a mystique all its own, borne of her quiet, reserved disposition. She had always been shy of cameras and the media, polite almost to a fault, unfailingly modest, and a little insecure. She didn't come across as vulnerable or fragile or weak, just not easily approachable. She was never convinced or satisfied that she was a good enough golfer, a good enough friend or daughter, and she'd had enough turbulence in her romantic life to create doubt in her mind that she was a good match for any man. She was certain it was because she lacked something, irrational as that may have sounded.

All of that just drove her with more determination to become better—at everything. It made her serious in her efforts to accomplish something more that day, that week, and for the rest of her life. Her accomplishments in the last two years had allowed her to come into her own. And she had met Eddie. Her self-confidence had grown and, maybe some would say, blossomed. Maybe that was a coincidence, maybe not. But her life had not been the same, nor would be after that fateful day.

She'd met Eddie two years before in what turned out to be a freak accident. Eddie, a pilot for a small airline that chartered planes for celebrities and business executives, was assigned to fly Tess from Harrisburg, Pennsylvania, to a photo shoot in the western part of the state. An hour after takeoff, the plane's engine failed in flight. The plane had just come out of an annual inspection, and the mechanics had opened the covers on the engine to inspect it. Afterward a service technician pressure-washed the engine, and water got into the magneto. Later in flight, turbulence splashed around some residual water from the cleaning and shut down the engine. The plane dropped from the sky, literally into the trees of the Tuscarora State Forest. Suspended thirty feet from the ground, at night, off the radar, with little hope of rescue and with Eddie trapped and injured, Tess was forced to call upon every ounce of physical and emotional strength that she possessed to survive. And save Eddie. It was an agonizing experience that lasted two days, but Tess and Eddie pulled through and were rescued.

A month later, they reunited for the first time since the crash for a celebratory dinner. That night, Tess and Eddie had to confront a stalker who had been following her since she'd won the US Open the previous year. It was another harrowing experience that bound Eddie and Tess into a relationship, and they'd been a couple ever since.

Eddie was irreverent, relaxed, comfortable in front of any audience, sarcastic, witty, a musician and self-educated well beyond his high school diploma. He was also an unrelenting risk taker, the quintessential type A personality. Even after the crash, he continued to fly small charter planes for a living and drove a race car for a hobby. He was serious about few things in life except Tess, his race car, and his dog Jack, a West Highland White terrier who at times Tess thought was the real love of his life. Tess and Eddie were very different in many ways, but he found her dazzling, and she found him funny and annoyingly entertaining.

She smiled, thinking back on one of his bizarre and ridiculous incidents, particularly the night they dined at Benihana. The Japanese chef and showman·was banging knives and spatulas in a percussion of metal on metal, creating volcanoes of fire, and flipping a shrimp into his hat. It was a good show, until he began flinging pieces of chicken directly into the patrons' mouths, a normal part of his shtick. Only Eddie would take one in the mouth and choke, requiring the Heimlich maneuver by the chef, after which Eddie had an asthma attack; later he vomited from too much sake. Only Eddie.

Tess developed a deep affection for him because, if for no other reason, he made her slow down, smell the roses, and laugh. Not long after they began dating, she realized she had to forego most serious conversations with him, which was a good thing because she didn't engage in a lot of idle chitchat. She was a matter-of-fact, no-nonsense person. Eddie was nonsensical and playful most of the time. He cooked, usually barbecue or Italian food, and she didn't, which made things interesting. He loved Mozart, and she loved Johnny Cash. Then there were the regional, ancestral, and religious differences. Without ever delving into the philosophical question of whether opposites attract, they had been pulled together like positive and negative ends of two magnets.

They were planning a future that would begin at Thanksgiving when she would accompany Eddie to New York for one of his infrequent trips to spend time with his family. That was the plan anyway. In the meantime, he asked his employer for a transfer to the Miami branch of the airline so he could live with Tess. It turned out to be easier for him to convince his employer of the transfer than it did to convince Tess to live together. She wasn't sure if her parents would approve, and although she conceded, she made him rent his own one-bedroom apartment for the sake of propriety. It might be 1978, but in many ways Tess's values were closer to her parents' and grandparents'.

He traveled constantly, flying charters, and she was on the road eight months of the year playing golf, which made romance challenging. They would cross paths for maybe a night and in Illinois for maybe one week a month when Tess returned to see her parents and Eddie was in Chicago. A future for them depended on a long-term commitment. Eddie had expressed numerous times that he was ready. Tess resisted. She wasn't ready. She was certain that the attraction was there, but having failed in romance before, she wanted more time. She had been uncertain about men for a long time, and for good reason. As a child, she had suffered a summer of sexual abuse from an older boy living next door. It had gone on for a summer, but the repercussions lasted a decade, and the healing had taken her years to accomplish. In her mind, at least up until now, she would never entirely put it behind her. Her trust in men was always tentative, fragile, and could vanish quickly on dubious grounds. Therapy had helped and she worked on these leaps, but there was too much history and trauma for her to extend open arms to anyone.

She approached a future with Eddie with the same modus operandi that she used when preparing for golf tournaments. Know the layout, plan the strategy, practice, practice, practice, and then execute. Rings, promises, and plans were not in the offing.

🍸🍸🍸

Tess made it a priority every summer to spend time in Champaign with her parents, grandparents, and friends despite the LPGA season. She always skipped a tournament she deemed less important during the season to go home to Illinois. It was a time to fall back into the comfort and cocoon she'd known as a child. To her roots. Here she could rebalance and realign herself, reconfirm her values and beliefs, and relax. Home. She wanted and needed to be with people like her.

She'd caught a flight to Chicago after a tournament in Palm Springs and came off the plane exhausted, sleep-deprived, and worn thin by the demands of travel, competition, and public life. Inside the terminal, standing at the end of a corridor, was her mother, smiling and holding out her arms as if her daughter were completing her first solo bicycle ride. Tess was home for a full, glorious week. Eddie might be back in Chicago by the weekend, but that seemed so far in the future that she didn't want to think about it. She was home where she could just be herself, be surrounded by her family, and relax.

At baggage claim they retrieved Tess's luggage, which always included her golf clubs, and they walked to the airport parking garage at O'Hare. Tess noticed that her mother, as usual, was well-dressed and spot-on in her fashion choices. Now in her early fifties, Betsy had gained only a few pounds from early adulthood. Her hair was always coiffed in a style found in current magazines, and her clothes were stylish and age-appropriate. Her makeup and perfume were just right. Tess thought that her mother was still a very attractive woman. Her white tennis shoes, salmon-colored shorts, and matching blouse made her look surprisingly elegant, even with Tess's golf bag thrown over her shoulder as they walked to the car. *You've still got it, Mom,* Tess mused.

"Tess, I decided to take up golf," she said. "I thought about joining the country club, but your father would have no part of that, so I signed up to play in a women's league at your old stomping grounds."

"You're playing at the University course?"

"Yes, and I have to smile every time I walk through that clubhouse and see your photograph and the signed scorecard from the day you broke the course record. They still have a copy of the newspaper article under the glass at the front counter, and the other one when your high school team won the state title too."

"Hmm. I wonder if anyone remembers the battles you fought to get me on that boys' team. It wasn't that long ago that girls only played soccer and field hockey."

"Oh I remember," said Betsy, "but Champaign High now has a girls' golf team, and I ... I ... ah ... made a promise to the new coach. She's such a lovely woman that I couldn't resist. And she's a big fan of yours."

"Mom, what kind of promise?" Tess asked, mocking exasperation.

They reached the 1976 Pontiac Grand Prix in the lot, and Betsy busied herself opening the trunk before responding. Tess's parents had driven the same model of car since its inception in 1962, and they were now on the third generation. The Kincaids would never consider buying anything but American. Buying a Japanese or German car would be counter to their sense of patriotism. Tess never gave their buy-American habit a second thought. It was just who they were: conservative, Christian, proud midwestern Americans.

"Tess, I know I should have asked first, but it just came out before I could think."

"Uh-huh." Tess put her suitcase in the trunk.

"I promised you would do a little one-hour clinic for the girls."

"Oh, well that's not bad at all. Of course I will."

"The girls in my club too," Betsy added sheepishly.

"Uh-huh. Anybody else?"

"No, no."

"Okay, I'd love to, but I can't possibly do it unless I'm properly taken care of with the right nutrition," she joked. Her parents' and grandparents' diets and the local restaurant fare were nothing like what Tess regularly consumed.

"What?"

"I'm going to need your fried chicken one night, Grandma's fried catfish and hush puppies another night, and an evening at Checkers Tavern with you and Dad for pool and burgers." She figured that alone would be about two pounds to work off.

"Deal! But don't expect to roll over me at the pool table. I've become a little bit of a shark."

"Mom, do you realize how weird that sounds? It's hard to imagine you in a pool hall, drinking beer, and actually playing pool."

They got in the car and buckled their safety belts, a new habit for everyone.

"I've got so much to talk about," said Betsy. "Are you hungry?" She exited the lot and headed north toward Interstate 90.

"I ate on the plane, but a little something sounds good before we drive home."

"Honey, have you been eating right? You look a little thin."

"Mom, I weigh 132 pounds, same as last year when you asked that question. And I've weighed the same since the day I graduated from high school almost nine years ago. I might say that you look great, though."

"I go to the gym three times a week. Aerobics."

"Mom, tell me you don't wear the tights and all that."

"Of course I do. And I sweat. Now if I could just get your father to do something besides mow the lawn once a week."

"Not gonna happen," said Tess. "His DNA makes him averse to exercising."

"That pipe will do him in."

"How is Grandpa doing with his oxygen?"

"White Castle okay?" Betsy asked. "There's one on the corner of Lawrence."

"Perfect."

They pulled in and parked. Tess knew that her mother avoided answering questions or discussing uncomfortable subjects until she was ready. She wasn't ready to talk about her father and his requirement for oxygen for a progressively worsening case of emphysema. They were seated at a gray-topped Formica table with red vinyl booths, and ordered coffee. Betsy decided to talk about the oxygen.

"Grandpa is doing all right as long as he uses his oxygen all the time," she began. "He doesn't, and he continues to sneak around the house and smoke those damned Swisher Sweets cigars. I can smell them on his breath. Yesterday your grandmother caught him out behind the car with the trunk raised up as if he was looking for something. Smoke was billowing out the back of the car. I'm really worried that if he doesn't stop, he could slide into full-blown emphysema, and that is a horrible disease."

"It may be too late already."

"He's been smoking for fifty years, and you're right. He probably won't quit, and his activity level is now limited to walking to the mailbox. Sometimes he rides his lawn mower to get the mail. He can hardly make it up a set of stairs. I want to cry when I see him struggle like that, but I suppose that's the way it's going to be."

Tess reached across the table and patted her mother's hand, knowing there were no words of consolation. She also felt the first stab of pain from what would be a deeply felt loss when her grandfather succumbed. He was a sweet man full of stories from a time long since gone. His speech was enriched by the use of colloquialisms so obsolete that explanations were required for youngsters. More than anything, Tess loved her grandfather because he was always there for her at every significant event in her life. Losses like this must add up, she thought, until the weight of so many drags someone down to the point where death seems a relief.

"Honey?"

Tess followed Betsy's eyes and realized the waiter was standing next to the table with his order pad in hand.

"Oh, I'm sorry. I was just thinking. Yes, I would like a piece of fudge-dipped cheesecake."

"How decadent! I will too. You only live once, right?"

4

WHEN THEY ARRIVED at her grandparents' house several hours later, Tess's father, grandparents, and the family dog, Stuck, were together on the front porch. Tess knew they'd be wait-ing for her arrival; they always were. This welcoming scene was so familiar to her that she didn't give it a second thought. These were the people who meant the most to her. They were always there in the good times and the tough times when she needed them most. As always, she felt a wave of guilt wash over her for being absent from their daily lives. This never failed to temper her excitement over coming home. Fortunately, Stuck interrupted her thoughts. The three-foot-long, overweight basset hound had an obnoxious habit of howling and getting himself trapped because of his short legs and wide girth. He greeted Tess with a mournful wail and was silenced in short order.

Usually when she returned home, Tess would spring from the car and sprint to embrace her family, but this time she hesitated. She stood next to the car for several seconds and stared at her family, etching a memory. It could be a Norman Rockwell painting, so classic, so iconic. These were down-to-earth people. There was never a hint of pretense or "putting on airs," as her father might say. They were averse to grandiosity, hyperbole, and extravagant shows of emotion—they were what they appeared to be, nothing more and nothing less.

And this was so comforting to Tess.

Her grandmother, whose given name was Cecil, ambled down the wooden porch steps and concrete walkway and met her halfway to the car. Grandma had been almost five feet seven inches in her prime but was now somewhat shrunken in height and, with almost eight decades of life, full figured. Some forty years earlier, she was driving a logging truck loaded with timber when it was involved in an accident. The truck rolled over, and she was pinned under the front tire, suffering a devastating injury to her spine and posture that impacted how she moved and shortened her at least two inches. She never complained about the chronic pain.

She embraced Tess for a long time. Inhaling the familiar fragrance of her grandmother, Tess fought tears of joy and sadness.

"Sweetie, you're skin and bones," Grandma said. "We're going to need to feed you."

Tess had heard the same comment every time she returned home since she left for Colorado State almost eight years before, and she knew then, as she knew now, that until she had plenty of body fat, the observation wouldn't change. It was just the way her folks greeted people, especially young people who had been away for some time; no malice, rudeness, or insult was intended.

"Grandma, you look wonderful. How are you?" Tess wiped a tear that had rolled down her cheek.

"Just about perfect, now that you're here."

Tess's lip quivered as she stepped aside and walked to the covered porch of the house her grandparents had lived in for the past three decades, a two-story square structure with white wooden siding. In the center of the yard of freshly mowed grass was a small berm where an antique water pump was perched alongside a flowerpot with a couple of purple petunias. A line of ceramic rabbits descending in size surrounded it.

As Tess ascended the creaky wooden steps, her grandfather stood up from his rocker. When she hugged him, she felt his bony ribcage and the vertebrae in his back protruding out like the knuckles of his hands. He seemed like a skeleton covered with skin. She inhaled the cigar odor that permeated his clothing and did what she'd done since her earliest memory: She touched her forehead to his and held it there for a long time. Now, she couldn't stop tears from rolling down her face. She swallowed hard, and she knew. She knew it was only a short time before his life would end. His breathing sounded like the wheels of a car driving over a gravel driveway. She pulled back, wiped tears, and forced a smile. *This is hard. This is the bitterest of the bitter/sweet part of loving people so much that the loss of them is incomprehensible.*

She pulled herself together and met her father as he stood up from the double swing that hung from the front porch ceiling. "How are you, little girl?" He'd called her that for as long as she could remember.

"Dad, I've missed you all so much. I hate that I have to live somewhere else and travel so much."

Franklin did what he always did: He hugged her gently while patting her on the back. "I know, me too. You look great. How was your flight?"

"Good. But I'm tired. I finished fourth yesterday, and that seems to take more energy than winning."

He nodded in acknowledgment. "Plenty of time to rest. I'll get your suitcase. Here, sit down on the swing."

"Iced tea anyone?" Grandma asked. Everyone wanted a glass, so Betsy and Grandma disappeared into the house while Franklin retrieved her luggage. Tess looked at her grandfather's mesmerizing blue eyes and wondered if she'd ever met anyone with eyes that color. There were no words to describe them. They still sparkled. Although his skin color was very fair, the flesh was so weathered from almost eighty years of outdoor work and activities that it had the texture of an old weather-beaten baseball glove.

"Grandpa, what do you say you and I go fishing tomorrow?"

He rubbed his clean-shaven chin. "I need to check my trotlines down at the lake. It's not like fishing for crappie, but we could bring dinner home. I caught a sixty-pound channel cat two weeks ago."

"I'm in. We'll make lunch and spend the day."

"I imagine your grandmother can rustle something up for us."

"Grandpa, I can make lunch!" She paused and thought better. "You're right, let's have her put something together for us. I admit I can only make peanut butter and jelly sandwiches, but someday I'm going to start cooking."

"I'm sure you will sweetie, and you'll be good at it. You know it took the old gal awhile to learn how to cook."

"Uh-huh. Old gal? You old fool," came from inside the house.

The front screen door opened, and Betsy and Grandma came out to the porch carrying a pitcher of iced sweet tea and a plate of warm brownies. Tess shook her head. "I'm going to gain ten pounds in a week if I eat like this." She was handed a brownie on a paper towel and a glass of iced tea.

Franklin joined them after carrying Tess's luggage inside. He sat in a straight chair and began packing tobacco into his pipe. Betsy stared at him for several seconds before he stuck the pipe back in his shirt pocket. Betsy nodded her approval.

"Tess, your father and I have big news!" She threw her hands up in the air to put an exclamation mark on the announcement.

"Oh?"

"Your father and I are going to build a new home!" Betsy gushed. "I've always wanted to live in a new house, and now we're going to do it. We've found a five-acre site a little ways south of town, and we're having plans drawn up."

Tess looked at her father and arched her eyebrows. Franklin nodded his agreement. He was seldom eager to change much in his life, but apparently this was one of those rare occasions.

"Mom, Dad, that's so exciting! When will you start building?"

"In a couple of months, once the plans are finished and the permits issued," Franklin said. "I should be able to pick up a preliminary set of plans tomorrow morning and show you what we have in mind."

Tess rubbed Stuck's ears as she listened, and he moaned with pleasure. Franklin continued, "I've been teaching at the university now for almost thirty years, and I'm thinking about just teaching a couple of classes a semester. I may start writing that geography textbook I've been talking about forever."

"Five acres, Dad. That's a lot of mowing. And writing a textbook to boot. You sure about that?" Tess teased him.

"I think it's time I get a riding mower. What do you think?"

Tess laughed. "I think it's just what you'll need."

The five of them sat out on the front porch until after five o'clock, catching up on news, the prospects of the University of Illinois football team, the extended family news, Tess's upcoming tournaments, the weather, and Stuck's latest antics. Curiosity and prowling for food had gotten the rotund canine into many distressing situations that usually involved being unable to extricate himself. He'd been stuck in a picket fence, the bathtub, and under the bed. His legendary howling always followed. Off-limits for discussion on a night like this were Tess's business interests, money, and politics. Even talking about the foundation's finances was not a conversation for immediate family members.

The women eventually migrated to the kitchen where they fried chicken, boiled corn on the cob, and made a salad. The men moved to the back of the house and spent the next hour hand-churning vanilla ice cream. After dinner, and when the dishes had been washed and dried, Tess and her grandparents settled in the living room. Her grandparents had the same routine five nights a week: They watched *Wheel of Fortune*. The show required players to guess letters missing from words of popular phrases, places, or things. Grandpa considered it a personal and serious challenge to beat his wife of fifty-five years in this game of spelling and wits. He tended to be a little quick on the trigger, and she had a better command of spelling, so epic battles ensued. Inexplicably, although his hearing was fine, Grandpa felt sure that having the volume turned up as loud as the television allowed increased his chances of success. This night was no different.

When the program began, Tess and her father sought a quieter and less contentious environment, and found some solitude on the aluminum chairs in the backyard. Stuck joined them. They couldn't help but hear "Wheel of Fortune" booming from the house. Game on, Tess thought.

Franklin could sit outside for hours in the summer engaging in only minimal conversation, listening to the buzz of cicadas. When they lived in the house Tess grew up in, he would listen to the Illinois football or baseball team practicing on fields not more than several hundred yards away. Betsy would join him for about five minutes before the mosquitoes, the chiggers, or Franklin's pipe smoke drove her inside. Tess had always loved this time with her dad, and although talking was sparse, what was said was usually memorable and meaningful. Tonight, Franklin relit his pipe and, as he always did, tapped the lid of his can of Busch beer before popping it open. Tess realized that she did the same thing for no discernible reason other than that she and her dad were very similar in many ways, even with weird quirky little habits.

"I'll bet you and Mom will be glad to get out of that rental house and into the new one when it's finished."

"Her more than me," he said. "That's a lot of yard to mow and a long driveway to clear in the winter."

"Yes, but a new house, new appliances, and air-conditioning!"

"I never really cared that much that the old house didn't have air-conditioning."

"Dad, it was impossible to sleep in the summer. It was torture."

"You get used to it."

"No you don't. Never." She laughed, and he smiled. *Yes even something invented fifty years ago, like air-conditioning, was moving too fast for him.*

"So how is it going with the young man from Chicago?" he asked.

"You mean Eddie." Not using his name was her father's way of reserving judgment, or maybe passing judgment. "Great. We don't have a lot of time together, but the time we do have is always wonderful."

"That's important. You have to like him and enjoy his company before you even get to the big issues."

They heard her grandfather bellow, "Checkers!" A moment later, "No, crackers!"

Her grandmother yelled in disgust, "Oh for goodness' sake, r and h have been used. Pay attention!"

Grandpa's response was inaudible.

"How's his transfer-to-Miami plan going?"

"Just waiting." Tess knew what was coming next, because her father never failed to ask the same question in conversations like this.

"Why don't you consider moving back to Illinois where he works and your family lives?"

Restraining her exasperation with the same comments each time the subject came up, Tess responded, "Dad, you know I need to be someplace where I can play golf year-round. I just have to. It's not that I wouldn't love to be near you and Mom and everyone else, but Florida is where I have to live, at least for now." She stood up and hugged him. "I'm beat and I'm going in. See you tomorrow?"

"You bet, sweetie. We'll take a drive out to the house site tomorrow when I have the plans, and show you what it looks like out there."

"Sounds like a plan. Love you. Goodnight."

As she passed him, he held her hand for several seconds and let it slide slowly from his, a gesture they'd practiced since she could remember. When she entered the back door, she saw both her grandparents sitting on the edge of their chairs, intensely focused on the television. Her grandfather snapped out "Dragonfly!"

"Dragonfly? You old fool. It's a place."

She kissed them both without interrupting their game and retired upstairs, where she found Betsy laying out towels on the bed in the extra bedroom.

"Honey, are you sure you don't want to stay at our house tonight?"

"Positive, Mom. I'm fine here, and I'd rather sleep in a bed than on the sofa."

"I'm so glad you're here, especially since there's been so much … ah … turbulence over the last couple of years. Oh, I told a few of the people down at the foundation that you'd visit for an hour or so in the next week."

"Definitely. I want to, but no newspapers or TV or any of that. Just you and me and the clients and staff. I hate those public shows. It's not about me, it's about what you do there."

"Absolutely." Betsy hugged her longer than Tess could remember her mother holding an embrace. *She's renewed and revitalized*, Tess thought.

"Good night, dear."

"Good night, Mom."

A few minutes later, Tess was sitting on the bed in ten-year-old gym shorts and an oversize T-shirt reading a magazine when the phone rang. She glanced at the clock. Eddie, just like clockwork. She picked up after the first ring, and they talked about the day and updated each other on the ordinary things in life before bidding each other good night. They did this every night without fail, regardless of time zones or schedules. It was the equivalent of a thousand-mile-away good-night kiss.

CHAPTER

5

TESS AWAKENED to the unmistakable clanging of pots and pans from the kitchen downstairs. She'd heard that comforting sound since she was a little girl—the best alarm in the world. She rolled over in her bed and looked at the clock, 5:50 a.m. She wondered if it was possible that her grandparents were getting up earlier as they got older, or did they always rise before 6 a.m.?

Tess inhaled the irresistible aroma of bacon permeating the house. She put her hands behind her head and stared at the ceiling sorting out the sounds, the smells emanating from the house, and her thoughts. She picked a point on the ceiling and focused on it, until she'd blocked out the rest of reality. It was her morning ritual. She'd prioritize, organize, and separate the important from the trivial. Today would be devoted to her grandparents and slowing down her life, which could run at the speed of light. *Reflect. Count blessings. Drive down the negative, the doubts, and let good thoughts rise to the top.*

She rolled out of bed, washed her face, and brushed her teeth. She pulled on an oversize Fighting Illini sweatshirt, a pair of gym shorts, and some white athletic socks, then softly padded down the creaky steps and into the kitchen. Her grandmother had a mound of biscuit dough on a cutting board, and flour covered her hands and her forearms halfway up to her elbows. The blue veins in the back of her hands shown through the flour as she massaged the dough. Tess smiled and stood in the doorway of the kitchen for a couple of seconds, memorizing the scene, before her grandmother looked up.

"Well good morning, sleepyhead," she said cheerily as she nudged her glasses back up onto the bridge of her nose with a flour-covered hand.

"Good morning, Grandma. How are you this morning?"

"Couldn't be better. How about a cup of coffee? I can't vouch for it. Your grandfather made it, and sometimes he forgets how much coffee he puts in the pot. Sometimes he forgets the filters, and now and then he forgets to put the water in. I've taken to putting the right size measuring cup right in the coffee so at least he gets close."

"I'm sure it'll be fine. Can I help with something?"

"No, just about got it." She pulled a baking dish out of the oven that had crackling, melted Crisco in it and set it on the counter. In a smooth and fluid motion, she began cutting the biscuit dough into neat circles with a glass and dipping them in the fat and flipping them over. "Grab a cup of coffee and join him out there on the back porch. That's where he always is first thing in the morning."

Tess grabbed a large mug with a faded "Branson Missouri" logo on it and smiled, remembering they had gone there when she was a little girl. She filled it with coffee and slipped out the back door. Her grandfather was sitting on the steps leading out to the yard, coffee in one hand and a cigar in the other. She sat down next to him and put her arm over his shoulders.

"How'd you sleep, Grandpa?"

"Oh, about as good as usual, which isn't that good. You?"

"Like a rock. I always sleep well in that bed."

They sat and listened to the sounds of birds chirping, a dog barking somewhere in the distance, and a garbage truck moving through the neighborhood.

"My favorite part of the day," he said. "Reminds me of when everything in life was a little bit more quiet and slower. Simpler."

"When you were growing up?"

"Yeah. You know when I was a boy, not a single person in town owned a car. Everybody had horses back then. In 1910 the doctor in town finally got the first automobile. That was a big deal. The old timers complained about the noise, how slow and unreliable it was, and the smoke."

Tess listened, knowing that this was a time for him to go back and remember the best parts of his past and grieve for the things, the life, and the people that no longer existed.

"You know what I think about sometimes?" he asked as he blew smoke away from Tess.

"What?"

"The winter of 1920. January to be exact. I'd gotten out of the army six months before and decided that before I settled down, I would go on an adventure."

"You did? I didn't know that. What'd you do?"

"I went with a couple of friends to Texas, to the King Ranch to be a cowboy. I couldn't hardly ride a horse, didn't know anything about cattle, and nothing about ranching. A real greenhorn, I guess they'd say. But they didn't know anything about me, so it was about even. They'd lost so many hands in the war that when it was time to move those big Brahman cattle north, if you could get on a horse and live on a dollar a day, you were hired. The King Ranch was famous for their Santa Gertrudis cattle that they created through crossbreeding to survive in the hot, dry country. They were a reddish-brown color and big, big animals."

"You were a cowboy?" Tess laughed.

"Not a good one, but after a few days if you stayed awake and stayed on your horse, you were fine. I can't remember now, but I believe that ranch was as big as a state. We moved that herd seventy or eighty miles north to market in San Antonio. And then went back and did it again. By the time I headed north, I had a butt as hard as steel and a hundred bucks in my pocket. I had a lot of time to dream, too. About the future. Now I dream about the past. Funny how that works."

The back door creaked open, and Tess's grandmother joined them.

"I had a little adventure like that a couple of months ago," said Tess. "I only rode a horse for about ten minutes, though."

"You did?" he said mildly surprised.

"Yeah, I did okay. At least I stayed on the horse anyway."

"You can tell us all about it over hot biscuits," said Grandma. "Come on, you two."

***

An hour later, Tess and her grandfather left on Interstate 74, driving east for Homer Lake where he'd fished since before Tess was born. She smiled when she looked at him behind the wheel wearing his worn-out baseball cap with the brim turned up and angled slightly to the side. She wished she didn't feel so compelled to adhere to the rules of fashion or style that would prevent her from doing the same. *If only I could be so free.*

With a twelve-foot aluminum flatbed boat in tow, he drove less than the speed limit, so the twenty miles took close to forty-five minutes. They pulled into the lake's recreation area and followed a gravel road to a small boat launch. Tess got out of the car and walked a few steps into the woods as her grandfather turned the car and trailer around 180 degrees and backed down the ramp slowly. The woods around the park smelled earthy and fresh, the dew on the ground cover still visible. She felt a gentle morning breeze coming in off the water and inhaled deeply. *I haven't been here in years. I'd forgotten how peaceful and beautiful it is*, she thought. She walked to the ramp and watched her grandfather deftly launch the boat into the lake.

He looked up at her and smiled. "Well, let's see how the fish are doing. Come on. You see, the way it works is you come to the boat. It doesn't come to you." He smiled. She ignored him.

Tess noticed that he didn't seem to mind getting his pants wet up to his knees as he walked the boat off the trailer and into the lake. "Pull the car up into the lot, will you Tess?"

She parked next to several old beat-up pickup trucks, locked the car, and headed back toward the water. Grandpa had walked the boat to the wooden ramp, where she could climb in without getting her white tennis shoes and socks wet.

"Hop in," he said. "How's that for service?"

"Excellent! Grandpa, this is a beautiful morning. Not a cloud in the sky, not that hot, and just a hint of a breeze. Can't beat it."

"We can, if we pull in a catfish or two."

Tess stepped over the side of the boat and saw a net with a handle around the size of a tennis racket, fishing gear, an old trotline, a rusted bucket, dried blood and perhaps fish guts, and junk littered about the bottom of the boat. She slid on something slimy, but nimbly found a seat on the forward bench. The boat smelled like dead fish and wet stinking mud. He pulled the engine starter cord several times, adjusted the choke, and tried again. The engine sputtered and coughed gray smoke before it spit out a puff of black smoke and began to run. She could tell the engine was old and tired. The boat was old too, and dirty, and seemed to have a slight leak—the bottom of the boat where he sat was already wet. He let the motor warm up and lit a Swisher Sweet, flicking the match into the water.

"Grandpa, I wish I liked those things well enough to smoke one with you."

Without a moment's hesitation, he leaned up toward Tess and handed her the cigar. She was taken aback, but reached toward him and gingerly held it with her index finger and thumb away from herself, like she would a nasty hypodermic needle. She wasn't sure if she'd meant what she'd said, but she was now certain that she had to indulge. He lit another and glanced at her. Slowly, she put the plastic tip between her lips, making as little contact with her mouth as possible, and inhaled ever so slightly. Her head moved back several inches in surprise. "It's actually kind of sweet."

"I've been trying to get your mom to smoke one for a hundred years. Never would."

Tess took a little longer and deeper pull on the cigar, as he turned the handle on the motor and steered the boat out into the lake. She smiled into the breeze. *Who would have thought that smoking a cigar in a stinky little fishing boat, puttering along to check trotlines for a stinky old catfish could be so relaxing, so invigorating, so revitalizing.* The wind blew her hair away from her face, and she inhaled the stench of dead fish, thinking that this morning it was as good as any fragrance. This was a memory. A good one.

Fifteen minutes later, they had reached the east side of the lake, where a series of old scum-covered, faded-white plastic bleach containers floated on the surface. "That's my line," he said as he idled the boat and drew closer to the floating containers. "It isn't legal to set trotlines anymore, but the one county ranger doesn't come over to this side of the lake, so me and a bunch of old-timers are safe. Look, see how those branches lay down over the lake? Well, there's branches under the surface of the water, too. When they built the dam, the water wasn't this high, but over the years it's come up and covered more trees. Fish love the underwater cover."

"Oh, they hide in the branches?"

"Uh-huh." He anchored the boat near one of the bleach containers and began pulling the line. A minute later, an empty hook came up.

"That's a big hook," Tess said.

"Big fish, since nobody fishes in here anymore. These suckers can go fifty, sixty pounds."

He used the line connecting the plastic containers to pull the boat. When he grabbed the line to the next container, he looked up at Tess with his million-dollar blue eyes and said, "Got something. Grab that net."

Tess moved to the back of the boat and knelt down, holding the net over the edge with childlike excitement. "This is so cool." As he pulled up the line, the water around it swirled in a circle, adding to the anticipation.

"Okay, honey, be ready. This is a big one. I can tell."

A moment later, Tess looked into the eyes of a catfish that barely moved as it was hauled to the surface. It was as big around as a fire hydrant, potbellied, and not more than three feet long. It had whiskers six inches long that poked out the sides of its mouth. "Oh … oh … Tess fell backward and plopped into muck on the bottom of the boat.

"Easy now, girl. Just slide the net under him and lift him into the boat."

Tess regained a kneeling position over the gunwhale and hoisted the fish up and into the boat, falling to one arm onto the seat. The fish flopped over once, splashing more muck from the bottom of the boat onto Tess. "Oh my God, it's so big. It's so ugly! We got him! We caught one!" She yelled with excitement as she stood up.

"Yeah we did, but he's probably been on the line for a day. They don't fight much."

"I don't care! Look at the size of him!" She threw her arms up in the air in celebration, literally rocking the boat.

"Never saw anybody so excited about catching a catfish."

"Grandpa, do you realize this is my first catfish?"

"Now that is something. Want to pull that hook out then?"

"No! God no!"

"Just like your mom. Never could bait a hook or take a hook out."

They checked several more trotlines and didn't find any other catfish waiting, so they headed back to the dock. Her grandfather pulled the boat onto the trailer and loaded the fish into a large, somewhat dilapidated white Styrofoam cooler. They were on the road back to Champaign when Tess realized that she had muck and mud on her arms, legs, and the seat of her white shorts. Her white tennis shoes were the color of the bottom of the boat, and her hands smelled like stinking fish, but that did little to dimmish her exuberance.

"Grandpa, this was great. Just great. This is way better than hitting a huge drive off the tee or sinking a thirty-foot birdie putt."

"Well, if you say so. I never tried playing golf. You ready to clean that fish?"

"Ah … no. I've got to go to the bathroom."

"Just like your mom."

Y Y Y

Forty-five minutes later, Grandpa was cleaning the catfish and filleting it, while Tess took a long hot shower.

Betsy and Franklin arrived around 5 p.m. just as Grandma finished frying the catfish breaded in cornmeal and some hush puppies. She'd made a pan of cornbread and a peach cobbler for dessert. As everyone took their seat, she set a pitcher of sweet tea on the table, took her seat, and bowed her head, leading them in grace. Tess thought about her world, where almost no one said grace before a meal.

When dinner was over and the dishes done, her grandparents settled in for another round of *Wheel of Fortune*. Betsy, Franklin, and Tess drove to the building site of their new home south and east of town. It was in an area of five-acre parcels where the city had installed sewer, water, and electric lines the year before. There was a small lake on the edge of the property on one side, a road on another, and woods surrounding the remainder of the property. Tess followed her parents, who she noticed for the first time in years held hands, and they walked to a slight rise on the site. Tess exhaled deeply. "This is absolutely beautiful, Mom and Dad. I love it. It's so quiet and peaceful, and the view is stunning. This is going to be just perfect."

Franklin unrolled the architect's plans and showed Tess where the house footprint was laid out. "The porch goes around three sides of the house so you have morning, afternoon, and evening sun and views. It's called a French country colonial style. Ever since we went to Cape Girardeau, Missouri, years ago, I've wanted a house with a porch like this." With his finger, he traced the eight-foot-wide porch on the plans and rotated his arm in an arc to show Tess. "It will be covered with an overhang so we can sit out here in the shade or if it's raining. It's what I've always wanted."

"Mom?" Tess looked at her mother.

"It's idyllic. I love the setting and the house. Best of all, we'll finally have air-conditioning."

CHAPTER

6

Sunday, four days before Thanksgiving, 1978; Chicago

TESS'S FLIGHT FROM MIAMI arrived at O'Hare Airport, and from her front-row seat in first class, she watched aircraft taxi up and down the runways as the plane headed for the gate. She wore jeans, a white button-down collar shirt, a light leather jacket, and tennis shoes, having read that the temperature would rise to about fifty degrees in the afternoon. Her attire displayed a balanced practicality with style for the day, no matter what activity Eddie had planned for them. She was second in line to walk down the jetway into the airport, and Eddie was waiting for her just a few feet from the gate. He wore a pair of white Converse sneakers, faded jeans, and a very worn Chicago Bears sweatshirt over a button-down collared denim shirt. She smiled and walked briskly to him. Tess dropped her carry-on bag, and they embraced.

He kissed her lightly. "I missed you," he said.

"I missed you too."

"You smell so good."

"Well, I am in the perfume business."

"Oh, I know. You ready? Let's get your suitcase."

She flung her small bag over her shoulder, and they walked through the jam-packed airport to baggage claim. Eddie stood by the carousel, watching for it to swing into motion, which gave Tess a few moments to study him. His jet-back wavy hair covered his ears but had been trimmed recently, and his olive-colored skin seemed to be tan even now at the beginning of winter. He'd pulled his sleeves up to his elbows, exposing bulging blue veins in muscular forearms. Eddie was five feet eight inches tall and, soaking wet, maybe 155 pounds, but he was strong and wiry. She thought he was cute, even handsome, but what made him attractive was his smile, his charming and infectious laugh, and his eccentricities. She also admired the fact that Eddie was organized and very neat, almost meticulous. The carousel jerked into motion and a few minutes later, he had retrieved her small suitcase.

They walked into a short-term parking area and passed by most of the cars. Eddie said, "I have a little surprise for today."

"Oh really."

"This way." He led her to the farthest end of the lot.

Parked in a spot at least ten spaces away from the nearest car was a bright red 1966 Chevy Impala convertible. Eddie waved at the car in a grand gesture. "I found this car several years ago, and I had a really good garage and body shop re-store it for my Uncle Tony. I gave it to him for his 50th birth-day. We're driving it today."

"Oh my God, it's beautiful." She admired how it glim-mered and reflected the sunlight.

Eddie waved at the car. "They did a great job on it. Take a look at the interior."

"Oh, I love the white. Is it leather?"

"Yes, and check out the four-speed transmission. That's original. So is the radio, the rear speaker, and the air-conditioning, which wasn't that common back in 1966. Let me open the hood and show this honker of an engine. Three hundred ninety-six cubic inches of raw power." Eddie walked to the front of the car and slipped his hand under the hood, releasing it. "And look at all the chrome."

"I like raw power, and it's certainly shiny." She chuckled at her own silliness. "How is Tony?"

"He's doing great." He shut the hood. "It's a little cool for the top to be down, so give me a hand to put it up, and let's rock'n'roll."

As they exited the parking garage, Tess asked, "So, what are we doing on this beautiful November day?"

"Well, are you hungry?"

"Nope, ate on the plane. You?"

"Me neither. So, I thought we'd start by doing something I haven't done in ages. Let's go to the zoo."

"The zoo! I guess why not."

"Yeah, I love the zoo, and I haven't been there since my brother took me to the Brooklyn Zoo a hundred years ago. I love the primates."

"Yeah, no surprise there," she laughed. "I love the elephants and the tigers."

"Now that figures, too. Elephants have great memories and are smart, and the tigers, well, everybody knows about tigers." He smiled, and they headed north for the zoo, which was on the shore of Lake Michigan. "You going to be warm enough?" he asked. "It is November."

"Absolutely."

They proceeded through the turnstile of the Lincoln Park Zoo after paying the $1.25 admission. For a reason Tess knew well, Eddie took it upon himself to act as tour guide and self-appointed zoological expert. She knew he loved to talk and probably would have conducted a full walking-talking tour even if he was by himself. They stopped in front of a directional guide, and Eddie furrowed his brow.

"Now let me get my bearings," he said. "Where are those elephants? Oh, okay, we have go to the right and past the serpent building. Alrighty, follow me."

Perhaps he was excited, perhaps he was just nervous, but for some reason Eddie stayed ahead of her by a couple of steps. He turned back to her and said with some authority, "Now Tess, you know that the elephant is the largest ..." And at that moment, as if he'd been hit in the head with a snowball, he staggered. Tess had noticed a flock of pigeons had lifted off just behind them and circled back. At least one of them had decided that it was the perfect time to relieve itself and had zeroed in on Eddie's head. It played out as if in slow motion: She watched the "bomb" drop and splatter over his hair. His hands shot up, his head recoiled, and, significantly, he stopped talking. Momentarily. "Oh God, Oh, God," he stammered.

Tess restrained herself for only a couple of seconds before bursting into hysterical laughter. She bent over at the waist, almost crying. Eddie tried to regain his composure but could only manage to utter, "Did you, did you spit on me?"

Tess couldn't answer and waved her hand dismissively in front of her face, watching Eddie as he looked around for an explanation. "What happened? Who spit on me?"

A small rivulet of white bird poop worked its way down the side of his head to his ear. Trying to provide some assistance to no avail, she made a valiant attempt to control wild burst of laughter and said, "It was a pigeon, Eddie. Go in the men's room there and get some wet paper towels."

Several minutes later, after a serious cleanup of Eddie's head, they resumed their trek to the elephant compound.

The episode had impacted Eddie's authority as a zoo guide and reduced his jocularity, but he marshalled on, his pride wounded. Tess made it through the rest of the tour with only a couple more bouts of uncontrollable laughter.

Later, as Eddie stared at an orangutan, he asked Tess, "What do you think he's thinking?"

"What's for lunch? What do you think?"

"I wish there were a couple of orangutan babes in this place."

"Uh-huh, show's you where your mind is and probably his too. Let's go and get some coffee, before one of you two loses control."

Twenty minutes later, after leaving the zoo, they were sitting in a small Italian bistro drinking coffee and sharing a cannoli. Eddie took a bite and asked, "Do you like the filling or the shell better?"

"The filling is pretty rich."

"That says something about you. You have unfulfilled sexual desires." He smiled devilishly.

"Uh-huh, and you will, too, when the day is over."

"Oh, come on."

"I've got a question for you. A real one, a serious one for a change."

"But I pride myself on not having serious conversations."

"Try one. What will it be like this week with me and your parents?"

"Oh, this is serious." He rested his elbows on the table and set his head in his hands. He stared at Tess for several seconds. "I guess they'll be fine. Polite and maybe a little reserved."

"You mean, maybe standoffish?"

"No, Tess. They'll be fine. I've told them all about you. Where you're from, your success on the golf course and in business, and of course how wonderful you are."

"Eddie, we have completely different backgrounds. That's what I mean. You haven't told them that the closest thing to me being Italian is that I own an Italian leather jacket. I'm not Catholic, and I've only been in a Catholic church once in my life. I'm not loud unless a bird craps on my head." She hesitated and smiled. "And the only authentic Italian food I've ever had, your sister made."

"There see." He interrupted and pointed his index finger. "They're going to love your sense of humor."

Tess nodded, just a bit more than dubious. "I'm not trying to be funny. So, that's it? That's all you have to say?"

"I don't know what to say. I haven't lived at home in ten years. I never brought anyone home except Mimi Fashoni, and they knew her family. They didn't like her, but my brothers *loved* her. I think everything will be fine." He held up his hands, palms out. "What are you gonna do?"

Tess shook her head and pursed her lips. She sighed and said, "Okay, where are we going Wednesday night in Albany?"

"Oh, you'll love it. The Dirty Martini Club. I already told you, my brothers and I will be performing."

"So you say. Should be something. So, you're leaving tomorrow morning, and I'm headed to my parents for a couple of days before I fly in on Tuesday. What should we do for the rest of the day, and where are we staying tonight?"

"Oh Tessy-Cakes, have I got a plan."

"Anything that starts with Tessy-Cakes cannot be good."

CHAPTER

7

Tuesday, two days before Thanksgiving; Albany

TESS LANDED IN ALBANY early Tuesday afternoon, picked up her rental car, and checked into her hotel. She had arranged to meet Teresa for some afternoon clothes shopping and dinner. Eddie was setting up equipment and running through some practice rounds with his band, so it was a girls' day and night out.

After they had browsed a couple of stores in the downtown fashion district, it became abundantly clear to Tess that she and Teresa had polar-opposite ideas about fashion and style. Teresa wore white high-heeled boots, a very short red miniskirt, and a small purple jacket.

Teresa held up a skin-tight sequined dress that would fit snug on a lamppost and gushed, "Tess, you've got to try this on. It's you."

Tess shook her head. "No, I think that's more your style, Teresa. But I do like this hat." She modeled a wide-brimmed gray fedora. "What do you think?"

"Awful!" Teresa said disgustedly. "It looks like something my father would wear."

"Oh. Oh." Tess quickly returned it to the rack.

As they wandered through more stores, Tess watched Teresa's exuberant response to outfits that may have been popular for a night at the disco or a date in a pool hall, but in her wildest dreams, Tess couldn't imagine wearing them. At one very chic store, La Femme Bien, they were immediately greeted by several well-dressed and attractive clerks. It wasn't long before Teresa was rushing in and out of a dressing room, swirling and swishing around to the oohs and aahs of the attending women. Tess found a comfortable chair and watched the exhibition. Teresa ended up purchasing several new outfits that must have cost her a month's salary, although Tess wasn't sure. The odd thing about Teresa was that although she worked, in her words, as an administrative assistant in the family business, she seemed to have the income of a highly paid executive—or at least she spent money that way. Tess found it amusing but didn't ask questions. It wasn't her place, as they said back home.

ỲỲỲ

After several hours of scouring Albany's high-end stores, Teresa proposed they have a cocktail before dinner. They found a table in the Capital Grill, and Tess ordered a Chardonnay, Teresa a highball. Teresa took a sizable gulp from her cocktail and said, "Now that's good. Thirst quenching. Well, as you probably guessed, I have no men in my life, no dating life, no fun, and zero sex."

Tess almost choked but managed to swallow her mouthful of wine. "Well, that's a lot of issues you've got."

"Oh, I got issues, and they are because of my family and how I am so stuck between a rock and a hard place that I couldn't get myself out if my life depended on it."

"You mean the dating thing or Albany?"

"No, I think it's pretty much the fact that my mother is a cold-hearted bitch who hates me, and my father is a wet fish who is about as much fun as a wet fish."

"I think you mixed up your metaphors there, but surely you're being a little hard on your parents."

"Well, let's see what you think after you meet them. So, when are you and Eddie getting married?"

This time Tess did cough through her Chardonnay. The question and the wine went down the wrong pipe. Tess had to cough, wipe her eyes with a napkin, and breath for several seconds before she could respond. "Ah, we're just starting to get there," she said timidly.

"Okay, well that's a start. You know you're going to have to push Eddie a little. He's always been, what's the word, coddled. He's got four older brothers and me, as well as my mother, who treated him like a baby until he was practically in high school. He was always so rambunctious. When he was a little baby in his highchair, he'd bang his head on the back of it until my mother fed him."

"Oh, he still does that!" They both giggled.

Teresa shook her head. "You know, he's always talked incessantly. On his first-grade report card, his teacher wrote, 'He walks around and talks a lot.'"

"Oh, he still does that unless a bird poops on him."

"What?"

Tess regaled Teresa with the zoo story, and they both laughed.

"You know how he loves sports, right? He and my brothers played that damned stoopball for hours."

"Stoopball?"

"Yeah. With one of those little pink balls about the size of a tennis ball, they'd throw it against the front steps. When the ball ricocheted off the steps, it would be like a batter hitting the ball. It would go on for hours and hours, and they would yell and scream and usually fight. Morons. If they weren't doing that, they'd play stickball in the street with a broomstick. And that BB gun, oh God. It was the same one he used to shoot the lunatic that attacked you guys in your apartment two years ago."

"I try not to think about that very much. Eddie was just helpless sitting there with his full leg cast. He must have hit the guy with three or four BBs before—"

Teresa interrupted her. "Before you teed off on him with Eddie's baseball bat and he ended up in the front yard, almost dead. Somebody ought to make that story into a movie."

"No thanks."

"You know, Eddie got really good with his gun while they played war. They'd build elaborate war scenes with hundreds of those little green plastic soldiers and then shoot them down. Lucky, they didn't shoot each other. If they weren't doing that, they were blowing stuff up with cherry bombs or whatever. And if they weren't shooting something or blowing something up, they were having ferocious to-the-death snowball fights in snow forts. Eddie has always had a lot of, shall we say, energy."

"His energy and zest for life is what I love about him. He's never dull."

"You're right, I guess. I can't blame you for being crazy about him. Almost everyone likes him. And you know really, Eddie is not that much of a ladies' man. You don't have anything to worry about there. Eddie is true-blue loyal, and I think he's absolutely crazy about you."

Tess smiled but felt her cheeks flush as the conversation had turned too personal. "Thank-you. I know. Can I ask you a question about your parents?"

"Sure. Fun subject," she responded sarcastically.

"I've heard some stuff about your family."

"Stop." She held up her hands, palms facing Tess. "I've heard the rumors about my family my whole life, but to be honest, Tess, I've never witnessed anything that would give any credence to those stories. But that's not to say I don't have my suspicions. I don't know, maybe. What I do know is that my father is like a character in a movie. He seems almost unreal. Distant, aloof, and detached would be how I'd describe my relationship with him, and probably the same for Eddie's relationship with him, too."

"What about your mom?"

"About as cool a cucumber as you'll ever meet. Never gives you a clue to what she's thinking or what she knows. Always calculating and manipulating. She and I are like water and oil."

"Oh, that's not good."

"This place, Albany, my family, and my parents make me want to move somewhere else. Somewhere warm and exotic, like California or Miami. Start my life over, or maybe just start my life period."

"You wouldn't miss them?"

"Not a bit, and they wouldn't miss me. Trust me. Another drink?"

"No, I've had my afternoon limit."

"A little more shopping before dinner?"

"I'm starving. I haven't eaten since the plane," said Tess. "You ready?"

"Let's do it. I made reservations at my favorite place, The Forum. Great Italian food."

8

The Dirty Martini Club After the Shooting

WITHIN MINUTES of the gunshots, the nightclub exits were sealed by police, and an ambulance had arrived. Two thick-necked club bouncers herded family members and others who'd witnessed the shooting behind a perimeter of yellow crime scene tape. Medical emergency personnel surrounded Frankie and soon moved him to a gurney, rolling it out to the waiting ambulance. Tess stood around with the family members and listened as the siren became faint.

"Everyone here move to the tables in front of the stage," bellowed a red-faced potbellied policeman, who filled out his uniform to a stretching point. "Don't even think about leaving. You can't. An officer will be interviewing each of you for your statement in due time."

"How long is that?" yelled someone from the thirty or so people herded together.

"When we get to it, smart-ass! And if you'd like to spend the rest of the night down at the station, keep talking."

Tess stood next to Eddie and Teresa, who appeared to be in a total state of shock. They stared vacuously at the policeman. Tess didn't attempt conversation. *What do you say when you witness an attempted assassination, a deliberate shooting of a person playing in a band at a family gathering?*

The people who remained after the mass exodus of customers stood around nearly silent, shocked in bewilderment bordering on disbelief. No one seemed panicked or acted hysterically, and that seemed odd, but then what were people supposed to do? To Tess, the incident was so foreign and so shocking that she couldn't put it in context of her life.

"Lady. Lady!" Tess looked up at the officer dragging her out of her thoughts and into his investigation. He asked her for identification, relationship to the victim, what she saw and heard. She answered honestly and with brevity that she had seen very little, heard very little, and knew almost nothing that would help with the investigation. As he snapped his notepad closed, he said sarcastically, "So, Miss Kincaid, if you really don't know any of these people, why the hell were you here in the first place?"

"I ... ah ... I ... am with Eddie."

"One of the Spinozza kids, right?"

"Yes, I'm with Eddie Spinozza as his guest and friend."

"How nice for you."

What a jerk. Why are they treating this like some bar fight?

An hour and a half later, they were dismissed. Everyone had been interviewed, photographed, and asked for a current address and phone number where they could be contacted, if necessary, in the near future. Eddie asked the policeman who seemed to be in charge, "Can we go now? I'd like to go to the hospital to see my brother."

"You're free to go, but we'll be in touch. Count on it," the cop said acerbically.

The family split up to leave. Eddie, Tess, and Teresa went to the front door, and Eddie's brothers and band members to a side door. Eddie pushed open the door and was greeted by a blast of snow that stopped him in his tracks. "Geez, now what? A freakin' blizzard!"

It had snowed so hard over the previous several hours that there were already a couple of inches on the sidewalk. Tess pulled on the light leather coat she'd worn to the club when it seemed balmy. Eddie pulled the collar up on his black topcoat and turned to Tess. "Look Tess, there's nothing more you can do tonight. Teresa and I will go to the hospital, and I'll call you as soon as I know something. Why don't you go back to the hotel and try to rest."

"Eddie, I want to come with you. I don't want to be by myself right now, and you may need something. Coffee or a Coke."

"Tess, they aren't going to let anyone in to see him when he gets out of surgery. And if—"

"Don't even say it!" Teresa said in a shrill voice. "Don't even think about if he doesn't make it. I don't want to hear it!"

Eddie closed his eyes and rolled his head back. "I can't deal with all of this and my family. It's too much."

Tess put her head down to shield her face from the almost horizontal snow. "Alright, but call me as soon as anything happens or you know anything. Promise?" She kissed him on the cheek and squeezed his hand. She hugged Teresa and said, "Call me if you need anything or if there is something I can do."

Teresa asked, "Where are you staying again? Sorry, I forgot."

"The Morgan State House."

"Nice," Teresa said.

🍸🍸🍸

Tess hunched up her shoulders against the wind and snow and walked to her rental car two blocks away, guarding herself with short, balanced steps. She slipped several times in her leather-soled cowboy boots. *How did I know there'd be a damned blizzard?* The red 1977 Chevrolet Malibu was her rental car of choice. It was the right size with enough trunk space for her clubs and a suitcase, reasonably priced by Hertz, and available everywhere. She stuck with the same model whenever she traveled from tournament to tournament, to avoid having to learn about all the gadgets that came with the newer ones. Always renting a red car, though, was pretty much a compulsive habit. She had many of those. What she didn't realize was that these cars had rear-wheel drive and, while that was fine in the South and during the summer in northern climes, they didn't perform well in snow and ice. She would learn what that meant.

When she opened the driver's-side door, snow instantly whisked into and covered the front seat. She closed the door, started the car, and turned on the windshield wipers to clear the snow. They didn't move. There was no scraper under the seat, in the glove box, or in the backseat. "Great service," she muttered. She left the car running so it would warm up, and got out of the car to look in the trunk. It was empty.

She got back in the car, opened her purse, and pulled out her American Express card to use as a makeshift scraper. When she got out again, her boot slid under the car and she went down hard on the curb, banging her shin on the car frame as she slid partway under the car. Her hands disappeared into the snow, and she had to roll to the side to extricate herself. The snow pelted her face, and her hands stung from the cold. Once she regained her footing, she cracked the frozen wipers free and scraped snow and ice from the windshield. The wipers were still on, and they scraped along the top of the ice on the windshield. The driver's side wiper caught her on the knuckle, and she grimaced from the pain. "I hate snow!" she said, getting back into the car.

She looked at her knuckle which was just beginning to bleed. Her face was wet, her leg was soaked, and her shin throbbed from what was probably going to be a bruise. The steering wheel felt like a frozen Popsicle, and she shivered as she waited for the windshield to clear. Plows hadn't been down the street yet. The snow was falling so hard that the streetlights across the street were barely visible. The lights cast eerie shadows that seemed to sway back and forth with the wind and somehow made the storm feel more ominous. Snow, night, darkness, and the shooting pain made everything so unsettling, so wrong. She had thoughts of bad dreams and terrible movies she'd seen. This was becoming both.

She waited several minutes for the car to warm up and wondered about the surly policeman. This was a horrific crime, attempted murder, maybe even murder. So why did the cops seem annoyed or irritated? It didn't make sense. The Spinozzas were all treated with what seemed like disdain and certainly insensitivity.

The snow began to melt as it hit the football-size area on the windshield that she had cleared, so she put the car in reverse and backed up. Then she pulled into the street, clunked over a rut, and settled into tracks made from earlier traffic, and drove to the hotel.

YYY

The sumptuous, exclusive Morgan State House was built in the 19th century and had been restored to its former glory. It was in the center of downtown Albany, in the historic Washington Park area. The parking lot and the surrounding neighborhood seemed deserted. No one had been out to shovel the walks or plow the parking area, so Tess was forced to slog through snow that reached halfway up her boots. Hers were the only tracks. It snowed in Illinois, but she'd never seen it come down this hard and accumulate this fast. She thought it must be snowing a couple of inches an hour, harder now than when she left the club.

The door of her room faced the outdoors, so when she entered, she stomped the snow off her boots and shook it out of her hair. "God, this is awful," she said out loud. She changed into sweatpants and a long-sleeved T-shirt, and called her parents. Her mother and father were astounded by the shooting and suggested that she come home. She told them that the police had instructed her not to leave town for a couple of days while they investigated, and she reassured them that she was safe. Although she didn't mention it to them, she didn't want to leave anyway, because she was here for a very specific reason: to learn if she could be a part of Eddie's family.

During the summer, she and her mother had talked about what it was like to be married, and she remembered her mother's words: "Yes, you marry your husband for better or worse, but you also, to a certain degree, marry his family. It's naïve to think that he is not like them in many ways. You will also have a lifelong relationship with his family. You'll spend a good deal of time with them. If there isn't some commonality in values, there will always be sticking points that come up over and over again. You'll argue about things and not even realize you're arguing over deeply ingrained family values and beliefs. It's so very important to know that you can at the very least abide and tolerate lifestyles, values, and core beliefs of the other family. Don't make that mistake."

Tess's thoughts drifted to Frankie. She tried to remember what Eddie had said each of his brothers did for the family business. She thought Frankie might be in charge of operations or something like that. This couldn't have anything to do with work. Maybe it was a love triangle gone wrong. That kind of thing happens. It's either love or money that makes people shoot each other, right? But why would someone shoot Frankie in a public place in front of two hundred people? Was the hand pantomime going on between Eddie's grandfather and the other older gentleman meaningful in any way? Surely not. It looked like two old guys upset about who won a game of dominoes. That didn't make any sense either.

She pulled the towel turban off her hair and turned on a blow-dryer to finish the job. She switched on the television to see if the local news had picked up the story, but remembered that the news on the East Coast started at 11 p.m. and it was only 9:30. Switching time zones with frequent travel was always annoying. She watched several minutes of *Dallas* before turning the television off and paging through the phone book for the nearest local hospital. She found Albany Memorial and recalled that name was on the sleeve of one of the EMTs at the club. She dialed the number, got a receptionist, and waited several minutes before being transferred to the surgical ward. She was then summarily dismissed by the nursing staff at that station.

She paced around the room, brushed out her hair, and then sat on the bed, flipping through the most recent copy of *Life* magazine. Mickey Mouse was on the cover, and there was an article on disco. She wasn't interested in disco in the least. The music seemed contrived and gave her a headache after about five minutes. It also made idiots out of perfectly normal human beings—the attire they wore to disco clubs would surely haunt them in photographs in the future. She decided to do her nails to kill time. She was on the pinky finger of her left hand when the phone rang. It was Eddie.

"How's he doing?" Tess tried to modulate her voice and seem calm.

"He's still in surgery, and the doctors haven't come out yet. We don't know anything. I suppose that means there's still hope."

"Of course there is, Eddie," she said with as much optimism as she could muster. "The surgery is going to take a long time. The bullet hit him in the chest so, I mean ... well, I mean that has to take a long time. Sorry that was awkward. Who is with you?"

"We're all here, my parents, brothers, and Teresa. And a cop."

"A cop? You mean in the room? Why? Do you think someone might try to attack him again? This is insane."

"I have no idea, and it would be weird to ask right now."

"Do you have any idea who fired the gun? Did anyone see anything? Did any of your brothers say anything about who might have done this or why?" She realized she was firing questions at him with the speed of an investigator.

"No one saw him or recognized him. The lights were shining in our faces. I saw the stage lights reflect off the gun just before he fired, but I couldn't see him. That's what made me feel like something was wrong. I couldn't really figure out what was happening at the time. I mean you never think that someone is shooting at you."

"Eddie, you don't think he was shooting at you?"

"No, no. He was only ten feet away. He shot Frankie, no question about it. He meant to shoot Frankie."

"Who were the four men who came in just before the shots? They came in just after your father, uncles, and grand-father."

"What men? I couldn't see anything and wasn't paying attention." His voice seemed agitated and edgy.

"Never mind. I'm sure a number of people told the police. You must be exhausted. Can I bring you anything?"

"No, I'm good. This whole scene here is strange. We're not talking about why or who. I don't know what to say. It's like my family are perfect strangers, so we're just waiting. My father has been on the hospital house phone the whole time, with his back to us. I have no idea who he could be talking to and about what. My mother isn't talking or moving, just staring straight ahead with this angry look on her face. My brothers, Teresa, and I are just sitting. I don't know what to do."

"Pray. Go to the chapel and pray. It's the best thing you can do right now."

"I don't know if there is a chapel."

"There is. Ask. Do you want me to come down to the hospital?"

"No, they're not letting anyone into this ward. I have no idea what's going on."

"Alright, call me as soon as you know something. I'm just sitting here. How's Teresa?"

"Crying constantly."

"God, poor thing. Take her with you and get out of the waiting area for a few minutes. I know what I'm talking about. Remember me telling you about the night my uncle and his family were in a car accident? Going to the chapel probably saved my sanity. Or go somewhere else."

He agreed to find the chapel, take Teresa, and call when a surgeon came out of the operating room.

Tess flashed back on the old man sitting at the table across the room at the nightclub. She knew he'd looked at Eddie's grandfather and mouthed something, but maybe her memory was playing tricks on her. Maybe she imagined what she saw. She hadn't mentioned that to the police because they had only asked her if she'd seen the shooter.

She sighed and got up. She walked to the window and pulled the curtain back. The cars in the parking lot looked like white whales surfacing in an ocean of white. Everything was white, even in the darkness of night. *This is a nightmare.* She rummaged through her suitcase and found the book she'd been trying to read. *Centennial,* by James Michener, had been published a couple of years before, and she'd picked it up because it was set in northern Colorado. She'd gone to school in Fort Collins and loved the state. *Centennial* started with the history of that part of the country millions of years ago, and it was fascinating even if the book seemed like it was about ten thousand pages long. She'd never been an avid reader, but her father was a professor, and his love of books had made her force herself to read. His advice about watching television killing creativity found a secure spot in her psyche.

She found her dog-eared place and read a couple of pages before her attention failed her. She realized that she'd only painted her nails on one hand, so she finished before turning on the television again. She watched the news; no coverage. She watched *The Tonight Show* and knew her dad was watching, too—he watched Johnny Carson and Ed McMahon almost every night. Joe Namath was on the show, talking about the ad he did for pantyhose. His next guest was a wildlife person who brought a ferret on the show. The ferret urinated on Carson's desk, then crawled up his arm and perched on his head. Carson's deadpan look as he tapped his pencil made her smile. She watched television for some time and again tried to read, but couldn't stay focused on prehistoric Colorado. She finally fell asleep.

CHAPTER

9

Thanksgiving morning; Albany

THE PHONE RANG, and Tess bolted upright. It took three rings before she oriented herself. *Where am I? What's happened? It's the phone ringing, not my alarm clock.* She grabbed the receiver on the fourth ring. "Hello." Her voice cracked and sounded hoarse. She cleared her throat. "Hello." Much better.

"He's out of surgery, and I guess he's going to make it."

"Oh Eddie, that's wonderful. Thank God!"

"I did. I'll do it again later."

"So what did the doctor say?"

"The bullet missed his heart and other vital organs and hit soft tissue. I guess that means muscle, and it lodged in his body."

"Really? I don't know what that means exactly, but it's good news, right?"

"Yeah. Apparently, that means it must have been a small-caliber bullet."

"Oh, I see. I know nothing about guns or bullets."

"I'm not sure of the significance of that either, other than the obvious. If someone wanted to kill him, I mean really take no chances that he would survive, they would have used a weapon with more lethal force and fired more than once."

"Eddie, I have to tell you, I can't make any sense out of this. Somebody, who none of you recognize, shoots your brother, for a reason no one understands, in front of hundreds of people, and really isn't trying to kill him?" She turned and dangled her legs off the side of the bed as she swept her hair back from her face.

"Tess, I can't think right now. I'm so relieved, so tired, and so confused. Can you come here? Do you know where Albany Memorial is?"

"Yes, and no, but I'll find it. Give me thirty minutes to an hour."

"Okay. Room 338. Believe me it's a circus here, but you won't have any problem finding me."

Tess hung up and fell back on the pillow. She closed her eyes and thanked God for Frankie's survival. She sat up and looked at her portable traveling clock: 6:30. "Arghhh!" She threw off the blanket and headed for the bathroom.

A half hour later, as she dressed, she thought about the snow and threw open the curtains. It was white on top of white, with the largest flakes of snow that must have ever been recorded falling on top of that. *Where am I? And how am I going to drive in this or even get to my car?*

She sat down on the bed and called the front desk. The hotel clerk assured her this was an extraordinary storm and the weathermen hadn't forecast it. Tess asked him where at this hour could she buy boots, gloves, a proper coat, and a hat.

"The only place open at 7:00 a.m. is the Army Navy store across the street."

"Army Navy? Even on Thanksgiving?"

"Yes, the owner is a fanatic. I think I can see the lights on in the store now. They sell surplus stuff."

"Surplus from what?"

"Not sure. I guess the Army or Navy," he chuckled. "Anything Army surplus, like knives, canteens, canvas bags, and I'm pretty sure hats and coats."

Tess was silent for a moment, mulling the concept of dressing herself with boots and clothes worn by a soldier. "Ma'am, are you still there?"

"Yes. Yes I am. Can I get directions from you to Albany Memorial?"

He gave her directions and told her that someone would be coming in soon to shovel the walks and plow the parking lot. She thanked him and looked out the window. The snow had to be at least a foot deep. She could see that plows had cleared the street sometime during the night and left three- to four-foot-high mounds on either side of it. She could vaguely make out the sign of the store across the street, Capital Army Navy. She thought about the alternatives. She could call a cab. She could call Eddie for a ride. She could stay in the hotel room and wait for the lot to be cleared. No, no, and no. She changed back into the jeans she'd worn the night before, knowing that by the time she returned from the store they would be soaked, as would her cowboy boots, which were wholly unsuitable for this weather. She took an unused towel from the bathroom and fashioned a hat out of it, made a scarf from another towel, and grabbed her wallet.

When she opened the door, snow that had piled up high against it fell into the room, and the wind blew in another blast that covered her and part of the room. "Oh! Oh! Oh my God!" She gasped and waited a moment before stepping outside, and promptly sunk into knee-deep snow. She felt it inside her pant legs and grimaced. What should have been a two-minute walk to the store took fifteen minutes, but she finally pushed open the door to Capital Army Navy and drew in a long breath as she stepped inside. "Whew! It's unbelievable out there. Unbelievable!" She pulled towels off her head and neck and shook snow off her pants and coat, unaware that the only person in the store was a clerk standing behind a glass-covered counter that contained an array of Swiss Army knives, hunting knives, and specialized watches for outdoor use.

"Cold enough for you out there?"

Tess looked up and saw a gigantic man with an extraordinarily large chest and black, shoe-polished hair walking toward her. He seemed to be the size and shape of a refrigerator. As he came around the corner, Tess knew from her own experience working out in gyms that this man was a serious weightlifter. She thought he must go 260, maybe 270 pounds.

"Can I help you?" he asked politely.

"Yes, please. I'm a little underdressed for the North Pole."

"You're not from around here, are you?"

"No, I'm from Florida and visiting, but I didn't expect this." She waved her arm at the glass window shielding them from the blizzard.

"Disney World! I'd love to go there," he said.

"Right about now, I'd like to be there myself."

"Let me guess. We need to properly dress you for this inclement weather. Correct?"

"Uh-huh. I need everything. I thought the fall weather was going to be cool and brisk. I didn't plan for an epic snowstorm."

"Well, epic is a little strong." She handed him the wet towels, and he set them in the corner by the front door. "Pick those up on your way back to the hotel. I can see the logo on the bath towel."

"Uh-oh … yeah."

"Since I've been here, we've had some big ones, 1950 and 1964. The huge storms have heavy snow, ice, and drifting. But this time we didn't get ice, and the wind hasn't started drifting the snow yet, but I believe later today or tomorrow it will." He pursed his lips and narrowed his eyes, considering his forecast. "Okay, come on, let's get you equipped." He held out a hand the size of a ping-pong paddle and as thick as a double cheeseburger. "Aristotle. I'm Greek. Call me Ari."

"Tess." Tess shook his hand, or, more appropriately, saw her hand disappear momentarily into his. Her arm moved up and down involuntarily as Ari robustly greeted her. "I obviously want something that will be suitable for the weather, but I'm also hoping to be even the slightest bit fashionable."

Ari bellowed with laughter and turned around, slapping his leg. "Follow me." They walked past bins of stuff, camp shovels, dried food, camouflage clothing, canoes, canteens, camping cookware, fishing waders, and nails in every size imaginable. They walked to the back of the store, and Tess assumed the clothing was in the rear, perhaps because she saw a single changing room. *How many women buy this stuff?* There were rows and rows of boots, racks of coats, and bins the size of coffins filled with hats, gloves, and mittens. A dozen wooden seats, with armrests that looked very old, were bolted to the floor and cut the room in two.

"Have a seat. We'll start from the bottom up. I'm all yours unless we have other customers and then I'll have to tend the register, but I bet we'll get you set up before anyone else walks in."

"Yup." Tess nodded as she eyed one of the archaic wooden chairs curiously, then sat down.

"They're seats out of old airplanes," Aris said. "Cool, huh?"

"Yeah, they are."

"Okay. Wool socks. Green, rubber, insulated, waterproof boots that tie off at the mid-calf. A Navy peacoat, double-breasted and worn by the Navy for over 200 years. I've got the perfect hat for you, aviator with earflaps and lined with rabbit fur. You'll look a little like Amelia Earhart meets a US Marine infantryman in Korea in the middle of winter, but warm. Heavy-duty woolen mittens that will keep you warm even if wet. And lined ski pants. And, oh, a green woolen Army scarf to cover your face."

Tess felt her jaw drop and forced it closed as Ari busied himself gathering the items. From two aisles away, he asked, "Shoe size?"

"Women's eight." She realized her fashions options were slim to none, but these conditions were not to be trifled with or she'd literally freeze.

"I'll grab three pairs of woolen socks for you. Never know, you might be here for longer than you think."

Tess rolled her eyes.

As Ari collected the necessary items, Tess perused the hundreds, if not thousands of items in the store. One particular article caught her attention: a pair of four-foot-long, oblong-shaped, flat, wooden-framed objects that were affixed to the wall. They had rawhide stretched across the middle and were shellacked, apparently to make them last and maintain their shape. They almost looked like pieces of ancient artwork. As Ari came around the aisle, he saw her studying them. He glanced up at the wall. "Snowshoes. They keep an average person on top of deep snow and allow them to cover a considerable distance much quicker and easier. Native American. I've tried them, but I'm ... ah ... I'm too heavy, and I still drop through the snow like a hot knife through butter. Don't worry, you won't need them," he laughed, "unless you're going to be out there in the snow."

"Don't think so. I need a scraper for my windshield, too."

"Yup, got it."

Thirty minutes later, fully equipped for the Iditarod and relieved of two hundred dollars, Tess shoved her wallet into her back pocket.

"Hey, Ari, quick question."

He looked up from the cash register. "Shoot."

"What do you know about The Dirty Martini Club?"

"The Dirty Martini Club," he snickered.

"Yeah, I was invited to go there."

"Who are you meeting, a Mafioso?"

"Really?"

"The place is owned by, and is the local hangout for known, shall we say, criminal elements."

"I didn't know."

"Small time, wanna-be gangsters. Don't go there."

Tess stared pensively at Ari and pursed her lips. "Gangsters? Come on, really? We all saw *The Godfather*, but this is Albany, and we're talking about a little dive. I'm not sure I believe it."

"Well, you don't have to take my word for it. Do your own research, but I'm telling you, around here, people know what they know."

Tess rubbed her eyes. "I can't believe this. Between the arctic snowstorm and all the rest of this, it's like I'm having a bad dream. Hey, thanks for everything and the heads up."

She opened the door and glanced back at Ari. He pointed a finger at her. "Be careful out there, and let me know if there's anything else I can help you with."

Tess smiled, walked out the door, and trudged back across the street to the hotel, at least feeling pretty good about her new gear. After depositing the towels in the bathroom, hanging her wet clothes in the closet, and straightening the room, she stopped for a minute in front of the mirror and had to smile at her appearance. The Abominable Snowman.

She made it to the car and began brushing at least a half foot of new snow off the windshield with her new scraper. It seemed lighter than the previous snow for some reason. She wondered if that meant the temperature was dropping. At least the wind hadn't started blowing. Not yet anyway. Didn't know what that portended either.

She started the car and felt warmer; the elements seemed far less consequential now that she was dressed properly. She heard an engine being gunned and glanced over her shoulder to see that a pickup truck with a blade on the front end had pulled into the lot. The truck's first run covered no more than twenty or thirty feet before it slowed from snow that reached the hood. She concluded that it was going to take awhile to push all the snow to the end of the lot.

A few minutes later, the plow had cleared a path for her to get out, but as she drove to the exit of the lot, she was stopped by a three-foot-high barrier of snow left by the plow that had cleared the street. She got out of her car and saw that the plowed snow was thick and crusty—and impassable. She turned and waved at the pickup truck. The driver waved at her and headed in her direction, plowing a pathway toward her. When he got within a few feet of Tess, he rolled his window down and said, "Hang on, I'll get you out. But in that car, I hope you don't have far to go."

"I don't, and thank-you for your help."

He made a circle and headed back at the exit, gaining speed. He hit the ridge of snow, and his truck rode halfway up and over it. Several runs later, he'd cleared an exit path for her to get onto the street. *Ridiculous,* she thought. *No, insane.*

She pulled onto State Street and turned left on Albany Post Road. Less than two miles and thirty minutes later, she turned onto Northern Boulevard and into Albany Memorial. *Enough! This is so awful.* She parked the car in a cleared parking lot and trudged into the hospital lobby.

10

SHE PULLED OFF her coat, hat, and oversize mittens, and clomped and swished to the elevator in her green boots and ski pants, feeling a little silly. She exited on the third floor and walked to the nursing station. Before she could say a word, the nurse on duty behind the counter pointed at one of the hallways, which were like spokes on a bicycle wheel all emanating from the nurses' station and going in half a dozen directions. Tess nodded and walked down the hallway to a lounge area where she saw Eddie, Joey, and Teresa standing in the center of the room. Tess walked to Eddie and hugged him, his arms barely moving.

"You must be exhausted," she said.

"I am, and you look like you just arrived from Fairbanks."

"You may have noticed the snow. It's like Alaska."

"Actually, I knew it was snowing but I didn't realize we were getting a storm coming off the Great Lakes. Uncommon this early in the year."

"Huh, I guess so," Tess mumbled, then turned and hugged Teresa. "There are no words for this. I'm so sorry. If there is anything I can do, just tell me."

Teresa closed her eyes and leaned into Tess's embrace. Tess was so much taller than her that her head came to rest on Tess's chest, like an adult hugging a child. "Okay, now. Okay. I'm sure we can sort this out. It's going to be fine."

Tess was beginning to think it was going to be anything but fine, anything but normal. This whole situation wasn't normal. She looked at Joey, who immediately averted his eyes, which struck her as slightly offensive, but perhaps he was just shy. *Nobody in this family is shy. Not one of them could even spell shy. It must be because I'm an outsider. Fair enough.* She pulled back just slightly from Teresa and held her face a few inches from her. "You're going to be all right now. Come on, let's all go downstairs and have some coffee. You're probably starving."

Eddie said, "That sounds good." Teresa nodded in agreement. Tess looked at Joey. "Would you like to join us?"

"No, I really should get going. Eddie, I'll be back after I get a little sleep." He hugged Teresa and Eddie and touched Tess on the shoulder before walking to the elevators. Tess watched him get on the elevator before glancing at Frankie's room, where she saw Tiziana sitting in a chair by the bed. A uniformed cop sat in a chair by the door, staring back at her. She knew not to ask about the cop, at least not here, not now.

"I think the cafeteria is in the basement. Let's go have some breakfast, shall we?" Tess said.

They joined the line at the cafeteria, pulling plastic trays off a stack. Eddie filled a plate with eggs, hash browns, and sausage, and placed a large mug of coffee on the tray. Teresa chose a cinnamon bun and coffee. Tess inventoried the offerings, trying not to seem like a picky eater, but she wasn't about to fill herself with a whole lot of fat and a ton of calories. Too hard to work off. She slid a bowl of oatmeal, a banana, and coffee onto her tray. They sat at a table in the corner away from the doctors dressed in blue scrubs sitting in pairs and from the tables filled with groups of nurses in white uniforms engaged in animated conversation. They sat in silence while Eddie devoured his breakfast and Teresa nibbled at the icing on her cinnamon roll. Tess realized that she was hungry, and the oatmeal and the banana hit the spot.

With elbows on the table, she sipped her coffee and stared at Eddie. "So what do we know about Frankie. He's going to be okay, right?"

Eddie answered. "He is. He's really lucky. I mean, if you call getting shot and not dying lucky. The surgeon said it was inches away from killing him. The bullet, I mean."

"Right." Tess nodded. She figured it was her place to be there, be supportive, and do anything to help, but not ask a lot of questions and not make any judgments. She was, however, forming judgments faster than the pages of a book turning in a high wind. "Your parents left." *Framed as a statement and not a question,* she thought.

"Yeah, everyone left but us, about an hour ago. Everyone was exhausted, and when the doctor told us he was going to make it, my mom really broke down. Dad took her home to rest for a few hours."

Tess didn't know what to say. It was all too strange. A baby hadn't been born, a voluntary operation hadn't been successfully performed, and cops don't stand outside the room of a patient. "Oh, I can only imagine," she said. "How long will it be before Frankie can go home?" A question without a lot of depth, keeping the conversation alive.

Eddie sat back in his chair and blew out a long breath. "Maybe a week," he said. "Look, Tess, you're probably wondering what's going on here. If I could tell you, I would, but I just don't know." His voice seemed defensive in tone.

Tess nodded and Eddie kept talking. "Frankie doesn't have an enemy in the world. He's funny, he's devoted to Tiziana, and he's hardworking." He started scratching his head vigorously.

Teresa grabbed his arm. "Stop that."

Eddie continued, "I haven't been told why he was the target, why there is a cop at the room, or anything else. Did you see anything on the news, Tess?"

Tess shook her head, no. She put her napkin on her plate and her coffee cup on the table, and leaned her chin on her folded hands. After a few seconds of silence, she sat back and said quietly, "Eddie, you and Teresa are very tired. This is incredibly challenging and extraordinary. May I suggest that you both get some sleep? It will help clear your minds and take the edge off the raw nerves."

Eddie exhaled deeply. "I know I'm tired, Tess." His voice carried an edge. "But I'm going back upstairs to sit with Tiziana for a while before I go back to my parents' place."

Tess wondered why he didn't mention joining her at the hotel. She was staying there because she had told him she would be uncomfortable staying at his parent's home; in fact, she was uncomfortable even being around them, although she hadn't said that. But she thought it was understood that she and Eddie would spend time, if not nights, together at the hotel. If a couple of hours' sleep was what he needed, then why not spend them with her in the relative calm and quiet of a hotel room?

"Alright," she said quietly.

Teresa took a deep breath and asked, "Tess, can you give me a ride to my parents' house? I can call a cab if you don't want to drive in this weather. I'll understand."

"Really the roads aren't too bad, at least not yet. So, sure. Let's get you home, and I'll come back and stay with Eddie.

Eddie, is there anything I can retrieve for you from your parents' house, anything you need me to do?"

"No, I'll be fine. Thanks."

They left the table and went back upstairs so Teresa could get her purse and belongings. She went into Frankie's room, leaving Eddie and Tess alone for a moment.

"I'll be back in an hour or so," Tess said and hugged him. She'd seen Eddie in extraordinarily stressful situations, in crisis, and even in danger, and he hadn't seemed as distraught as he did right now. Frankie was going to recover, but Eddie wasn't holding up. He had the weight of the world on his shoulders. Tess could not think of a single thing to say to him, so she stood there awkwardly in her arctic garb, wondering what would happen next in this fiasco.

"Okay, I'm ready." Teresa walked out of the room and kissed Eddie on the cheek. "See you in a while."

Tess touched his face and said, "I'll be back as quick as I can."

He nodded and walked into Frankie's room.

☙☙☙

They took the elevator to the main floor and walked from the building through a covered area into the hospital parking garage. As they left, Tess paid the attendant $2.00 at the gate and she pulled onto Northern Boulevard and back into the unrelenting snowstorm. To the credit of the city maintenance crews, the streets were relatively passable. They had kept two lanes in each direction open, but the piles to either side of them were beginning to resemble hillsides. The tops of parking meters poked up through the snow like little mile markers on a highway. A white crusted residue of salt glazed the street, perhaps keeping fresh flakes from turning to ice.

They passed hundred-year-old store fronts that had once been thriving businesses but now appeared to be on hard times, with many seemingly vacant. A pool hall with a flashing neon sign, two pawn shops, and a thrift shop stood among nondescript buildings that may have once been warehouses with storefronts. A stately granite building that might have been a nineteenth-century hotel had a sign advertising rooms for rent by the week. And there were numerous vacant lots where the owners had apparently given up any notion of constructing new buildings and instead rented parking places. On another block, rising above the commercial riffraff, were newer buildings that housed what she assumed were government offices.

They stopped at a light. "Everything is so deserted," said Tess. "There isn't a car on the streets."

"I'd almost forgotten. This is Thanksgiving," said Teresa. "This is a hell of a storm, though. How much have we gotten?"

"I'm not sure, but I bet it's close to two feet, maybe more by now. That reminds me, I have to call home and wish everyone a happy Thanksgiving."

Tess was watching the wipers clear the windshield when she noticed in the rearview mirror a large black vehicle pull up close behind them. The vehicle was high profile and close enough to the back of her car that she could only see the grill.

"Geez, are you close enough?" she said throwing up her hands.

Teresa turned her head to look back, and as the light changed, Tess started through the intersection. The vehicle stayed on her tail.

"Oh man!" Teresa yelled.

Tess accelerated but the vehicle stayed inches from her bumper. She peeked in the rearview mirror and still could only see the big silver grill. She put her hands in the two and ten o'clock position and leaned forward into the wheel.

"What's the deal?" Tess bellowed as the vehicle bumped them hard enough to jerk her head forward. "Are they nuts?"

She stared into the rearview mirror trying to gain perspective, and then a second vehicle pulled out of an alley running perpendicular to the street and stopped in the middle of the street. She jammed her foot on the brake, and her car slid sideways, turning almost parallel to the vehicle in front of her. The big black vehicle stopped inches from Tess's door, making it impossible for her to open it. Before she could react, the passenger door was jerked open, and someone violently pulled Teresa from the car. Teresa screamed, and Tess tried to open her door anyway, banging it into the black monster's chrome grill. Tess slid into the passenger seat to get out of the car, but that door was quickly slammed shut. Before she could open it, she saw two men wearing ski masks throw Teresa into the backseat of their vehicle. Their car doors slammed as she got out, leaving her standing there helplessly.

Tess threw up her arms in panic. She turned to see the vehicle that had pinned her into her seat back up and swerve back into the oncoming lane and take off in the opposite direction. The roar of engines and the cold mechanical sound of shifting gears and acceleration threw her into a momentary lapse of focus. She was stunned, unable to move or think. Her hands were trembling. *I should have looked at the license plates or the make and model of the vehicles.*

The smell of exhaust permeated the air around her car like poisonous gas. There were no parked cars and no pedestrians.

There was no one, only a sea of white covering everything. She felt the wind begin to blow, like the awakening of a silent, foreboding, and menacing giant. The wind would make everything more dangerous, more threatening, and possibly more frightening.

She heard a clanking sound and saw an orange plow turn at the corner. She stepped into the middle of the street and waved it to a stop.

CHAPTER

11

A POLICE OFFICER arrived and parked at the corner, with lights flashing, to divert any cars that might want to drive by. A second car arrived minutes later, and while one policeman took a statement from Tess, another took photos of the scene, which didn't amount to much since there were no skid marks and new fallen snow had covered the vehicles' tracks. She was asked to sit in the back of the police cruiser and wait for a detective, who showed up later and asked about the details of what had happened. It was more than an hour before Tess was brought to the police station, a large, nondescript edifice that had probably been built decades earlier and now looked grimy, gray, and weathered. It made her feel even more powerless and depressed.

She was ushered into a large waiting room and told she could use the phone but not leave the room. She called the hospital and to her amazement, she was connected to Frankie's room. Tiziana picked up, and Tess blurted out, "They took her. They pulled her from the car. I'm so sorry, but it happened so fast I couldn't do anything. I'm so sorry."

"Tess, what are you talking about?"

"They took Teresa!"

"Oh God, this just keeps getting worse. Eddie!"

Eddie got on the phone, and Tess briefly recounted what had happened before a detective tapped her on the shoulder and motioned for her to follow him. Exasperated, she said to Eddie, "Come here to the station, please."

"I'm on my way."

Tess followed the officer into a large room that held a dozen desks lined up in symmetrical order. Each one was identical and, except for the different stacks of folders and files, was indistinguishable. The room seemed old, smelled like stale coffee and cigarettes, and was poorly lit by incandescent lights hung too high from the ceiling. The room buzzed with conversations as detectives interviewed people seated adjacent to them. She was led to a desk where a plainclothes detective stood up to greet her.

"Morning, Miss Kincaid. I'm Detective Keibler. Have a seat," he offered with a slight wave of his hand.

"Thank-you. Listen, I really don't want to waste your time, but I already told you people everything I know, which isn't much."

"I understand, but this is procedure," the detective answered. "I just want to review everything one more time."

An hour later, Tess was still sitting in the same hard, wooden chair, thinking this was so cliché: the balding middle-aged, paunchy, no-nonsense detective with his stale, smelly coffee and half-eaten doughnut on the desk. *This is another scene right out of a television crime show. I'm living in an episode of* Kojak. Several feet away, another detective was interviewing a young bedraggled-looking male, perhaps twenty years old. Tess had overheard part of that conversation, which apparently involved the possession of narcotics. The man's legs bounced up and down so fast they seemed to vibrate.

Tess had tried in vain to get up and go to the waiting room to find Eddie, but the detective wouldn't allow it. "Lady, you're not leaving until I get a full finished statement."

She reviewed the statement she had made verbally and then had written out in longhand. She handed it to the detective, who scanned it quickly and took a gulp of the old coffee. He looked at Tess. "So, just to be clear, you can't really describe the vehicles involved nor did you see any of the faces of the perps?"

"Yes, that's correct. I can't tell you anything about the vehicles except that they were large and black. I'm sorry, but I just couldn't think and react fast enough."

"Understandable."

"This has to be the same people who shot her brother at The Dirty Martini. It's all tied together, right?"

"Miss Kincaid, I can't discuss an ongoing investigation. I need your contact information and where you're staying. I need to also tell you that we're going to want to talk to you again as this investigation develops, so I need you to understand that you cannot leave town for at least several days. Are we clear about that?"

"Yes. Can you tell me what you're going to do about protecting the other family members? I mean, you have the one cop at the hospital, but what about everyone else?"

"No, I can't tell you what the department is doing, and that officer is off-duty. He isn't working for us right now. He's working for the Spinozzas."

"Oh … Oh, he is?"

"Yes. Here's my card. If you hear anything, see anything, or need to talk to me, you have my direct line. Don't hesitate to call. You're free to go."

He stood up and walked across the room, leaving Tess sitting there feeling like a lost child. She stood up, slipped Keibler's card in her pocket, exited the pit area, and walked into the waiting room.

Y Y Y

Eddie was sitting on a bench, his chin resting on his hand. He looked up and walked to Tess, shaking his head.

"Tess, I'm sorry. I'm so sorry. I should have seen this coming. I should have driven Teresa home. I should have been there. I should—"

"Eddie, stop! You would have been better at the wheel, but then maybe *we* would have been ... taken or something worse. There was no way to stop this. They had the advantage of apparently knowing my vehicle, where we were going, and the element of surprise with overwhelming force."

"Jesus, help us. If they hurt her, then I will kill all of them."

"Eddie, come on, let's get out of here. You can't say stuff like that in here. I think it's time you go home to your family anyway. You've got to talk to them. This is now a police matter."

Before he could say anything more, she guided him out of the office and into the main lobby. "Eddie, do you feel like it's safe to drive to your parents' house, or do you need someone from the police to come and escort you there?"

"I'm fine. I need a gun."

"No! You don't." Tess felt a wave of panic rush over her. *A gun!* This was spinning out of control. Eddie was losing it and acting oddly, and she understood, but he wasn't a part of this. He wasn't prepared for this. She wasn't prepared for this. Who would be? You're visiting for Thanksgiving, and one family member is gunned down in a public place and another kidnapped in broad daylight.

"What are we going to do? What is your family going to do? Does somebody have a plan?"

Eddie shrugged. "I don't know. I just don't know."

"I'm thinking I should go back to the hospital," Tess said. "Maybe I can give Tiziana a break or at least sit with her for a while. There's nothing we can do to help the police with Teresa. I mean we can't drive around in a blizzard looking for her. Besides, somebody must know what's going on. Won't they demand something like a ransom?"

Eddie seemed demoralized and disgusted. He answered sharply, "I have no idea what anyone wants. Nobody has told me anything. I can't believe we would just wait. I'm going to talk to my father."

"Your father? You think he knows what's going on?"

"He has to know something."

"Hmm. Okay." She blew out a long breath. "Call me if anyone needs me to do anything or if you hear anything. Go to your parent's house and get some sleep, and I'll talk to you soon." She reached for his hand, and they hugged.

She watched him leave the building, suddenly realizing that she'd just sent him away and didn't have her vehicle. The police had towed Tess's rental car to the lot adjacent to the station. But she learned that it was not being impounded, so she was free to take it. She retrieved the keys from a police officer at a desk in the basement.

Tess walked into the holding yard and discovered what Ari meant about the combination of wind and snow. With the wind blowing much harder now, the snow was now drifting on the streets, the sidewalks, the cars, and even in the covered areas. As she made her way to her car, she flashed on scenes of lifeless, bitter cold Siberia depicted in the movie *Doctor Zhivago*. It was turning into a death struggle to move anywhere.

It was all so frustrating, but nothing compared to what the Spinozzas must be going through. *What in the world is going on?* She couldn't leave this frozen wasteland, couldn't help Eddie, couldn't help Teresa, and was in a virtual blackout of information—and she was sick of it all. *What kind of way to live is this? Who kidnaps a young woman for some game of intrigue that involves some business interest or vendetta or who knows what? I'm sick of it all. Just sick of it all.* She started the car and scraped windows for five minutes in a losing battle with the elements. Finally she got in the car, threw the scraper in the back seat, and put the car in drive.

The ice beneath the tires crunched as she drove onto the deserted street. With the wind blowing snow from the piles along the streets and the continuing snowfall, the plows weren't keeping up. The Malibu lost traction with even the slightest acceleration and slid sideways before moving forward. And the wind whipped snow off the roofs of buildings, reducing visibility to nearly zero. The ten-block trip back to the hospital took her a quarter of an hour, and she was very grateful to find a parking space inside the hospital's garage, which provided at least some protection.

As she made her way to the entrance, she felt some comfort that no matter how bad the wind and snow were, she was warm and dry. She reminded herself to call home, where her mother and grandmother were probably busy in the kitchen cooking a turkey and setting the table.

Ari had made the right choices for her clothing, but she felt anything but safe and secure in general. Maybe they'd take her next. She stomped herself free of snow in the lobby and swished to the elevator, catching herself looking over her shoulder and down the corridor.

    ***

A different off-duty cop was now sitting at the entrance to Frankie's room. He scanned a list of names and waved her in. *Some security. He doesn't know me from Adam.* Tiziana was sitting in a chair next to Frankie's bed with her eyes closed. Frankie had tubes in his nose, an IV attached to his arm, and wires connected to a monitor. He was sleeping or resting. He didn't open his eyes. Tess gently tapped Tiziana on the arm, and she sat up with a start.

"Tess! Oh my God, has anything else happened? Has anyone heard from Teresa or the Cuchinellis?"

"Ah … no. Not that I know of, but I'm completely out of the loop. Who or what are the Cuchinellis?"

Tiziana looked puzzled and sat up in her chair. In a quiet voice, she said, "You don't know anything, do you?"

"Apparently not. I'm from the Midwest. I play golf and go to barbecues and have turkey with my family on Thanksgiving. I don't live like this. No one ever gets shot or kidnapped!" Tess caught herself sounding judgmental and derisive. "I'm sorry Tiziana. May I buy you some breakfast or lunch? Maybe you can enlighten me a little."

"No, I'm not hungry, but let's go into the waiting room. I think he's resting pretty comfortably."

"Looks like it. Everything okay?" Tess nodded at Frankie.

"They say he's going to be okay."

They sat down in the empty waiting room on cushioned chairs separated by a coffee table littered with old magazines, newspapers, and stained paper coffee cups. The wooden arm on Tess's chair stuck to her sleeve. She grimaced. The room needed to be cleaned.

12

TIZIANA BIT HER LIP and stared at Tess for a few moments before beginning. "Tess, I like you. You're honest, straightforward, and you seem genuinely nice. The only reason I'm talking to you right now is because you still have time and a choice."

Tess was confused. *Time and a choice. A choice about what?* She didn't interrupt.

"You have no idea who the Cuchinellis are, and probably only a vague and inaccurate perception of the real Spinozzas. I know Eddie doesn't, so I need to ask you something."

"Okay," Tess said hesitantly. She felt a wave of anxiety wash over her.

"I need you to promise me that you will never tell anyone, ever, about this conversation. It would seriously damage my relationship with my husband and with my in-laws. I can't tell you how bad it would be for me and Frankie. Can you make that promise?"

"I can keep a secret. Believe me, you can trust me." Tess nodded an affirmation and continued, "I'm not sure why Eddie and I aren't having this conversation, or why we haven't had it before now."

"I can answer that. First of all, Eddie has always been protected, shielded, and absolutely off-limits from his father."

"Off-limits?"

"Connie wouldn't allow Vinnie to, ah, recruit him."

"Recruit him for what?"

"You have to understand how all this works. Eddie's father is as close to a tyrant as you can get. He's old world and yet American. He believes in old-world traditions and American business realities. He's in between the two cultures."

"Not sure what you're saying here."

"Connie allowed her family to be like the rest of them, the Spinozzas." Tiziana's tone dripped with disgust as if she'd just gulped sour milk. She held up her index finger and sniffled. "But in one case, the one case I think that defines her as a strong woman and someone to be respected, she drew the line, and that was with Eddie. She said no to her husband, that Eddie was not going to be involved in the family business at any level like his brothers."

"Involving him in the family business?"

"That's right, or at least involving him in the way they do business. They don't import olive oil and anchovies and crap like that as their primary source of income. They run the trash hauling business in Albany County without competition."

"So?"

"So, it's not because they wouldn't have competition. They get a contract from the county every year for a monopoly, and they charge a significantly higher rate for people to have their garbage hauled away."

"How? I mean how do they get that contract?"

"You really don't know how they work, do you?"

"I guess I'm just a small-town girl, so maybe I don't know how this works."

"Let me start at the beginning. Eddie and Frankie's grandfather was born in Sicily."

"Eddie told me that."

He grew up near Palermo, which is like the center of the Cosa Nostra world. The Mafia." Tiziana arched her eyebrows. "As a kid, he played with old man Cuchinelli and a couple of other kids with names like Gambino and Genovese. I'm not saying those people specifically because it's all so secret, but you know what I mean. You know those names."

"You mean the names of the people who run the major crime families in New York. I'm familiar with them. They're in the paper all the time with stories about some kind of war that's going on between them."

"Right. They are. Sixty or seventy years ago, they all came to New York, Chicago, and Philadelphia from Sicily. Something like that, anyway. But there wasn't room in New York for all of them. The Spinozzas and the Cuchinellis had to find someplace else to start their racketeering and bootlegging. So, they 'got'"—she held up her fingers to form imaginary quote signs—"Albany. They were spin-offs, small-time secondary branches of the New York families. I'm not going to sit here and pretend like I know very much, but I know a little.

"I know this sounds like I'm telling you the script from *The Godfather*, but I'm not. This is about penny-ante mobsters that don't kill people and all that stuff. There's no Luca Brasi and all that. But Eddie's grandfather called on his connections in New York decades ago to bribe and coerce Albany County into an exclusive contract for trash hauling. The Cuchinellis got the concrete or cement business with the city and county in the same way. I don't know those details either, but everybody was happy for a long time. All through the 1940s, '50's, and '60's, life was good."

Tess interjected, "But the Spinozzas own a food business, right? I thought they do import olive oil and stuff like that."

"They do. That started at the same time, and that was the"— the quote fingers again—"'legitimate' part. That's how they got all those excessive profits from charging people, say, twenty dollars a month to haul garbage when at the same time for the same service outside the city, it was ten dollars. With that many customers, over that amount of time, it was like printing money. Think about it. Twenty-five thousand customers, paying an extra ten dollars a month is a quarter of a million dollars a month, or millions a year. Subtract out what they paid city officials and the union officials who are in charge of the people who pick up the garbage, and you still have a ton of money."

"I'm following you."

"They laundered it into legitimate business, like catering, the bakery, and the stores. The Cuchinellis did the same thing in the construction business with all the public projects over the last thirty or forty years. Except old man Cuchinelli is kind of a pervert and couldn't help himself when it came to some of the sick stuff, like prostitution and loan sharking and then drugs. His sons are greedy and sickos, too. You saw them last night, right?"

"Yes, I did, but to be honest they didn't look that much different than the Spinozzas."

"They are different. The Cuchinelli stories are sickening. But all this is just standard Mafia stuff. The real point is this. Old man Cuchinelli and Eddie's grandfather knew how they ran each other's businesses, and it was okay with both of them. They figured, hey, I grease this palm and they rub my back and nobody gets hurt. To them, coming from the old country, it was normal, and for the most part it was just garden-variety graft and corruption. Nobody got hurt.

"But the sons, the next generation of Spinozzas, Eddie's father Vinnie, and the Cuchinellis wanted more. They wanted more of everything. The Cuchinellis problem is that there aren't that many public buildings being constructed, so they don't have cash flow. Acting as pimps and petty loan sharks is dirty business and not as easy or lucrative. The drug business got away from them, too. It stays in the ghetto, at least it does in Albany, for now."

"I get it. So this is about taking the Spinozza garbage contract."

"Exactly. At least part of it. They have been having meetings. Can't imagine how that goes. The old men live like they are working-class men. Eddie's grandfather dresses like a guy who shines shoes, his house is a small ranch, and his car has got to be ten years old. Cuchinelli is the same. It's the next group, it's Vinnie, that lives in a big house, drives a fancy car, and lives the lavish lifestyle. They are, at least for the most part, running the show. Frankie and two of his brothers and cousins work like they are employed at IBM or GM. They sell stuff and do accounting and all that business stuff like a million other big company people."

"And Eddie?"

"His mother said no, never. Eddie was never even aware or a part of anything in the family business. He had a paper route and then a job at a grocery store as a teenager. Then he left home right out of high school, so he was never part of any of it."

"Tiziana, if you don't mind me asking, how do you know so much? I thought everything was hush-hush. Did Frankie tell you all of this?"

"Yes. Yes, because he wants to get out before it's too late. Move to Chicago or Phoenix and start a new life where his kids and me are not part of this. Now it's too late."

"Did they mean to kill Frankie? And why him?"

"Who knows?"

"Is Teresa really in danger, or is she just being held as a pawn?"

"That part I don't know. A million years ago, in a turf war in New York, Eddie's grandfather was kidnapped and held for the same kind of deal. He was released when the mob got what they wanted, so maybe he thinks Teresa can be used the same way. I mean—"

"I know what you mean."

"But the Cuchinellis are thugs, and this isn't 1910, so I wouldn't be surprised if they hurt her, like cut off her hair, then a toe, or a finger."

"Oh my God! Will the police help?"

"Depends on who is paying them and whose pocket they are in. They hate dealing with this stuff. There are never any busts, no one is ever indicted, and their bosses are the ones taking bribes."

"You mean the police chief?"

"I don't know about him specifically, but maybe some of the higher-ups."

Tess stood up and walked over to a nearby counter. She sloshed the coffee around in the glass coffeepot and concluded that it must have been made by the night shift. It looked toxic. She returned to her chair. "Tiziana, I absolutely believe everything you've told me despite the fact that Eddie has a different version of his family history."

"When did you talk to him about this?"

"Two years ago. You know, he was the pilot of the small plane that, ah, transported me from a tournament to a tree." She cracked a smile. "I don't want to go over all the gory details, but after we crashed and we were sitting in the tree for about twelve hours, he started talking about his life and his family history. And it's a very different story. He spoke about an indigent immigrant's life, escaping the crushing poverty and lack of opportunity in a caste-like society in Sicily, and coming to America. He talked about his grandfather basically being abandoned as a young child and having to make his own way in New York. How he overcame great obstacles to find steady employment, buy a home, and raise a family. His children would have unlimited opportunities compared to what he had in Sicily. It's a wonderful story of the American dream."

"That's true except he left out the part about the dark underbelly of the Mafia," said Tiziana. "He traveled a route that included breaking all the rules and laws, for that matter. He used his contacts from the syndicate to bribe officials, he hasn't paid taxes, and he's hidden everything he's done. They do that, you know. The syndicate never talks or reveals anything to outsiders of, for the most part, even the women in the family. I think that's overplayed a little. They know a lot more than they let on. I'm talking about the wives. Connie knows. She's lived in this life for thirty years."

"But now it's gotten nasty and violent," said Tess.

"Yes, and to my knowledge, for the first time. The Spinozzas have never been involved in any kind of violence, no murdering people, no kidnapping, and no *Godfather* stuff. In a lot of ways, they are lightweights. I guess that's a good thing. But this new round of tactics is bad. Desperate. And the next generation has a different code of ethics than the old guys from Sicily. The old guys would never target anyone but men directly involved in the business. No women or children."

"Well, that's changed."

"I've heard his grandfather talk, and he would never have gotten involved in the drug trade, either. His version of the world is about surviving in business. It's business, and he can go to church every week and think that he's done good things for his family."

"Ah ... that's a little different. It's a lot different than church back home in Illinois. There's a lot of things that are different. But I have a question that's bugging me. Why would the Spinozzas have a meeting, a negotiation about this garbage thing, and then all meet at the Dirty Martini Club last night?"

"That's bugging me too," said Tiziana. "I think it's a disconnect. I don't think the old guys were aware or would ever consider shooting a family member. I think old man Cuchinelli and Eddie's grandfather may be just as stunned as everyone else. I believe this is Eddie's father, Eddie's uncles, and their Cuchinelli counterparts. I'm afraid it may be coming to a point where neither side will compromise and give in. Neither of the old men is totally in control anymore, and there's a vacuum as to who is in charge. A standoff. I don't think there is the same orderly structure."

"So, if nothing has been resolved, both sides are still looking for an advantage, so to speak. The stakes are pretty high, and, worst of all, the police aren't doing squat," said Tess. "What happens next? And what happens to Teresa?"

Tiziana sighed and sat back. She shook her head in disillusionment. "Don't know."

CHAPTER

13

TESS AND TIZIANA continued talking for a while longer before they both succumbed to fatigue and fell asleep on the couches in the waiting room. Several hours later, Tess awakened with a start and sat up abruptly. She shook her head to clear the cobwebs and walked to the restroom to rinse her face with cold water. By the time she'd returned, Tiziana was in Frankie's room. Tess quietly slipped into the room and stood behind Tiziana and rubbed her shoulders as she studied Frankie. "He seems to be resting pretty well. They must have his pain meds right. Is there anything I can do for you?"

"No, I'm good, but thanks."

Tess heard a rustling sound and looked over her shoulder at Connie standing inside the doorway. It was like a blast of arctic air, similar to what she felt when she opened her hotel door the day before. The expression on Connie's face was severe and communicated clearly that Tess was unwelcome and out of place, an interloper. It was the same look that Tess would have given her dog, Stuck, if he'd relieved himself on the kitchen floor. Tess composed herself and stood up straight. She inched her chin up slightly and said, "Good morning. I was just leaving. How are you?"

"Fine." It was like an icicle dripping.

Tess stared at her for just a moment too long and knew. She knew then without a doubt that this woman may not have been involved in a single business transaction, a single illegal act, but she presided over a galactic-size cover-up. She'd sold her soul for the lifestyle, the possessions, and the family by looking the other way. She was as rotten and hollow as the rest of them, and her capacity to justify, overlook, and rationalize was disgusting. Tess slid past Connie and headed for the elevator.

She walked through the garage and climbed into her car. As she waited for the car to warm up and the defroster to clear the windshield, she tried to construct a plan. She knew she was way out of her element—a galaxy away. She knew that all of this drama was none of her business, but for the part that involved her relationship with Eddie and her deep concern for Teresa. Her mother's words about marriage weighed heavily on her: "You marry the family." But reaching decisions about the future and her relationship with Eddie going forward had to wait. They weren't nearly as crucial or urgent as doing whatever she could to help Teresa. Teresa had become more than a future sister-in-law; she was a good and loyal friend. She was bright, funny, practical, and feisty. Tess enjoyed her company and her sarcasm, although Eddie was the target of most of it. She couldn't just leave, get on a plane, and go home to Florida. It wasn't in her nature, and besides she now had become involved with the police. She had to stay, but by God, she wasn't going to sit in the hospital or the hotel and wait for something to happen. She put the car in drive and headed for the exit.

The entire landscape was white—blowing snow, mounds of plowed snow, drifts exceeding four feet, snow-packed streets … and it seemed to be getting worse, if that was possible. Parked cars looked like moguls on a ski hill. Icicles that looked like glass daggers dangled from ledges and downspouts. It all made her feel insignificant and vulnerable. The plows had officially lost their battle, so Tess had to put up her own battle as she navigated the rough stretches of road.

As she pulled into the visitor parking lot of the police station, she hit a two-foot wall of plowed snow that stopped her car. She put it in reverse and heard the whining buzz of the spinning tires. She put in drive and accelerated. More spinning. She turned and was about to try again when she saw the flashing lights of a police cruiser a few feet behind her. She opened her door as a uniformed officer did the same. "Put it in neutral and I'll give you a little nudge," he called out. Tess waved and followed his instructions. She felt a slight thump, and the car jumped over the ridge and into the plowed lot. She opened her window, waved, and parked.

She entered the station and stopped at the dispatcher's desk. "Is Detective Keibler in?" she asked. The dispatcher waved her to a row of chairs, and Tess sat on a discolored green, plastic seat that had lost its vertical spring and banged against the wall behind her. Keibler came out and stood in front of Tess so close that she couldn't stand up. *An aggressive posture.* Talking down to her, literally, he said, "Miss Kincaid, what can I do for you?"

"Is there any news? Anything?"

"No, we haven't located her. At this time, I'll tell you we're looking at some leads, some information, but nothing I can discuss. Not sure why *you're* here."

Tess was just as frustrated and becoming irritated. "What *can* you tell me?"

"Nothing at this time."

Tess felt the color rising in her cheeks. His attitude was dismissive and rude. She started to snarl but stopped herself. *It won't help.*

In a tone meant for a parent speaking to a child who'd spilled milk on the kitchen floor, he said, "It would very helpful if you could give us any more information on the vehicles involved, but since you have no recollection, we're really looking for a needle in a haystack, aren't we?"

She snapped. "I don't have a loss of memory!" Her voice carried through the lobby, ricocheting off the walls. "I didn't see the vehicles or I'd remember them. Why don't you visit the Cuchinellis? That's who took her, and you know it. That's where she is, and you know it!" Tess snarled. Keibler grabbed Tess by the arm in a strong grip, lifted her out of the chair, and pulled her through the doors into the pit of desks now occupied by several detectives talking on the phone and interviewing people.

He seethed as he walked her to his desk. With clenched teeth, he said, "You shut your damned mouth right now. I don't know who the hell you think you are, but I'm about to throw your ass in jail. And I don't even need a reason." They reached his desk, and he pushed her into a chair next to it. "I don't know what you think you know, waltzing in here from wherever the hell you're from and telling me how to do my job. You don't know anything, and I suggest if you'd like to get out of here in the near future, you keep out of this, go back to your hotel, and let us do our jobs!" His lip curled, and he glowered at her.

She took a deep breath and waved her hand. "Okay, I'm sorry. You're right, I don't know anything, and I am getting into something I know nothing about. But I'm really afraid that something is going to happen to Teresa. And there seems to be nothing anyone can do, nothing I can do, and time is ticking away."

He didn't respond. He removed his shoulder harness and gun and opened the top drawer of his desk. He stared at Tess as he dropped them in with a thunking sound. *Another aggressive gesture.* "Look, I can't discuss this with you, and even if I could, I wouldn't. I suggest you go somewhere and wait for us to call you. You'll be out of Albany in twenty-four to forty-eight hours, I hope. Don't even think about *doing anything* because whatever you do, *it* will be wrong. And if you do something stupid, you'll end up spending some time in our jail socializing with a couple of hookers, a couple of drunks, and a couple of drug addicts thrown in for entertainment. Am I making myself clear?"

Tess imagined herself reaching across the desk and smashing his face with her fist and then kneeing him in the groin, before telling him to have a good day, even though she'd never struck another human being in her life. "Yes sir, you're right. I'm sorry about the outburst. You'll call me, right?"

"Sure." He said exhaling through his nose.

She got up and left the pit area, despite wanting desperately to tell him he had mustard on his shirt.

🍸🍸🍸

By the time she got to the Morgan State House, fatigue, lack of sleep, stress, and anxiety were piling up like the snow. The walkway to her room hadn't been shoveled and was again knee-deep. She unlocked her door, but it wouldn't budge, stuck from frozen moisture in the jamb. She was in no mood to go look for a hotel employee, so she reared back and kicked the door just below the knob. It cracked loose, and for a moment she felt the most satisfaction she'd experienced in two days. Now if she could just kick a few people into action. She turned the wall-mounted heater up to high and began pulling off the Army Navy garb. She spread it on the chair and table to dry, and laid her woolen mittens directly on the heater. She dialed her parents' home, and it rang six times before she hung up.

It was time to just lie down, think things through, and wait for Eddie to call. *I'm sure as hell not calling his parents' home.* She doubled over one of the pillows and propped her head up as she lay down to strategize. *It's hard enough to form a cogent strategy when you know all the variables, but exceedingly difficult if the parameters of a problem are unknown.*

Twenty minutes later, she had a plan, and she began flipping through the yellow pages of the Albany phone book. There were a dozen Cuchinellis in the white pages and three concrete companies in the yellow pages. One company was in Schenectady, wherever that was, and another was in Troy, which according to the map in the front of the phone book was ten to fifteen miles away. So the third, Ideal Cement Company on Empire Avenue, had to be the Cuchinellis' enterprise. She thought in a town this size, which had to be at least 100,000 people, it was really unusual to have only one major concrete company. Even in Champaign, which was not even half the size of Albany, there were two plants, one owned by the father of one of her high school classmates and the other one north of town. She guessed it probably wasn't smart to operate a concrete plant in competition with the Cuchinellis. She made some notes on the complimentary hotel notepad and made a map with directions to the plant.

The Cuchinellis listed in the white pages had only five different first names, like the Spinozzas with their tradition of naming everyone after the father, the uncles, and when that list ran out, saints. Eddie had told her about this tradition, and it seemed to ring true with the Cuchinellis as well. There were three Anthonys, three Franks, two Josephs, two Vincents, and one Robert. *Bob Cuchinelli couldn't be related.* She needed a family tree to figure out who the old man was that Tiziana referred to, his sons, and their sons. Another thought came to her: Who was Eddie named after and why? She hadn't heard about anyone else named Eddie. Hmm ...

She guessed that one of those Cuchinellis, or most of them, knew where Teresa was being held captive. Okay, maybe not Bob, who was probably a dentist or a chiropractor. If she could do any of the work the police detective should have been doing—that is, if the Cuchinellis hadn't already bought him a boat or a trip to the Bahamas—then maybe Teresa could come home with her hair and digits intact. What else could she do? Sit in the hotel room and watch television? Watch the snow fall? She didn't consider herself an act-first, ask-later kind of person, or the kind of person who was willing to just do something, anything. But somebody had to do something.

She flipped her mittens over on the heater and turned on the television to kill some time as her mittens dried. She watched a football game for several minutes, then the phone rang. It was a relief to hear Eddie's voice.

"Tess, how are you doing?"

"This is incredibly frustrating, but I'm okay. Did you get some rest?"

Eddie told her it was nearly impossible to sleep when the phone continued to ring off the hook, the doorbell rang multiple times, and family and employees were spread out all over the house.

"They've gone to the mattresses!" Tess said.

"Tess, that's not funny. This isn't *The Godfather* and that's not what's happening."

"Well, I saw the movie and I was trying to lighten it up a bit. I'm sorry. That was insensitive and rude." *It was a little funny.*

"Forget it. I really want to see you, but I don't think coming here is right. On the other hand, the weather is so bad."

"Eddie, we need to do something."

"Do something?"

"The police aren't doing anything, and the Cuchinellis are probably paying them and everyone else off."

There was silence on the phone for several seconds. "The Cuchinellis. How do you know that name?"

"I … ah … I talked to the police and that's … uh. You know I can't remember."

"The Cuchinellis are not discussed in my parents' house, and don't ever talk about them with a family member." His tone was abrupt and defensive. "It goes way back."

Tess sat quietly trying to assess what she'd just heard and decided that either he was being extremely frank or someone was listening. She went in a different direction. "Has anyone heard a ransom demand?"

"Not that I know, but I'm not in the circle that knows anything. My mother said my father is handling the situation."

"Eddie, come here and we'll talk. I don't care how bad the snow is. Teresa needs your help."

"What can I do?" he asked.

"I have an idea."

"When do you want me to be there?"

"An hour. I have to do my hair and get dressed."

"Don't eat," he said. "We'll go out for something."

"See you about four then?"

He confirmed, and Tess hung up the phone thinking that not only does he not know anything, they're not telling him anything. *I think.* He's in the dark and always has been. *I guess.*

14

TESS THOUGHT ABOUT changing her clothes but reconsidered. What difference would it make with outerwear that made her look like *Nanook of the North*? She put a bit of makeup on and brushed out her hair, which resembled "hat hair" thanks to her rabbit-fur-lined aviator hat. Lipstick seemed to be helping with lips that were becoming chapped. The cold was drying out her skin, so she reapplied lotion, and just for good measure spritzed a bit of perfume on her neck.

She called her mother again, but there was no answer. It was frustrating not to be able to communicate when she needed to reach people in an emergency. It was, after all, Thanksgiving, and her parents were probably at her grandparents' house, but she decided not to call them there and talk about what was going on. It would only upset everyone and disrupt the holiday. She flipped on the television and rested until she heard knocking at the door. She pulled the curtain back and saw Eddie.

They hugged and kissed. He stepped back, and she felt that he was retreating in more than just a physical sense. *Imagination? Overly sensitive? Come on, get a hold on yourself.* "Well, look at you," she said.

"I know. I look like hell, but this seems like hell. This storm's coming off Lake Erie."

"Actually, I meant you're here, and you look pretty good. Lake Erie, you say?"

"Yeah. Cold air comes across the lake, which is relatively very warm this time of year, and picks up a huge amount of moisture. Buffalo will get five or six feet. We may get a ton of snow and wind, too. This is a big one."

"I can't imagine anything worse," she said. "Something to eat?"

"Let's go. My car?"

"Please. There's a diner about two or three blocks up the street."

Minutes later, they were seated across from each other in a blue vinyl-covered booth that Tess guessed was older than her. The Formica-covered table was scarred and chipped, but the waitress wiped it down vigorously before leaving menus. Tess smiled and said, "I'm glad she didn't ask if it was cold enough out there for me. I don't know why people always do that. It makes no sense."

Eddie nodded and made a good-faith effort at a smile, but it disappeared quickly. She sensed the conversation would be deadly serious and direct. He cleared his throat and rubbed his forehead. "Tess you said on the phone something about the Cuchinellis. What do you know, and how do you know anything about them?"

Tess sidestepped her conversation with Tiziana and pointed to the detective as the source of her information. Covering the highlights of what she knew and skipping any reference to Eddie's grandfather, Tess painted a broad picture. She did reveal that Tiziana had said that she and Frankie were considering moving to Chicago. "But that could have been just a reaction to everything going on."

Eddie rubbed his eyes before beginning. "I didn't realize that Frankie was that serious about leaving New York and the family business. We had talked the day before yesterday, and that's when he gave me more details about stuff I should have known for years. I guess I just didn't want to know. I didn't want to see what was right in front of me. It was chicken-shit of me, and I'm sorry. I'm sorry that I invited you to meet my family. I am ashamed. I'm sorry that this all happened now. I'm sorry about my family. I'm sorry—"

"Eddie, stop! I believe you. I believed you the night in the plane in the tree. In my own life, there are things that have happened to me that have been overlooked, side-stepped, and swept under the rug by people very close to me. People do that. It's human nature. You can't let it be a measure of who you are or what your life has become. You are not your family." Tess flashed on her mother's advice about marrying someone along with their family. But marrying the family and being your family should be two different things.

"You're wrong," he said. "We are, for the most part, who we come from. We have their values, their genes, their tendencies, and the same background. There is no escaping it."

"Eddie, you're being way too hard on yourself, too judgmental, and you're drawing conclusions that are illogical. You're also being overly dramatic."

"No, I'm not!" Eddie raised his voice. "It's the truth, and you're doing it yourself."

"Doing what?"

The people sitting in the next booth turned to them. Tess motioned to Eddie to lower the volume.

"Making excuses, rationalizing, and explaining away the simple truth. We both know it now, although I'm surprised Tiziana wasn't more forthright with you."

She held up her index finger. "First of all, I'm not rationalizing or excusing anything. I don't know what the hell is going on, *and* it's really none of my business. Secondly, Tiziana is scared more than anything. For God's sake, her husband was shot."

"Do you really think I can divorce myself from my family and their business activities? I am them, and they are me."

"Yes! Yes, you can, and you will. You will if you want to be with me. Now Eddie, I'll be blunt. You need to pull yourself together and be the person I know you are, not this whining, mealy-mouthed wimp that you sound like right now."

He looked through the window that had fogged up, the moisture on the inside of the glass turning to ice, and shook his head and closed his eyes as he rested his head back on the seat. He exhaled deeply. "I didn't see this coming. How could I not know this? How could I not know my family?"

"Here you go, folks." The waitress placed a steaming bowl of stew in front of each of them, and laid another plate of hot French bread with a half dozen pads of butter in the middle of the table. "Can I refresh those coffees?"

Tess answered, "Yes, thank-you."

"More cream?"

Tess restrained an urge to lose her patience with the woman, who was only doing her job but interrupting one of the most important conversations in Tess's life. "Yes, thank-you."

She swung by a minute later and poured coffee to the brims of their cups and left another miniature stainless steel pitcher filled with cream. Tess smiled and nodded.

"Eddie, here is the important thing right now. You, your life, and your future life—even the future of our lives together—aren't as important as doing something about

Teresa. I know the police are shushing this away like it was a case of pickpocketing or jaywalking or vagrancy. I'm also beginning to think that this isn't a no-harm no-foul game of chicken between the two families. It appears that there is a lot of history and a lot at stake, and I don't know if that means Teresa is in serious trouble or not. But it doesn't take a rocket scientist to see that Frankie could have been killed, almost was killed. If they'd kill him, they could and may hurt Teresa."

"It's different with girls and women."

She looked at him as if he had two heads. "Eddie, you can be so naïve sometimes."

"Says who?"

"Eddie, it's not Sicily or Brooklyn, 1915. I have no idea what I'm talking about, I'll grant you that, but I do know what I saw. I was there when they kidnapped her. I do know that I may not have very much information at all, but I've got enough. I do read the paper and watch the news. Are you kidding? This is real. It's real life and death."

"So what are you and I supposed to do, huh?" he asked curtly. "We're two naïve outsiders that don't know a damned thing about this whole business, police activity, or anything else. I own a BB gun, and you can barely drive in the snow, and we're going to bring down the Cuchinellis? Stop with the delusions."

She sat quietly cradling her coffee cup. "I have a plan."

Eddie bowed his head and pooched out his lower lip. He looked at her. "You have a plan?"

"I do. And by the way, I'm doing just fine driving in the snow."

Twenty minutes later, after Tess had laid out her strategy, they paid the bill and left the restaurant. Eddie cleared the snow off his car, and they drove back to the hotel.

Tess said, "I'll be back in a few minutes. I'm just going across the street."

"For what?"

"We need some field glasses."

"What!"

Ignoring his comment, she said, "Eddie, while I'm gone, you call Ideal Cement and ask for Tony or Frank or some Cuchinelli."

He agreed as Tess left for the Army Navy surplus store.

15

AN HOUR LATER, they were driving through the inhospitably white city. Cars were randomly stuck, and plows had cleared the main roads but trapped more cars behind the snow barriers; it would take days and herculean efforts to clear them. With street signs covered, Eddie was only able to navigate to their destination because of his familiarity with his hometown.

Tess had learned from the phone book map that Ideal Cement was just inside the city's southern boundary. After a half-hour's drive, they went slowly past the front gate of the facility and down the street. The front of the property was enclosed by a six-foot chain-link fence topped by barbed wire. It reminded her much more of Joliet Prison in Illinois than a cement company. The large lot held dozens of cement trucks parked in lines that looked like rows of enormous white teeth, smaller pieces of equipment scattered about, and half a dozen cars parked close to an office building. A tall menacing structure that looked like a guard tower rose up behind the building. The plant back in Illinois had one just like it, and she thought it must be a part of the cement-making process.

Next to the office building and for as far as she could see into the darkening sky were small mountains. She assumed they were working piles of sand and gravel and whatever other raw materials were used in the production of concrete. Her entire life experience with cement was watching street crews form and pour concrete into sidewalks in front of her house in Champaign. She'd never really thought about cement or concrete or whatever you called it, and come to think of it she didn't really care much about it.

It was close to 5 p.m. on Thanksgiving. The cars there must belong to employees because they were only covered by a few inches of snow, which meant they'd probably been moved since lunch. Why were they working on Thanksgiving?

Eddie drove past the plant a quarter mile and the street dead-ended. He turned the car around and drove back toward the tower and parked a hundred yards from the gate, directly in front of the company's lighted office. "Most likely anyone exiting the lot will turn in the opposite direction and not notice our car. Those three parked cars in front of us on the street are going nowhere. That ridge of plowed snow makes it impossible to move without about an hour of hard work."

"I think we're good. We just have to wait."

Tess used her newly purchased field glasses to watch the people moving around the office from one room to another and wondered what on earth they were doing there on Thanksgiving during a dangerous snowstorm. *Could anything productive be happening outside the office? No. What could they be doing inside? Paperwork? Billing? Plotting?*

"I don't even know why we're here?" Eddie asked. "This seems so stupid. And who are you, Sherlock Holmes? What could you possibly see with your little opera glasses?"

"Here's the way I see it, Eddie. I could sit in my room waiting for the airport to open, the roads to clear, and for this bogus investigation to come to a conclusion. I could then just get on the next plane and fly the hell out of this shithole. You could be standing around your family's home fretting, worrying, making plans for revenge, and waiting for something to happen when the Cuchinellis decide your family has sweated enough and are willing to concede something. What, I don't know. You'd eventually leave, too."

"And this is better because we're going to sit here and freeze and see what?"

"I know it's a long shot, but what if just maybe that thug in the black utility vehicle who trapped Teresa and me pulls in to chat with somebody. Maybe he needs to find out what he's supposed to do or pick up his payoff for kidnapping her and is holding her in some crappy apartment or wherever. I know I'll recognize the vehicle or at least the grill and the back of the vehicle."

"And we'll do what?"

"We'll follow him and then go to the police with Teresa's location."

"You watch too many movies. A stakeout? Come on, Tess. This has about as much chance of working as a snowball in hell."

"Well, drive me back to the hotel and go sit at home, and *you* come up with a plan. We are doing something. Just leave the car running and watch. We're going to learn something."

They sat silently with the car idling for fifteen minutes. Tess peered through her glasses for any movement or clues. Several people came out of the office, started cars, and cleared snow off the front and back windshields, before going back inside; within minutes, all the cars except one had driven out of the lot.

"Well, maybe I was wrong," Tess said, "but then again, maybe this is the one guy waiting for everyone to leave."

"Maybe. We'll see."

"Eddie, I want to ask you something. We're just sitting here with time on our hands, so here goes." With her field glasses still affixed to her face, Tess said, "What is it with your mother, or maybe more accurately, your mother and me? I am becoming convinced that she dislikes me intensely. She also seems very bitter, even angry about the world around her. I'm not looking for a big psychological analysis, but maybe you could tell me about you and her, and it will explain how she feels about me."

"You want the long version?"

"Sure, why not?"

"I was maybe nine or ten years old when I realized that my mom really did love her children and care about us, or at least me. She may not have been the most affectionate person in the world, but she had a place in her heart that was warm and protective and loving. It balanced out the rage and bouts of violence that erupted out of my father like Mount Vesuvius.

"One of my chores at that age was to wash the dishes, and my father was a stickler about using hot water. He was on one of his tirades about discipline and respect and disobedience or some fabricated cause to teach me life lessons. It had little to do with me and a whole lot to do with doors slamming in his head. Anyway, he thought that the temperature of the water that I was rinsing the dishes in wasn't hot enough to properly clean them. It wasn't a matter of water temperature but disobedience and disrespect or some such thing. So, he hit me on the back of the head with an open hand. But I didn't react, and that made him even angrier. He hit me three or four more times and had me hunkering down, shielding myself when my mother stepped in and pushed him away. She wrapped her arms around him and said, 'That's enough!' in a loud voice. I'm not sure what he would have done if he'd lost all composure, but I know in my heart that she saved me from what might have been a real serious beating. As violent and mercurial as my father was, my mother was just as calm and restrained in a polar-opposite way.

"She also had a soft side. That's when I knew how much she loved me and liked my company. In the summertime, I would wake up early and find my mother sitting at the kitchen table just after sunrise. Everyone else would still be asleep, and she'd whisper for me to quietly get some clothes on, and we would go outside. There were blueberry bushes across the street and along the road, and we would pick a big bowl of fresh blueberries. She told me how she loved that time of day, loved blueberries and cream, and, although she didn't say it, I knew she meant that she loved me too. We'd come back in the house and eat blueberries and cream and drink coffee. Mine would be half evaporated milk, half coffee, and two saccharine tablets for sweetness. Probably lethal if consumed regularly for a long period of time, but it was so good.

"It was also a time in my mother's life when she talked a lot more. I mean, she was never loquacious, but she was sociable and likable. I would go on errands with her, and we would talk to all kinds of people about their families, the weather, the Brooklyn Dodgers, or whatever. People liked her, and it was because she seemed to genuinely care about them and expressed that caring. I remember fondly on many occasions we would go to the supermarket or hardware store, but we invariably ended up at Walgreens. They had a real old-fashioned soda fountain and counter with stools that swirled around like tops. There were balloons taped to the top of the wall behind the soda fountain, and in each balloon was a price for a banana split. I love banana splits to this day. Anyway, the idea was to pick a balloon and hopefully get your banana split for less than the regular price of thirty-nine cents. Over the years, I must have picked dozens of balloons and never got anything less than thirty-nine cents, but every time she would still get me a banana split. She would drink coffee and smoke her Lucky Strikes and watch me devour the ice cream. She spoiled me.

"You know she taught me how to read before I went to kindergarten, and that's saying something. I wasn't the smartest kid in the world, I'm sure, but she wanted me to have a head start on the other kids. So, we sat at the table for what seemed like hours learning letters and words and reading those primer books. And, by God, I could read in kindergarten! It would be years later before the teachers concluded that I wasn't the sharpest pencil in the drawer, but I'd had a really good preschool education. That was my mom for you.

"Maybe because I was the youngest, or maybe because my mother fawned over me, it seemed to make my relationship with my father worse. Could it have been jealousy? He's a weird, vain, arrogant guy, no question about it. I don't know the answer, but I do know that my mother cared deeply about me, and it made me hopeful. It all became crystal clear the day I graduated from high school. My father had some emergency that came up an hour before the ceremony, and so only my mother attended. I saw her face when they called my name. I could see her smiling when I walked up to the stage and got my diploma. She was beaming with pride and grati-fication. She hugged me so hard afterward—I felt like I was on top of the world, and maybe I was for a few brief hours.

"When we got home, my father was in his study, and my mother and I walked in and stood in the middle of the room. My father came from behind the desk with an unusual bounce in his step and a smile on his face. I thought to my-self, 'This is all I needed to do to gain his approval and maybe his affection—graduate from high school?' He reached out his hand, and I shook it with a feeling of great accomplish-ment, maybe my greatest success in life up to that point. I remember what he said as if it was yesterday: 'Congratula-tions Eddie. Good job.' I beamed and said, 'Thank-you.'

Then he said, 'You did well, but we are going to need you to leave tomorrow morning.' I asked him, 'What do you mean?' He said, 'Oh, come on. You and I both know that you can't wait to get out of here.' It was as if I'd been struck by lightning. I couldn't move, couldn't speak, couldn't think. I looked at my mother, and I knew. I knew at that point that she had been defeated as much as I had. It seemed as if she had just been figuratively thrown overboard. Her face con-torted into absolute despair and surrender. Her spirit was crushed, and a little of her soul evaporated into the ether at that moment, never to be recovered. I left the next day for Uncle Tony's place in Chicago with a wad of money in my pocket—my father's graduation gift and his way of solving everything. My mother's decline into the hardened, cold, bit-ter, and cynical person she is today began the moment my father executed my banishment."

Tess inhaled a breath and said, "Ah, that definitely was the long version. I don't know what to say. I'm sorry. I'm so sorry that all happened."

"It's just the real-life deal. I'm okay with everything. I don't believe my mother hates you. I just think she doesn't like much of anything or anyone. She's the one I feel sorry for. Hey, Tess, I'm going to close my eyes for a few minutes, okay?"

"Oh, sure."

"That rehash took it out of me. Wake me up if anything happens."

An hour later, both Tess and Eddie were asleep. Exhaustion forced them to sleep like the dead and only the lights from a sedan that parked in front of the gate and faced them awakened Tess. She nudged Eddie. "Look!" she whispered. "I don't know how long we've been asleep, but all the lights are out in the office. Who's this guy?"

They watched as someone got out of the car and walked to the gate, swinging it open. "Did you see that? The gate wasn't locked. He just pulled it open. That's preplanned," Eddie said.

They watched the dark four-door sedan turn off its lights and drive into the lot. It did a half circle and then parked with the front of the car pointed away from the office. "I knew it. I knew it," Tess said as she watched through the glasses.

"Know what? This could be the janitor or an employee who forgot something. Maybe he just backed in to load something up."

"Like what? The trunk isn't open. It's a little late to be loading up frozen turkeys for the employees or paperwork to do over the weekend. No, this may not be the vehicle, but this isn't right. It's a holiday and the middle of the night."

Eddie looked at his watch. "It's 8 p.m. You watch too many television shows, and this is way too exciting for you."

"Okay, but there's nobody in there, and this guy is picking something up. Wait, they wouldn't have her here, would they?"

"No! It'd be too obvious, and we're not breaking and entering to find out."

They both watched intently as the man entered the front door. "He's got a key, and he didn't turn on the lights," Tess said. "I think I can see a beam of light. A flashlight."

Eddie said dismissively, "He's got a key because he works here. I don't know. Wait, here he comes. Stay low when he comes out of the gate in case he turns this way." They ducked down and then peered over the dash as the car approached the opened gate. Instead of stopping to close the gate, the car zipped through it and turned away from them.

Eddie started the car and put it in drive when the flash struck. It was an explosion that made Fourth of July fireworks look like child's play. The car shook from the blast that mushroomed up and shone brilliantly against the darkened sky. Eddie held his foot on the brake, stunned into immobility. Pieces of insulation and debris cascaded down in the lot. Smoke and fire billowed out of the top of the building, making the tower look like a volcano. Shattered glass skidded through the parking lot. A single office chair landed on top of a pile of snow.

"Holy shit!" Eddie yelled. "Holy shit! They blew up the fucking building. Jesus, I hope nobody was inside because they're dead now."

Tess was speechless. She'd never seen a bomb explode, never witnessed destructive power with this kind of force. They watched the falling debris continuing to cascade down onto the lot, until Eddie suddenly said, "We have to get out of here. The police will be here in minutes."

He hit the gas, and the car slid sideways before gaining traction. He immediately turned left. "I don't want to meet any sirens coming in this direction," he said.

"Oh my God! Oh my God! What if someone was in there? I'm freaking out!" Tess yelled. She put her hands on the sides of her head.

Coming through the intersection perpendicular to Eddie was the car that had only moments before come out of the gate. "That's him!" Tess yelled. "Follow him!"

"That guy watched the explosion. He stopped on the street and watched. Has to be, or he'd be gone. The bastard watched," Eddie said as he turned the car in pursuit of the vehicle.

Tess focused on the car in front of them. It spit up chunks of snow each time it accelerated, fishtailed through intersections, and then slid sideways almost colliding with a snowbank. The vehicle struggled to gain speed, slip-sliding, gaining traction, and then getting out of control again.

"His rear windshield is covered with snow," Eddie said. "The only way he can see us following him is through his side mirror, and he's probably completely focused on the street in front of him. I'm going to stay a half block behind. I can't lose him."

Tess took a deep breath. "We need to call the police. We just witnessed a bomb, right? I mean that couldn't have been an explosion from some gas leak or something right?" She could hear her voice, high-pitched and staccato.

"Tess, if you call the police, you put yourself at the scene and me at the scene. I become an instant suspect. I just hope nobody saw us. Those houses up the street were not in our line of sight, and we turned before they could see us."

"We can't just drive away! What if someone was in there or is still in there?"

Eddie started to speak but was drowned out by a siren from a fire engine turning onto the street at the intersection they'd just passed through. "They're on the way. Somebody called it in. God, that was fast. Maybe planned. Maybe an alarm."

Tess put her hands on the dash and tried to think. The world was spinning ten times faster than normal. She was running on adrenaline again and just trying to put the pieces together. *What just happened? In the span of forty-eight hours, I've seen a man gunned down, a woman kidnapped, and now a bomb explode. This wasn't a prank, an accident, or an act of God. It was full-blown terrorism. It was meant to inflict penetrating, overwhelming fear for the victims. This is terror in the truest, ugliest, and most horrifying sense.* "What are we trying to do, following this guy? Aren't we putting ourselves in more danger?" she asked.

"We can find out who did it?"

"Who did it!" she yelled as she threw her fur-lined hat to the floorboard. "Who do you think did it? Your family did it! This is revenge. This is payback. This is the return volley. This is how warfare goes until somebody surrenders. I can't believe I'm witnessing this."

She realized the moment she said it, that it sounded like an indictment of Eddie as well as his family. She backpedaled. "I mean to say that this is the turf war stuff that happens in New York City that I've read about in the paper. I don't mean you, Eddie. I don't mean you're part of this."

"Yeah, you did," he snarled.

"No, really, I didn't, and I don't mean to start a fight about this."

"Well, it's my family, and I'm in it up to my ass. I'm following this guy so at least we know who planted the bomb."

"So you can tell who? Your father? He already knows. He probably paid someone to do it." Her tone was accusatory, and she realized she was spitting as she said it.

"You don't know that!" he bellowed back at her. "You don't know anything about my father or my family."

"You're right, and I don't want to know them. They're crim ... they're mob ... they're ..." She stopped herself.

"They're what? Huh, Tess? What? You want to say it. Go ahead and say it!" he said in a raised voice.

She looked out the side window into the darkness that was punctuated by shrouded streetlights flashing by. The blowing snow made it seem like she was looking into a gigantic larger-than-life snow globe. The weather was breaking her. Her nerves were like the icicles hanging from the eaves of every house they passed. She was so far from home, so far from her comfort zone, so far from what she knew to be normal in life that all she wanted at this moment was to wake up from this nightmare. To wake up in her bed, in her Florida home, and make a pot of coffee. To go out into the backyard at daybreak, in shorts, into the humid warm air and pick a couple of oranges for a glass of juice. To feel safe.

"He's turning. He's heading back toward my part of town. Who is this bastard?"

"Eddie, don't follow him anymore. Nothing can be gained. You already know everything you need to know. Let's just drive out of here and go south, catch a flight in New York. You're being pulled in, pulled into something you can't escape from. Eddie, I'm asking you to stop. Stop now."

"Jesus, we're going right by my neighborhood. This is my home turf. This is right where I grew up."

"Eddie, you don't want to know anything more about this. If this is the guy who just blew up that cement plant, he may have also murdered someone. There might have been an innocent clerk or janitor in there."

Eddie ignored her. "He's breaking. He's turning on Norge Road. Look, he's turning into Otto Vitello's house. I went to school with him. His dad worked for the Spinozzas back then. I think he was in catering or the bakery. He used to give me stuff at the bakery."

As Eddie slowly passed the house, the garage door closed. "Do you think they can, uh, trace him to the bomb. I mean, what if he has bomb-making stuff in his house or bomb residue on his hands or something like that?"

"I'm sure they can, Eddie, but you already know that he was at the scene. You know that he probably works for the Spinozzas. The question now is, what are you going to do with the information you have?"

"Well, I sure as hell can't tell the police anything. This could lead right back to someone in my family."

"This whole thing is crazy," she said. "What was I thinking, that we could follow some guy from the cement plant to where they were holding Teresa and that we could just stroll in and rescue her."

"Actually, that was your plan, Tess, and it was workable. So, where should we go?"

"My hotel."

They drove mostly in silence. The hotel's parking lot was fairly cleared of snow when they pulled in.

"Now what?" she asked. "Are you coming in?"

"Tess, I think the best thing I should do right now is go back home. My mother will be worried, and I need to tell them what we saw."

There's that word, "home," again, she thought. "You mean tell your father? Don't tell them I was with you. Will you call me in the morning?"

"Yes, I've got to tell my father. I'll call you early in the morning."

They bid each other weakhearted goodbyes, and Tess climbed the stairs to her room, thinking about home. Home is where you go to watch a football game on Sunday afternoon and have a family dinner. Home is where you sit on the back porch and listen to your grandfather's stories from half a century ago and drink coffee. Home is where the biggest argument is about whether everyone should watch *Jeopardy* or *Hawaii Five-O.* Home is where you kick a soccer ball around with kids, play cards, eat corn on the cob and barbecued burgers. This place was hell.

She dialed her parents' home phone number, and her mother picked up.

"Hello," her mother said in a voice that was so soothing it made Tess take a deep breath.

"Mom, I've been trying to reach you all day!"

"Well, honey, we were where we always are, at your grandparents. What's wrong? You sound very upset."

"No, no. It's just that it's been a long day and a lot has happened."

"So, you met Eddie's family and how did that go? Are they nice people?"

"Umm, different. Mom, ugh, well they're not like us, but we can talk about that later. There was an accident last night and, um, well there's been several accidents and ... umm—"

"What kind of accidents? Was someone hurt? Are you okay? What happened?"

"No, I'm fine and Eddie's fine. Just there's been so much snow, like three feet and there's accidents everywhere." *Oh my God, I'm lying to my mother.*

"This sounds terrible, Tess."

"It's been hard, Mom. How was Thanksgiving?"

Her mother launched into a recap of the food, the card games, the weather, and family news. Tess wondered how or even if she should tell her mother more about what had happened over the last twenty-four hours.

"So, what did you have for dinner?" her mother asked, changing topics. "They're Italian, and we were thinking maybe they don't eat turkey and sweet potatoes?"

Tess had already decided it was time to end the call and save the details for another time. "Mom, I'll tell you all about it later, but I'm so tired I've got to go to bed. Tell Dad I love him, and I'll talk to you soon."

"Well, okay. Drive carefully in all that snow."

They bid each other good night.

CHAPTER

16

TESS TOOK A HOT SHOWER for warmth and comfort, then fidgeted with her clothes and other belongings until eleven o'-clock when the news came on TV. The lead story was the explosion and fire at the cement plant. The station cut to the scene and a reporter, who's every exhaled breath looked like he was blowing cigarette smoke. He described the incident as an explosion of unknown causes, and said the fire had been extinguished. The fire chief and a team of investigators were inside the plant looking for clues, and, the reporter continued, "It appears that no one was inside at the time of the explosion, and there are no witnesses."

No witnesses, no known causes, no suspects. Tess thought the report would seem to many viewers like just another garden-variety explosion. They might think it was a natural gas explosion. There were no victims, just property damage.

Maybe the message from the Spinozzas was supposed to be symbolic: You come after our business, and we'll come after yours, or at least your capacity to do business. Or maybe the Cuchinellis blew up their own place to collect insurance. *I really have no idea how these people think. I can't even imagine doing things like this or being a part of this life. I need to leave.*

Leave everything here. She flashed back on the detective's warning not to leave town. *What could they do to me? Arrest me for what? I haven't done anything.*

Not long after the report, a woman who looked young enough to be in junior high school, stood in front of a weather map. She indicated that the storm had not yet passed through the Albany area and was going to dump at least another foot or more of snow. *Unbelievable!* Most areas had already received thirty-two to forty inches of snow, and now more.

As Tess watched the commercials before *The Tonight Show* started, she had another insight. Maybe the kidnappers, the guys who were actually holding Teresa, would make contact with the Cuchinellis somewhere other than their office, if they had an office. It certainly wouldn't be the plant. If it was the plant, it was rubble now. Maybe they'd meet somewhere and get additional instructions, money, or whatever mobsters do at a table in the back of a restaurant or nightclub. The top people in the Cuchinelli family didn't work in that grungy cement factory. Surely the police are tapping their phones and watching these guys with undercover investigators.

Then she thought about what was really happening. She and Eddie were the only people watching the cement plant. This wasn't New York, and this wasn't the big-time Mafia. She reminded herself that her frame of reference was unrealistic dramatic television shows that depict an entire story in less than an hour. There was probably no surveillance going on, no phone tapping, and probably no real motivation by the police department to give this investigation more than a whitewash. This was a world so unfamiliar that reality and fantasy were becoming intertwined and interchangeable.

Tess was sure that Teresa was stuck in some shabby room that smelled like cigarettes, probably restrained and frightened to distraction. Would they hurt her or violate her? Who knows what demands, if any, were being made. She was thinking less of Eddie and herself, and more and more of Teresa. She could leave town now, sure she could. She could catch the next flight out of Albany, leave Eddie, leave the Spinozzas and Cuchinellis, and leave this damned snowstorm. But she couldn't leave Teresa. She had become a friend and had been her ally in the past. Teresa was indefatigable, outspoken, and feisty, but she'd be no match for armed thugs; she was now helpless and vulnerable.

Tess decided she wasn't going anywhere. There had to be something she could do. It was a drive in her that came from an ancient past, one that placed loyalty to the family, the tribe, the clan above all else. Maybe a thousand, two thousand, or more years ago, her Scottish ancestors had survived because of this ingrained trait. She would stay to the finish.

For the first time since her college days, Tess left the television on all night. She would periodically awaken, watch for a while, and fall back asleep. It was the worst sleep possible. She finally dozed off for a couple of hours before dawn. The crushing feeling of sleep deprivation hit her like a brick when she decided it was time to get out of bed.

CHAPTER

17

IT WAS FRIDAY MORNING. Eddie hadn't called, so she decided he must finally be getting some much-deserved sleep. It was time to get on the move. She pulled on her arctic outerwear and walked into the icebox world outside. It was considerably colder than the past couple of days, and the snow under foot now crunched like she was walking on gravel. The chore of cleaning snow and ice from her car took longer than it did for the engine to warm up and defroster to work. *Somebody should invent a car with a defroster in the rear windshield.*

Her first stop was the police station to gather any information. The dispatcher behind the glass at the front of the station disappeared, looking for a detective or any information about the explosion the previous night. She returned several minutes later, drinking coffee and indicated no one was available. Tess wanted to ask how that was possible, but decided not to get on anyone's wrong side this early in the morning. That settled it: The police worked behind closed doors and spoke only through talking heads at briefings. No need to waste any more time or energy looking for answers from them. She trudged to the car and headed for the hospital, hoping that she would find only Tiziana.

When she reached the surgical ward, she saw that the rent-a-cop was gone and only one nurse was on duty. The nurse waved Tess through, so she walked right into Frankie's room and saw that he was awake. "Well, how are you today? I'm glad to see you sitting up and with the living." She smiled at Tiziana in a chair on the other side of the bed.

He laughed. "No joke." His voice was hoarse from having tubes stuck in his nose and throat for the past two days. "Close call."

"I'll say."

"I don't even know what happened. It was like I got hit by a rock. A big rock, and then it all got foggy. Thank-you for coming to see me and spending time with Tiz."

"You're welcome. I'm not sure anybody knows what happened, but at this point you need to just rest and let the police sort it out." *Like they're doing anything.*

"Do you feel like eating a little something?" Tiziana asked Frankie.

"I could, yes."

"I'll order it. What would you like?"

"Pancakes."

"Pancakes!" Tiziana and Tess said in unison.

"I'm sure they have them," Frankie said weakly.

"Okay, I guess you can have that or anything else you like. It will take forever for them to deliver them. I'll just go get them. I'll be right back. Tess, would you like to come with me?"

Tess looked at Frankie. "I'm so, so happy you're going to be okay. We'll talk later."

"Nice outfit."

Tess laughed and thought, *the Spinozza trademark, charm.* They could be charming in the face of death, on a deathbed, or in bed. *Don't go there.* She joined Tiziana in the hallway, and they took the elevator to the basement cafeteria. "Let's have coffee before we order his pancakes," Tiziana said.

They got coffee and sat at a table away from the rest of the patrons. Tess studied Tiziana's face. She had darkened circles under her red eyes and appeared to be exhausted. Tiziana added cream to her coffee and paused before asking, "You heard?"

"About the explosion at the cement plant? I saw it on television." Tess decided it would not be prudent or in Tiziana's best interests to tell her she had witnessed it, assuming Eddie would feel the same.

"Tess, this is degenerating into full-scale war. Someone is going to get killed. They almost killed Frankie, and only by the grace of God did someone not get killed last night."

"What can make this stop? When do they call a truce?"

"I have no idea. I haven't seen anything like this since I've been married to Frankie. I can't see either side giving in to the other. They'd lose face."

"Lose face! You're kidding me. I do not understand these people. No offense, but kidnapping people, blowing up buildings, and for what? For a cement business or a garbage business! This is not how the rest of the world lives."

Tiziana was silent for a few seconds. "I know," she said softly.

Tess sipped her coffee. "I've reached the point where I really don't care what happens to them. I mean, you know, whoever is in this business. I think they're all a bunch of criminals and thugs, but I do care about Eddie and Teresa. And you two. I just don't know what to do. The police are sitting on their thumbs—"

Tiziana interrupted her. "They will only be involved afterward. They will not solve this mess."

"What about Teresa?"

"I don't know what to say. I've been dating or married to Frankie for twelve years now, so I hear snippets of what goes on. I hear stuff from behind closed doors. I hear secondhand versions from Frankie and his brothers and other outsiders. But you and I will never know how this works, what motivates them, the Cuchinellis and the Spinozzas. I just know Frankie wants out." She spoke rapidly and nervously.

Tess nodded.

"You won't ever understand and you shouldn't," Tiziana said. "You should go home, now."

"I can't." Tess hesitated. "I've been crazy about Eddie since the night I met him. I don't want to just walk away because of his family and this debacle. I still believe he is not part of this or ever was. Am I right?"

"Yes. As soon as he graduated from high school, he moved to Chicago to live with his Uncle Tony."

"How could he not know? And another question, how come the family leaves Tony alone and out of everything?"

"Come on Tess, give Eddie a break. Nobody wants to think the worst of their family. As far as Tony is concerned, there's history between Tony and the family that's dark. Nobody talks about him, like he is banned. Mentioning his name is taboo. I heard that he had it out with Eddie's father in some kind of power struggle, and Tony would have done something terrible, so the grandfather made them agree to a truce. No way will anyone in this family cross Tony. He's really a nice man, but he's untouchable. I think they are afraid of him for some reason I don't know."

"Hmm. Seemed like a giant Teddy Bear." Tess flashed on Tony. He was the original black sheep of the Spinozza family, having moved away from New York twenty years earlier. He drove a cab and not only provided a landing place for Eddie, but had in a way mentored him and become a big brother and father to him. The way Tony sang Frank Sinatra and Dean Martin songs, laughed easily, and loved sports reminded Tess of Eddie.

"Let me ask you another question," Tess said. "What about the next generation's involvement?"

"Most of the third generation, Eddie, his brothers and cousins really aren't involved in anything illegal. It's his father and his brothers, and of course, his grandfather. As I told you, his grandfather started the business, and he keeps everything at arm's length. He doesn't get directly involved. He doesn't tell anybody what to do and they don't report to him. That way when the FBI or the police question him, he can say honestly that he doesn't know. But he didn't get to where he is without doing some pretty nasty things. Believe me, he has blood on his hands."

"It seems a little cowardly."

"I suggest you never say that again. It's their code. They never rat out each other or even their enemies, and they never tell anyone outside the family, and by that I mean the men in the family anything. Nothing!"

"Tiziana, you know a lot."

"Well, when Frankie decided to get out, he had to tell me more than I already knew. Frankie is a good man, and so is Eddie. All his brothers are. It's just so hard to break out and leave. It has to be a complete and clean break. Think about it. Could you do it with your family?"

"But my family—"

"Tess, I know. They're not mobsters. But if that's all you've known, then it really doesn't matter, does it? It's still *your* family. You're still someone's son or father. There is no point in judging them. It won't change anything. You can't change anything here, and you shouldn't try. I think you should just leave."

"I don't want to just leave Eddie, and there has to be something I can do, or that somebody can do, to help Teresa."

"Not you."

They sat in silence for a few minutes, and Tess digested what Tiziana had said. She watched a group of nurses break into laughter. How much of their lives at the hospital could be funny? Nothing seemed like it could be funny right now. Laughing seemed unnatural.

"We better get those pancakes," Tiziana said.

Tess and Tiziana returned to Frankie's room with a tray full of pancakes for him, and scrambled eggs and more coffee for them. They ate breakfast, while making conversation with Frankie about the latest news. Tess thought he seemed to be making remarkable progress for someone who had a hole the size of a dime drilled into his chest less than forty-eight hours before.

🍸🍸🍸

Later, she took the elevator to the lobby and tried to decide who to call, what to do, and how to occupy herself while the powers-that-be sorted this mess out. There seemed to be no sense of urgency by anyone to resolve this matter so they could move on to the ordinary and normal things people do in their everyday lives, like go to work and take care of business. Gray clouds seemed to envelope her life, and real clouds of snow continued to pummel the city.

She drove slowly past the Albany Police Department and was about to turn to make her way back to the Morgan State

House when she saw a sign for the Albany Public Library. The library was only two blocks away, and the road seemed manageable, so she decided to go for it. Maybe it was the comfort and familiarity with an institution where she'd spent a lot of time as a child that drew her there, or maybe it would hold information if not answers. Libraries are filled with knowledge. She wanted to know more and had virtually nothing else to do.

The parking lot had been cleared by a plow, and she took that as a sign and pulled in. There were only two other cars there, so she guessed it was closed, but when she trudged up to the front door, she was surprised to find it unlocked. She pulled off her outer layer of protection and her boots, and bundled them into an armful, and walked to the main desk in her woolen socks. A woman who had been doing something underneath the counter popped up like a jack-in-the-box. She wore a bright sweater that featured a turkey and a pilgrim in bright colors. Her reading glasses hung on a bright blue necklace dangling from her neck. She was startled for a moment, but regained her composure.

"Well, good morning, I think."

"Pretty bad out there," said Tess. "I'm sorry if I snuck up on you."

"Oh, don't worry about it. I was just fiddling with this little electric heater down here. It's freezing in this building in the winter, and my feet are cold all day. My name is Mrs. Moncrief, but you can call me Wendy. How can I help you this morning?"

"I wasn't really planning to stop at the library today, but I'm here now and I'd like to do a little research."

"You'd be surprised how many people will trudge in here today, what with no school, most people not working, and no one able to shop or go to the movies, and just about every-one sick of being cooped up at home." She pulled her sweater into place, and Tess saw that the pilgrim had a devious smile on his face and that he was holding an axe.

"Love the sweater."

"It's the stupidest thing in the world, but I wear it one day a year to please my husband who thinks it's hilarious. Next thing you know, people will be wearing ugly sweaters during the holidays just to be different. Now, what are we re-searching? Let me help you get started. I've got very little to do, and moving around will warm me up a bit." As Wendy stepped out from the desk, Tess noticed that she was wearing what appeared to be snow pants and house slippers with fur lining.

"I'd like to look at some newspaper stories over the last thirty to forty years about local, uh, businesspeople."

"Okay. Let's look at the *Times Union* and *The Knicker-bocker News*. We have only last year in actual paper format. The rest is on microfilm. Let's go to section A, down this way. Follow me. So, which businesspeople are you research-ing on this horrible day?"

"A couple of local families, the Spinozzas and the Cuchinellis."

Wendy stopped and abruptly turned to face Tess. "You're not from Albany, are you?"

"No, Wendy, I'm not. I'm from Illinois, but I live in Florida."

"You seem like a nice young girl. I have three daughters myself, probably about your age. All of them went to school with boys from both those families. The boys were all nice enough, but their families don't have, shall we say, a very good reputation. Let's sit a moment and chat, shall we? I

might be able to give you some insight before you start." She
pointed to a large wooden table and pulled out a chair. Tess
sat across the table.

"What's your name?"

"Tess. Tess Kincaid."

"Tess, the people you're asking about are members of
local," she hesitated and whispered, "*crime* families." She
continued, "I've lived here all my life, and it's understood
there is a whole other world that operates outside and maybe
underneath what you see in everyday life in Albany. It's interesting that a young girl from Florida is researching these
people, the day after Thanksgiving, in the middle of a blizzard." She waited for Tess's response.

Tess waited several seconds before making eye contact.
She bit her lower lip and said quietly, "I know."

Wendy waited for more, but Tess averted her eyes and
shrugged.

"Okay. In that case, you'll find 1977 newspapers in those
racks. You know how to use the Dewey decimal system to
fine-tune your search?"

"Yes. I spent a lot of time in the library in school."

Wendy pointed at some racks holding newspapers. "I'll
show where you can look at microfilm of papers going back
to the 1930s." They walked to a room containing a dozen
machines with small screens and viewfinders where a person
could rest their chin to ease the neck muscles. "Okay?"

"Yes, thank-you very much."

Wendy stopped at the door and turned back to Tess. "If
you need anything else, let me know."

"Thank-you."

Tess was soon flipping through the pages of *The Knicker-
bocker News*. There were a few articles, but they were not in-

structive. The newspaper appeared to have never done an investigative story on the local crime syndicate. She switched to the *Times Union*. She easily found family member names regarding marriages, high school graduations, and very general articles about the business enterprises. Staring into the machine-made Tess sleepy, and she stopped and rested her head on her elbows on the table. Wendy had reminded her that the day before had been Thanksgiving. She'd only thought about the holiday when she called her parents.

Thanksgiving back home was like most of the holidays— lots of family, food, and card games. Her Uncle Tom and his family would come up from Carbondale and stay in her grandparents' home. Tess and her parents would stay there too, even though they lived in the same town. Her mother's sister and her family would come down from Chicago, and invariably a great aunt and uncle, her father's parents, and at least one family friend with no place to call home would all pack into the house. Every bed was taken, and the living room floor would be covered with people sleeping in rows in front of the fireplace. Some lucky person would get to sleep on the couch, and someone might even try to sleep in the oversize recliner. Her grandfather built such raging fires that the temperature in the house approached sauna levels.

Sleep was nearly impossible. The giggling and laughter continued into the late hours of the night and broke early when her grandmother began her trademark banging of pots and pans at the crack of dawn. For breakfast, they'd eat sourdough biscuits with honey and jam, pounds of bacon, and gallons of coffee. Afterward, the men would migrate into the living room or the back porch, depending on the weather, and the women would congregate in the kitchen. The kids would separate by gender: The girls would play in a bedroom, and the boys would make mischief anywhere they could. Shortly after breakfast, preparations for the big Thanksgiving meal would begin, with her grandmother in full command. Tess loved it all. The laughter, the food, and conversation seemed like only a dream now.

Several years ago, she and Uncle Tom had won the family card tournament. They played pitch, a trick-taking game that involved an element of luck and a lot of skill. They played viciously, with the two winners keeping the table until they lost. The game started at sunset with pitchers of iced tea and leftover dessert, frequently cobbler, and carried on well into the evening. These were not battles for the faint of heart—culminating in someone "shooting the moon" in a "do or die" play. The howling and screeches of laughter rattled in her head. The year she and Tom won, he'd "double-shot the moon" and miraculously pulled it off. She wondered if she hadn't developed some of her skills on the golf course from these card games.

Then she recalled the year her grandfather forgot to thaw the turkey and had to cut the frozen bird with a chainsaw as Tom held it. ... Her head slowly dropped to the table. ... She started reading another article and fell asleep.

CHAPTER

18

TESS AWAKENED to tapping on her shoulder and turned around to see Wendy standing next to the table. She wiped a dribble of drool from the side of her mouth with her sleeve and attempted a smile. "Oh boy. I can't believe I fell asleep like that. How long have I been asleep?" *That's Eddie's line,* she thought. *He never wakes up after a nap or in the morning without asking the same silly question. Funny how many expressions and thoughts of a person you love become part of your own, even stupid ones like that.*

"I don't know, but I think you must be very tired. How about taking a break? Since it's you and me and only a couple of people in the library, why don't we have a cup of tea?"

"I'd love that. Thank-you."

Tess followed Wendy back to the front desk and noticed an elderly gentleman sitting in an overstuffed chair reading a newspaper, a clerk taking books from a cart and returning them to shelves, and a young man, fully dressed in his outdoor clothing, with oversize textbooks spread out on a table. "The hard-cores," Wendy whispered as she nodded at the young man. She slipped behind the counter and turned the switch on an electric hot plate. She placed a teakettle on top of the hot plate. "Earl Grey okay?"

"Oh, that would be perfect." Tess sat on a wooden stool and looked around the old, stately library. "I used to spend time in the university library when I was in junior high."

"You did? And where was that?"

"I grew up in Champaign, Illinois, where my father was, and still is, a professor at the University of Illinois."

"That's impressive. What field is he in?"

"Geography."

"I always wished I could have gone on with my education, but I got married and had my first girl when I was twenty-one, and never was able to go back to school."

The teapot began to gurgle, and steam trickled out of the spout.

"Did you grow up right here in Albany?"

"I actually was born in Troy and lived in Latham and Cohoes most of my life. Now I live in Delmar. It's only a few miles from here."

"You're pretty dedicated to come in on a day like this," said Tess.

The teapot began a full boil and just began to whistle when Wendy pulled it off the hot plate.

"I have a four-wheel drive Jeep, and since no one is on the roads, it's not as bad as you'd think."

"I think it's unbelievable. Back home, we get ice storms and some snow, but never anything like this."

"I love the sound of that."

"What?"

"'Back home.' It speaks of such longing and familiarity and comfort. You must have a big family that lives there, and I'll bet you're close. Sugar? No cream available, sorry."

"Yes on the sugar. Well, I don't have any siblings, but my parents and grandparents and many of my aunts, uncles, and cousins live close by. We always celebrate the holidays together, and my whole family always came to my local tournaments. So, yes, I'd say we're close."

Wendy poured a mug of tea for Tess and put it on the counter. "Tournaments?"

"I played golf in high school. Actually, I still play golf."

"You mean you play an occasional round at the country club?"

"Ah no, I play for a living. I play on the LPGA tour."

"You're a professional golfer?" Wendy asked excitedly.

Tess nodded. "It's a lot of travel and a lot of pressure. If you don't win, you don't make any money."

"Do you? Win, I mean."

"Yes, sometimes."

"Well, that's fantastic. You know, you look familiar to me. I have to read or file a lot of magazines, and I swear I've seen your face before, but not on a golf magazine."

Tess felt color rising in her cheeks as a rush of lifelong embarrassment that accompanied talking about herself came on like a wave, as if playing golf or selling perfume meant more than just that. "I have a perfume line, and we did a back cover photo for a popular golf magazine two months ago."

"That's it." Wendy pointed at Tess. "You're *that* Tess!"

Tess managed a smile and nodded.

"Well, it's certainly a pleasure to meet you."

"Thank-you, Wendy, but really it's not a big deal. I'm just a girl who can hit a golf ball a long way and make an occasional putt. In the grand scheme of things, many people do things that are so much more important. My mother, for instance, runs a safe house for abused women and their children. Now, that's someone who has great character and

purpose in her life." Tess didn't mention that it was her foundation, funded and supported by her, or that she'd bought
the family home for the foundation.

"She sounds like a wonderful woman. So, Tess, why are
you here of all places and not home with your family for
Thanksgiving?"

"It's a long story."

"I have plenty of tea, not much to do, and I think you
want to talk. Am I right?"

"Yes and no. I hate to talk to people I barely know, but I
would like to have someone give me some answers that I
can't seem to get from anyone around here."

"I'll share if you will."

Tess nodded in agreement.

"What would you like to know?"

"I am romantically involved with someone who is from
here." Tess laughed and covered her eyes. "I can't believe I
just said, 'romantically involved.' It sounds like something
some Hollywood movie star would say. Okay, let me start
over. I met a guy about a couple of years ago on a plane. His
plane. He was flying a charter for me from Harrisburg, Pennsylvania, to ah … God, where were we going? Oh, Altoona,
Pennsylvania. And we crashed."

"Oh my God. You crashed and lived?"

"Amazingly, yes. It was a small plane, a Cessna something
or other, and we had some kind of trouble with the engine.
A part, and I don't remember which one, maybe a magneto?"
Tess shrugged. "Anyway it got wet from an engine cleaning
and failed."

"Causing the crash?"

"Yes. But we didn't exactly crash crash. We landed in a
tree."

"Well, that sounds like a crash."

"The plane came to rest in the branches of the tree. It was badly damaged, and Eddie Spinozza, the pilot, was trapped in his seat because the fuselage just caved in."

"So that's the connection. The prodigal son returns."

Tess smiled. "Luke and the parable of the lost son. I'm not religious, but I remember that from Bible studies."

"I am religious, and yes, there were two sons and one returns to his father, and it causes quite a stir. But go on. I've known Eddie since he was born. I've known his mother for forty years. You were in a plane, in a tree, and Eddie was pinned in."

"You've known Eddie his whole life?" Tess asked incredulously.

"Yes, I have because his mother has been coming in here for decades and he often accompanied her."

"Oh! Okay, well, to make a long story short, we got out. Eddie was injured, and I wasn't. We met months later and started dating. We've been a real couple for a year, I guess."

"That's a very exciting and quite a romantic start," Wendy said. "So you're here to meet his family and something didn't go right, from what I've seen in the *Times Union*."

"That's putting it mildly. The first night, well Wednesday night, his brother was shot at The Dirty Martini, and then yesterday his sister was kidnapped."

Wendy added, "And then there's the explosion at the cement plant. Pretty much everyone knows that's part of this turf war."

"Now, we're coming to the part I'd like to know more about. Earlier this year, we had a nightmare experience that ended in a bizarre way. It was in Denver, at the end of a long, whirlwind car ride that had a scary ending. Just as it looked like we were in really big trouble, two guys who looked like hit men from a mobster movie showed up and bailed us out. Big, burly guys who had to be gangsters. Anyway, Eddie was genuinely shocked when they told us they'd been sent by his grandfather to look out for him. I think that's when he began to realize that his family did a lot more than sell salami and olive oil."

"That would be an understatement. But maybe I can help here. His mother, Connie, has been coming to the library ever since I've worked here. That includes from the time Eddie was born. She only brought his brothers in once in a while, and that wild one, his sister, once. But she and Eddie would come in once or twice a month. They would look at books and photos of planes and so on, until he went into junior high school. He was a sweet kid, polite too. Connie kept coming in after Eddie wouldn't come, and we got acquainted. I'm not sure why she wanted to talk, but I guess for the same reason you and I are talking. She didn't have anyone else to talk to."

"Hmm, didn't think about that. She hasn't been very … ah … welcoming."

"People from here have known for decades about the underworld connections of the two families that are in open warfare now. They're just part of the fabric of life around here. Everyone who is not in the businesses they're involved in stays clear of them. It's like the IRS: If you don't cross their paths or get in their way, they leave you alone. But if the IRS audits you, or the Cuchinellis drop in on you, big trouble. Maybe real danger. My kids knew kids from both families from a distance. They never associated with them. I haven't seen Connie in a couple of years, but I can tell you for a fact that the woman is ferocious in her own right."

"What do you mean?"

"Combative."

"Wendy, that sounds about right."

"Growing up where you did, when you did, explains your perception. Most people didn't know very much about the inner workings of the Mafia until Hollywood made it popular. The FBI made them"—she made quotation marks with two fingers from each hand—"Public Enemy Number One."

"I did see *The Godfather*, but I haven't read the book."

"You need to, now. By Mario Puzo. Pick up the paperback. The Mafia is built around family, secrecy, and rebellion against the system. Yes, that involves a lot of criminal behavior, and yes, they are ruthless. I think a lot of them are sociopaths, but what do I know? I'm a librarian!"

"So is it possible ..." Tess hesitated to finish the question, so Wendy did.

"Is it possible that there are a whole lot of bad apples and one good one? Is it realistic that Eddie went away after high school and never really knew about his family? Is it possible that Eddie is different and that you and he could be a happy couple someplace far away? Is that what this is all about?"

Tess inhaled deeply and fought tears. She looked at the young man sitting at a table across the room with his head buried in textbooks. She returned eye contact with Wendy. "Yes."

Wendy took a sip of tea and with a look of appraisal stared at Tess. Tess looked away and felt about as foolish as the day she threw up in church. It wasn't like she could pretend someone else had vomited. She couldn't hide it. It was just there next to the pew. A pile of puke.

Wendy put her hand on Tess's hand and nodded gently. "Honey, you seem like a wonderful girl. You remind me of my daughter, so I'll tell you my absolute, most honest opinion."

Tess closed her eyes and waited for the inevitable.

"Connie is formidable. She's a force not to trifle with, and this would be true even if she didn't have thugs drive her around and a husband who would have your face bashed in for insulting her. Eddie went to a high school way across town in Delmar—Bethlehem High School, same as my kids. She personally drove him there every day, which is saying something in itself. He didn't work in the family business. I recall her proudly telling me that he delivered newspapers, shoveled driveways in the winter, and in high school worked at a small private airport as an apprentice mechanic. So, believe it or not, he may be one in a hundred. A small miracle."

Tess couldn't fight it any longer and began to cry. "I was certain you were going to say that only a fool would believe him," she said in between sniffles.

Wendy patted Tess on the cheek. "I didn't say I *knew* anything, but based on what I've seen, there is a chance that Eddie is cut from different cloth. But there may be enormous pressure on the poor kid to choose between you and his family now. That's a bargain with the devil, if you ask me. If I were you, the easy thing would be to run as far away as possible, today. But something tells me you don't give up or quit easily."

"I just don't know what to do. I can't talk to my parents or they would just die. I can't talk to anyone in Eddie's family, except Eddie, and I have to admit I am beginning to doubt him."

"I understand."

"We've done so well together. He's smart, ambitious, and so wonderfully considerate. He's generous. He's really cute, funny to an annoying fault, and he's so self-deprecating that

I can't stay mad at him for more than a day. But maybe this is all an illusion."

"I guess that's what this story is all about. Is he really who you think he is and will he end up, when the chips are down, choosing you and another life, or going over to his family?"

"I can't afford to make a mistake. I can't put myself or my family through another crisis. I've already done that. I can't put my golf career or my business in danger."

"If I recognized you, you really are a public figure, and that puts more scrutiny on you."

"Most of all, I can't take another blown-up romance. It happened in high school. Well, it started in high school and lasted seven years, and then blew up like a bottle rocket."

"You want some advice?"

"Yes, desperately."

"Do the right thing. It almost always turns out right if your motives are true, if your heart is in the right place, and you do what you know is right."

"How do I know all of that?"

"When things have been going badly, when you need guidance, who have you used as a role model? Who have you thought, 'What would he or she have done?'"

"My mom. My dad. Well, my dad most of the time."

"Uh-huh."

"My mother is not like Connie, and of course my dad doesn't deal with loan sharks and pimps, just pushy students, an annoying dean, and term papers. My mother is steel tough, though. When I was a sophomore in high school, I wasn't allowed to play golf on the boys' team. I know this sounds trivial, but it wasn't then. My mother went into the principal's office and faced off with the coach and the principal. I ended up playing on that team, the first girl in Illinois. Ever! So, I don't live in this mobster world here in Albany, but I was taught to never give in and never shy away, especially from the good fight, if it's someone or something I care about deeply."

"You care deeply about Eddie."

"I do."

"Then give him the benefit of the doubt. If he's true to the core, you'll know it. If he's one of them, then get the hell out of here and don't look back."

"How will I know?"

"You'll know. There will be two paths to take, and he'll have to choose one, if he hasn't already."

Tess thought about that one. She hadn't seen Eddie for more than a few hours in the three days she'd been in Albany. He continued to go to his parents' home, and he was acting strangely, or at least he'd been distant. *Maybe family trumps love. There are a million examples of that in fiction and history. Maybe I'm a fool. On the other hand, I can't leave Albany for another couple of days or whenever the cops finish their investigation, so it's not an option. I don't know what they'd do if I left. Maybe arrest me in Florida or something? Doesn't matter. No flights are leaving, and I'm not driving out of here. And then there's Teresa.*

"Okay, I hear you, and I'll think about it. Can you help me with one more thing?"

"Perhaps."

"Can you show me on a city map where the Spinozzas and Cuchinellis live, where their offices and businesses are located, and where they hang out, like restaurants and bars?"

"Why? Tess, a word of advice. Don't do this. You're a nice girl from a place where corn grows, and you play golf for a living. These are guys that carry switchblades, guns, and brass knuckles. Right now, you're a curiosity, a nobody. Don't become a nuisance, or they will hurt you. It may seem comical compared to New York City, but they are violent, guilt-free animals without consciences. Go back to your hotel and work things out with Eddie."

"Just show me. I'm not going to do anything except look."

"Look for what?"

"Teresa."

"To what end?"

"So, I can tell the cops."

"The cops are not part of the solution. Everyone knows that. They care and serve the private citizens, but they're almost delighted when one of these people kills another. It's no-man's land out there as far as the police care."

"Wendy, please."

Wendy shook her head as she got up and went to a reference desk and extracted a city map from a rack. She laid it out on a table and began giving Tess points of reference. Fifteen minutes later, Tess had drawn a map for herself with directions and the locations of Spinozza and Cuchinelli places of business, homes, offices, a pool hall, and several restaurants that Wendy felt fairly confident were local hangouts. Tess thanked Wendy, bundled up, and headed for her car.

🍸🍸🍸

Her car was still one of only three cars in the lot, which had been plowed again and was now covered by a layer of hard-packed snow. The sky was still slate gray, and the clouds looked like they hung a few hundred feet from the ground. The snow was still flying but only sparsely, and the wind had died down to a few miles per hour. It wasn't pleasant, but it wasn't the hellish conditions of the past two days. As she walked to her car, she realized that all normal life had ceased to exist. No traffic, no pedestrians, no lights in any stores, and the traffic lights weren't working. The power had been on in the library, but when she turned to look, she saw that it had darkened as well. "If it's possible, this is going to get worse," she said, and the words formed a small fog of breath in the frigid air.

With light traffic and plows working diligently on the streets, her drive back to the hotel was surprisingly manageable. Traffic lights had become four-way stops, but there were so few cars that she only had to slow at each intersection. Ten minutes later, as she pulled into The Morgan State House parking lot, the car heater was finally spitting out warm air. The windshield had a frozen ice coating inside and out, except for the area the size of a dinner plate where she had scraped. There were at least a dozen cars in the lot which, all things considered, gave her a little bit of comfort. Being trapped in hell somehow felt better with other poor souls nearby. The lot had been plowed and stairs had been shoveled. There were piles of snow the size of dump trucks on each corner of the lot and plowed mounds the size of cars near the end of the sidewalk.

With the work that had been done, she was able to quickly walk to her room. She had to work the key in the frozen lock and saw the curtains of the adjoining room flung open. No maid cart, so probably someone just waking up and trying to make sense of the weather. The lock stopped resisting, but the door didn't budge. She put her shoulder against it and threw her weight into it like a football player throwing a block. It cracked as it opened, sounding like shattered glass from the frozen moisture around it.

Tess stepped into the room and saw the light blinking on her phone. "Eddie, thank God." She pulled off her coat and gloves and picked up the phone and dialed 1 for messages. It was just the hotel manager's voice on the message, apologizing for the lack of room service. The maids weren't able to get to work, and he and the staff were trying to keep walks and stairs cleaned. She was asked to understand. No message from Eddie.

Tess understood and exhaled a long breath. She flipped on the light switch next to the bed and did a fist pump when it beamed on. The heater was working. In this frozen wasteland, she had heat and light. "Thank God for small miracles!"

🍸🍸🍸

The phone rang.

"Eddie! My God, it's so good to hear your voice."

"I'm so glad to know you're all right. I'm sorry about everything. I can't even begin to apologize for the weather, Albany, my family, the nightmare of what's happened. You must hate me."

"Stop being crazy. You can do a lot, Mr. Spinozza, but control the weather and your family are above your pay grade. When can I see you?"

"Well, that's why I'm calling."

"Oh good."

"Not so good. My father and family would like to meet you."

"Eew. I mean, oh. When?"

"I'll be there in thirty minutes."

"No you won't. I can be pushed a little, but I'm not a pushover. Make it an hour. I need to paint my fingernails.

They can wait. Hell, I've been here over two days, and no one seemed anxious to even say hello."

"Tess ..."

"Eddie ..."

"Okay, see you in an hour."

Tess hung up and rubbed her chin. *How do I dress for this occasion?*

19

TESS WENT THROUGH her normal routine, putting curlers in her hair and painting her fingernails bright red. *Why not? If they cut my fingers off, at least they'll look good.* She had a limited selection of clothes hanging in the closet. She studied her inventory: jeans, black slacks, gray slacks, a white blouse, a cream-colored blouse, a red cardigan sweater, and a dress. The dress was black, sleek, and cut with a V-neckline. Beneath it, on the floor, was a pair of black three-inch heels. All very classy if she was going to a cocktail party in decent weather with friends or professional associates, but not particularly appropriate for meeting the potential future in-laws and other random gangsters, especially in blizzard conditions. On the other hand, a blouse, jeans, and cowboy boots seemed weak and contributed to the notion she was a farmhand, a hick, a country girl who shouldn't be with Eddie and shouldn't be here. *Screw them!* She laid the dress and sweater out on the bed.

She had just finished putting a second spray of her own line of perfume, Tess, on her neck—and, for good measure, dabbed it behind her ears—when she heard more of a thump than a knock on the door. She peeled back the drape and saw Eddie standing at the door blowing on his hands. She opened the creaking door and threw her arms up in dramatic fashion. Eddie's mouth fell open.

"Wow!" Eddie said.

"Too much?"

"Maybe for them, but not me. You look good enough to kiss all over and eat."

Tess made a face.

"You're right. That didn't sound right. But you look fantastic, and you smell really good. What perfume are you wearing?" Eddie asked, attempting to recover.

Tess made another face. "Eddie, I sell perfume, remember?"

"Yup. I forgot momentarily because I was dazzled. Ah, Tess, you can't wear those shoes in this snow. If you go down, I can't be responsible for what happens if I go down on top of you."

"Eddie, in your dreams, and I'm going to wear my boots to the car. I'll put these on inside the house." She sat on the bed, pulled off her shoes, and put them in her bag, then slid on her Sorel boots. She pulled and tugged her light leather jacket over her sweater. "Tight and silly looking, but I'll take it off inside the house before I go in. I'm ready."

They descended the stairs carefully. Parked perpendicular to the other cars was a large black utility vehicle, the exhaust billowing clouds behind it. Eddie opened the rear door for Tess rather than the passenger door. She put her gloved hands face up and made a quizzical face. Eddie said, "No one is going anywhere without, ah, accompaniment." She got in, and he closed the door. He joined her in the backseat.

"Panda, this is Tess. Tess, this is Panda."

Panda, the driver, turned his bowling ball-shaped head around and smiled. His neck was only slightly smaller than his head, his shoulders looked like basketballs, and his shaved face looked almost black below the eyes. Tess guessed that he was one of those guys who needs to shave at least twice a day. "Nice to meet ya." His voice sounded like he had both a frog and gravel in his throat.

"Likewise," Tess responded.

"Lady, you really smell nice."

Tess cringed. The creepiness of it made her stomach lurch. She managed a wave that Panda saw in his rearview mirror.

The monster-size, black GMC Suburban with oversize wheels pulled away, and they turned south on Highway 9.

"Where exactly are we going?" Tess asked.

Panda answered, "Other side of Albany."

Tess whispered, "Why do they call him Panda?"

"Because he looks like a Panda bear, and he's about as hairy."

"Good to know. Pandas are gentle vegetarians."

"I said he looks like one, that's all. So I've heard anyway," said Eddie.

"Have you heard anything more about the explosion last night?"

"No one seems to know anything."

"Will we be having lunch, dinner, what?"

"I actually don't know what the plans are. I was working on the band equipment when I got called in to my father's office. When he told me it was time to meet you, I raced up-stairs, changed clothes, and Panda and I left."

"Sounds like an executive order," Tess said sarcastically.

"Well, I don't know if he intended it that way."

"What's the news on Teresa?"

"Nothing. The police are investigating and looking. I can't sleep or eat, I'm so worried about her."

Tess said, "I can't believe nothing is being done."

"I don't know what's being done, but I didn't say nothing was being done."

They rode in silence through Albany and into the suburbs. Conversation seemed inappropriate and brittle. Tess stared out the window and fought the urge to tell Eddie what she really thought. *Not the time or place.*

When they turned onto Wedgewood Lane, they were greeted by a Dead-end sign that had an addendum beneath it, no turn-around. *Appropriate* she thought. The homes were gigantic, some Tudor, others contemporary style. They all had formal gates that appeared to be more than decorative, several with lion or gargoyle statues guarding the entrances. One had full-bodied Roman god-like statues on the sides of the gates, all of them partially concealed by snow-covered vegetation and drifts. They slowed and pulled into a driveway without statuary but buttressed by a stone guardhouse and a black wrought-iron gate that was at least ten feet tall. Eddie forced a smile and said, "Home sweet home."

A man emerged from the guardhouse toting what looked like her grandfather's shotgun. His face and head were completely covered in a ski mask, with only his dark eyes showing. As the guard walked toward the vehicle, Panda rolled his window down and waved. The guard nodded and signaled to the guardhouse. The gates opened slowly, swinging into the property. Panda put it in park, and the guard walked a circle around them. He motioned for Panda to step out, and both of them walked to the back. Tess heard the trunk door open but didn't look back. It slammed shut, like a prison gate, she thought. *Don't these guys work together? Didn't he leave there an hour ago? Why the inspection?*

The guard disappeared momentarily, and Tess assumed he was looking underneath the vehicle. *A bomb? Oh my God,*

I need to get out of here. Now. She was sliding into full panic mode. Burning bile came up into the top of her throat.

The guard stood up and stared inside. Tess looked down at her boots. He tapped on the window, and Tess jumped. She glanced up and saw him making a circular motion with his gloved hand. She rolled the window down.

"Name." *Not really a question and a stupid statement at that.* "Tess Kincaid."

He looked at Panda, who nodded and got back in the driver's seat. The guard made a dismissive gesture with his hand, and Panda put the vehicle in gear and drove toward the front entrance. Tess rolled her window up. The house was several hundred yards ahead, and only the roof was visible from this vantage point. She saw what looked like a turret and several rooflines cutting in different directions. The driveway was semicircular, and the grounds were hidden by snow that was piled higher than the tank she was riding in.

They came to a slow stop in front of the house, which was enormous, bigger than any house in Champaign, even the old Victorians on Green Street. There were two men standing on either side of the steps leading up to the front door, both dressed in black topcoats, no hats. One of them walked to the car and opened Tess's door. He said nothing. She felt like a helpless child as she got out and stood waiting for some kind of inspection. She looked down as the guard patted her waist and lower back. "May I look in your purse?"

Eddie came around the corner of the car and yelled, "Hey, what the hell are you doing? She's with me." The guard held up his hands and gave them the same dismissive hand gesture as the guard at the front entrance. Tess pulled her tote bag close to her side and grabbed Eddie's arm, and they proceeded up the steps to the front entrance. Eddie stopped and said, "I'm so sorry Tess. I've never been around this before. My father is just so paranoid right now with everything going on. I've never seen these guys before. I'm so embarrassed. I don't know what to say."

"Then say nothing, Eddie. Let's get this over with. I have no idea what they want from me or why I'm here."

Panda drove away, and they stepped across a large S on the slate-tiled entrance to the front door. Spinozza. Another man wearing a black topcoat stood by the door and opened it for them, and even managed a meager smile.

The foyer was at least two stories high with yellow-tinted glass that let what little light there was from outside create an eerie glow inside. Her eyes fell downward to the marble floor, then back up to the wood-paneled hallway in front of her. Mirrors hung on the walls on both sides. Several dark wooden doors, at least nine feet high and all closed, lined the hallway on the left. A large entryway into a sitting room on the right was only partially visible.

There was a small seating bench and table on the side of the foyer, and Tess sat down and slipped her shoes on and left her boots under the bench. She laid her jacket on the bench, stood up, and took stock of herself in the mirror, physically and mentally.

"Ready?" Eddie asked.

"Not really."

"Tess, less is better. This is not a good time for my family. If my father or uncles ask you a question, answer it with as much brevity as possible. My grandfather is the one who wanted to meet you, but he won't speak. He forgets English when it's convenient and almost always speaks Italian to strangers or has someone speak for him. My father or uncles will talk for him. Don't stare at anybody or make extended eye contact. Don't comment on anything. Don't ask any questions. They're really not like this, but everyone is on edge."

I bet they're not. I bet they're usually much bigger assholes.

"Okay. Do I shake hands, hug, or just stand still like a mannequin?"

The absurdity of the question made them both smile for just a moment. "I guess just stand there. Probably no one will approach you."

"Such wonderful, friendly human beings."

"Tess, this is my family, not me."

"I know that, but I'd be lying if I didn't say I think they're just awful, and I haven't even met them. Let's go."

As they walked past the arched entryway to the sitting room, Tess touched Eddie's arm and they stopped in front of the unoccupied room so she could look. It was large with high ceilings and seemed comfortable, with two leather wing-backed chairs positioned diagonally from each other; a beautiful gold and red area rug; rich, dark, wood-paneled walls; hardwood floors; shelves filled with hardcover books; tables beside the chairs, holding small antique-looking lamps; and a large fireplace at the opposite end of the room, with a fire blazing. *Very pleasant and tastefully decorated,* she thought. Above the fireplace was a portrait of a stern-faced man wearing a gray fedora seated at a table against a backdrop of what appeared to be olive groves. Tess asked, "Who is that?" and pointed at the portrait.

"That's my grandfather's grandfather from Sicily. Actually, he was born in Ireland and lived in Sicily. My grandfather still wears that fedora on occasion."

"Impressive."

They continued walking down the hall to a partially opened door, and Tess heard men's voices coming from the room. Eddie turned to her as she inhaled deeply. She closed her eyes and calmed her nerves.

YYY

Eddie led, and Tess followed two steps behind. When she entered the room, she saw four middle-aged men, and a young man about Eddie's age. All of them wore black suits, white shirts, and differing solid-colored ties. She recognized Eddie's father sitting on the edge of a large wooden desk, and vaguely remembered seeing two of the other men who were approximately his age. *His brothers.* She'd never seen the other man or the younger member of the group. They ceased talking and stared at Tess for a couple of seconds before anyone moved or talked.

Vinnie Spinozza spoke. "Come in, Eddie."

Eddie took a couple of steps and turned and waved his hand in a sweeping motion toward Tess. "Tess, this is my father. My Uncle Joe," he pointed to his uncle. "My Uncle Frank," Eddie nodded at his uncle. "My cousin, Joey," another head nod. And this is Ernie Steinberg, the family consigliere ... ah, lawyer and advisor." Ernie nodded.

No one moved or said a word. Tess blinked and in an instant became something different than the shy girl from the Midwest, the girl who spoke only when spoken to, the girl who was self-conscious. She became someone else, someone with her mother's moxie. Her self-esteem skyrocketed, her strength multiplied tenfold, and she felt all trepidation fall away. It was like being on the first tee of a big tournament, when all thoughts of failure found no room in her psyche. She was Tess Kincaid. She was bigger than these game-playing, overblown, two-bit, narcissistic, macho, rude, pompous asses.

She smiled, blew out a breath, and strode purposefully to Eddie's father and extended her hand. She sensed the others in the room vibrate in place with this unexpected and bold overture, and she thought she could hear a faint murmur of voices. Eddie's father was caught off-guard and seemed to retreat into his own space.

Vinnie slowly extended his hand. His face was distinctly unfriendly, hardened by strong features. Dark, penetrating, close-set eyes now fully locked onto hers. A prominent nose, hooked at the end, and green-brown-olive-colored skin dominated his visage; his black, receding hair was streaked with gray. Perched as he was on the desk, his posture was slumped, and his shirt, although buttoned at the collar, seemed to fit loosely in the neck.

Tess smiled broadly. "Hello, Mr. Spinozza, it's a pleasure to finally meet you. I've heard so much about you it seems like I know you already."

She grasped his hand in a strong handshake and gave it an extra shake. He tilted his head and arched an eyebrow. He waved her to the others, and Tess moved from one to the other until she reached the consigliere. "Mr. Steinberg, my pleasure." He gave her a short, abbreviated nod and stepped aside.

Tess turned to her right and saw Eddie's grandfather sitting in a chair behind a coffee table. She now faced him, and they stared at each other for what seemed like an eternity. He was an old man with just a wisp of gray hair, thick black glasses that hung on the end of his nose, an old, rumpled shirt covered by a plaid sports coat, and baggy brown corduroy pants. His skin was very white, almost pale, and his eyes were as blue as hers.

Before Tess could move toward him to shake his hand, he slowly stood up. Again, she could feel the other men in the room vibrate with energy and just the slightest rumble of undertones, like a train in the distance. When he stood, Tess realized that with her heels she was at least three inches taller than the old man. His posture was also slumped, not like the curvature of his son but certainly not erect.

He reached across the coffee table and firmly clasped Tess's hand with both hands. It was a strong, domineering, controlling gesture, but in some way it felt genuine, unlike the others. When he pulled his hands away, he motioned for her to sit in the straight chair opposite him and across the table. He sank back into his overstuffed chair and motioned for Steinberg to come close. He whispered in his ear.

Steinberg looked at Tess. "Don Spinozza would like to welcome you."

"I'm very pleased to be here."

The old man said something to Steinberg through a hand cupped over his mouth. Steinberg looked up and addressed Tess. "The don would like to know if you could recognize any of the men who abducted his granddaughter, if you saw photos of them."

"Maybe, but I doubt it. I didn't get a good look at anyone, and it happened so fast."

More whispering. Steinberg asked, "Did the police ask you about this family?"

"Yes."

"What did they ask you and what did you say?"

"I told them that I'd never met any of you, didn't know anything about your family, and that I was here to see Eddie. I'm from Illinois and I play golf for a living, so I don't know anything about anything like this." More murmuring. The men seemed to move their attention and heads back and forth like seals at a waterpark following the conversation.

"And ..."

"And I didn't tell the whole truth because I know a lot more about your family than I told them."

All of the men moved closer, forming a semicircle around Tess. She addressed Eddie's grandfather. "When Eddie and I were trapped in the plane that crashed, he told me a lot about you. He told me about Sicily and your family and your parents."

Don Spinozza rubbed his chin and studied her. Steinberg glanced back and forth, waiting for instructions. Tess looked at the table and saw a checkers game sitting to the side and asked, "Do you play checkers?"

There was more murmuring, and she could even sense trepidation behind her. He made the slightest gesture with his fingers and had Steinberg's ear for more than ten seconds. Tess wondered if she had committed the final and fatal faux pas. Safe for now, the don slid the checkers game to the middle of the table.

Eddie stepped to Tess and whispered in her ear, the whole scene taking on the appearance of some high-level international summit. "You've got to lose. He never, ever, ever loses. It would be a bad show to win. You win you lose. Just play and stop talking so much. What's gotten into you?"

Tess nodded and pulled the checkers from the wooden box. The don whispered again to Steinberg, who looked at Tess. "The don would like to bet. He always bets on friendly checkers games."

"And the horses too? At Saratoga Springs. Eddie told me you love to go to the track."

The old man smiled. Steinberg was about to speak when Don Spinozza waved him off. He stared at Tess for what seemed like an eternity and finally spoke. "I do," he said.

"Actually, so do I. I go to Hialeah a couple of times a year. I also bet on golf games quite a bit," Tess said enthusiastically.

He tilted his head. "You live in Miami?"

Tess was surprised at his English, realizing that his unwillingness to speak English was a power play. "Boca Raton."

"I visited a friend in Florida many years ago. He was retired there after a time in prison."

"Oh, I see." It was phrased as a question.

"Al Capone."

Tess didn't react. "White or black for you?"

"Black."

"Okay, what's the bet?"

The don opened his hands and narrowed his eyes.

"I'll bet you a hamburger and a Coke," Tess said impulsively.

The don signaled for Steinberg, who listened to more whispering, which was beginning to annoy Tess. *Childish.*

"Mr. Spinozza doesn't shop, go out much, doesn't eat anything but Italian food, and doesn't know much about pop culture. He hasn't eaten a hamburger."

"Great, then it's a good bet."

Tess pushed his checkers across the board and laid hers in place.

"Would you like coffee?" the don asked.

"Sure, sounds great."

In a gesture she was becoming accustomed to, he flicked his fingers and seconds later two demitasse cups with saucers were placed on the table. The cups were half filled with jet black coffee by Eddie's cousin, whose name she'd forgotten because they all seemed to have the same three or four names. Frankie or Joey or whoever it was sat back down.

The don picked up a bottle that was sitting on the table. "Anisette?"

"Love some. Please." *I have no idea what that is.*

He filled the cups and held his up. "Salute!"

"Cheers." Tess sipped the anise-flavored spiked coffee and smiled. "Exquisite. Please make the first move." *Always better with overconfident competitors to give them honors. Throws them off slightly.*

Tess looked to her side and swore that half a dozen pairs of beady eyes were darting back and forth like one-eyed cats in a fish store. The game began.

"I've played a lot of checkers with my grandfather," Tess said.

He made the move, a perfunctory one. The silence in the room was deafening.

"Don Spinozza, what was your wife like? Eddie said she passed away several years ago, and I'm very sorry for your loss." *Distraction is my friend in golf and checkers.*

He stopped studying the board and looked up. "She was like a saint. I miss her every day."

"She had black hair, dark eyes?" Tess said, remembering what Eddie had told her.

"Yes, and the skin of most Sicilians. Very dark. I have my mother's skin, very light. My mother's eyes were very blue. She had blonde hair. She looked like you." Tess was certain that a tear began to form in his left eye. "She was beautiful and full of life, but they sent her back."

"To Sicily?"

"Yes, sick in the lungs."

"Tuberculosis?"

"Yes, and my sister."

"What were their names?"

"Carolina."

"Both of them?"

"Yes." He wiped a full-blown tear from his eye.

The conversation subsided as both players began taking checkers from the board. The play continued until they were both down to several checkers and two crowned kings. Tess thought about what Eddie had said. *Lose. You lose if you win. He never loses.* She thought if he never loses, then he'll be overly aggressive because winning for him isn't about actually winning, but how fast he wins. That's how he impresses on-lookers: with his guile, skill, and instinct.

Tess retreated and forced him to chase. After several minutes, she caught him in a trap and hesitated. *I can lose and walk away feeling good that I actually got the all-powerful don to speak in English, and call it a moral victory. Or I can play the way I was raised. Play fair. Play hard. Play to win. I always play golf to win.* She pursed her lips. She made eye contact with the don. She sat back in her chair. She inhaled and then she trapped him for the win.

The room was hushed. Don Spinozza looked around at his sons and at Steinberg. He slowly stood up and walked around the table as Tess stood. He approached her and pulled her to him, hugging her. In a quiet voice, he said, "You are a strong one. You are a brave one. Eddie is good, and you will be good for him. If you *choose* him, as a matter of respect, I will pay for your honeymoon to Italy. That was my bet."

♈♈♈

Tess sat on the bench in the foyer and pulled on her boots and coat as Eddie left to find Panda and retrieve the car. She looked up, and Vinnie Spinozza was standing over her. She raised her eyebrows, waiting. He seemed to be glowering down at her.

"We're glad you came," he said disingenuously. "We're happy to have met you, but this is a very hard time for the family. Eddie needs to be with his family now, and you need to go home to yours."

"Mr. Spinozza, I can't go anywhere until the police say I can. I'm a material witness to a kidnapping, and besides I can't drive or even fly out of here for a couple of days."

"Don't worry about it. I'll arrange for travel."

"I don't think—"

"Don't think about it. It will be done." He turned and walked away.

Tess wanted to scream, "You ass! You complete ass! I'll leave when I want to, not when I'm dismissed." She shoved her arms into her coat and stormed out the front door, forgetting her black heels.

20

EDDIE AND TESS slid into the backseat of the car, and the guard closed the door. She seethed and spit out, "Your father just told me to get out of town. What is wrong with him"

"Tess, are you sure you heard him? Are you maybe over-reacting?"

"No! Are you kidding me? Are you freaking kidding me? I just went through a creepy, bizarre experience, and you ask me if I'm overreacting?" She was yelling at the top her lungs. She threw her bag at him, which he deflected.

"Tess—"

"Don't!" She held up her hands. "You're going to have to choose between them and me because I'm not going to deal with your family. It's them or me. Period!"

Eddie looked out his window.

"Where to?" Panda interjected.

"The hotel!" they said in unison.

Eddie scratched his head vigorously during the ride, and Tess stared out the window. There was no conversation; only the sound of Frank Sinatra on the 8-track tape player kept the tension from becoming explosive.

When they reached the hotel, Tess opened her door and said curtly, "Eddie, I need to do some things that don't include you."

"Like what?"

"Like figure out why I'm here."

"Tess—" She slammed the door and walked to her room.

Eddie opened his door and said over the roof of the car, "Tess, come on."

She waved dismissively without turning around as she crunched over the snow-packed sidewalk.

Tess found two clean towels on her unmade bed from the staff who had made it to work. "Great. Not that it matters."

She changed clothes, sat on the bed, and pulled a yellow pad of paper from her suitcase and decided to make some notes using her favorite analyzing tool from college: a "Ben Franklin" list. She called it that for a reason she'd long since forgotten, but it was the best way she knew to analyze her thoughts. She started with the most pressing and important issue currently in her life, Eddie, which she wrote in all caps across the top of the sheet. She drew a line down the center of the pad and wrote "Positives" at the top of the left side and "Negatives" on the right side. She was still fuming, so she started without hesitation on the right side. All the problems with Eddie started and ended with his family. She listed fourteen items before she threw the towels toward the bathroom.

There was a knock at her door. She bounded off the bed, thinking it was maid service, and opened the unlocked door. As she turned the knob, the door came back at her, and only her quick reflexes allowed her to get a forearm up before the door slammed into her face. A man with a ski mask covering his face and black gloves shoved her toward the bed. She screamed.

"Good luck with that. Nobody is here but you and me."

"Get out!" she screamed as she tried to kick him. She turned and made a move for the phone, but he beat her to it.

Tess backed up in a defensive posture. No way was she going to let anything happen without one hell of a fight. She hesitated as he stopped in the center of the room. As he stood there, his body loosened somewhat. Through his mask, he said gruffly, "This is a courtesy visit. I'm here to warn you to stay out of police business and forget about Teresa Spinozza, unless of course, you'd like to join her. GET OUT OF ALBANY!"

Even as he demanded that, the way he spoke made him sound like more of a college prep than a thug. Tess regained her composure, concluding that there was no imminent physical danger. A wave of anger and frustration grabbed her like a rogue strike of lightning, and she straightened up. Pointing at the intruder, she seethed fearlessly, "Who sent you? Take off the mask, chickenshit!"

"You've been warned," he said walking toward the door.

She moved toward him, ready to pull him back and yank off the mask, but in an instant, he was out and slammed the door behind him. She yanked it open and looked for the vehicle that must have been in the lot, but the lot was empty, and he was gone. She raced inside and called the front desk and the police.

An hour later, after explaining what happened to two uniformed officers and having her hotel bill canceled by the management, she sat down hard on the chair in her room. The warning could have come from either family or, for that matter, the police. The guy seemed almost professional, but he was a lousy excuse for a thug—his performance was more theatrical than frightening, and after the initial shock, she hadn't felt extraordinary fear or panic. She glanced at her watch: just before 8:00 p.m.

She finished her "Ben Franklin" list with only six positives for continuing her relationship with Eddie. She realized this might not be entirely reasonable at the moment. She watched television and tried reading *Centennial* late into the night before finally falling asleep.

YYY

She pulled open the curtains the next morning and thought she saw a slight change in the weather. The cloud cover, which had kept the sky a battleship gray for days, had improved to the color of dirty dishwater, transforming the mood from that of a migraine to dull forehead pain.

Tess packed her bags and dropped off her room key at the front desk. There was a different clerk on duty, and she made sure her bill had in fact been paid, which when she thought about it, was one of the only good things that had happened on this adventure. She saw the headline of *The Knickerbocker News* laying on the counter: "42 INCHES ENOUGH!" She'd had enough too.

She pulled onto Route 9, and as she approached the police station, she made the snap decision to check in with Detective Keibler. As she pulled into the snow-packed lot, she wondered what the point was in stopping. It appeared Teresa was mere flotsam in the ocean of corruption, crime, and lowlife activity she'd witnessed the past couple of days. All the players seemed to lack moral conviction, decency, and civility. She'd had it with two-bit punks and cops that cared more about their doughnuts than resolving the crimes. It was time to call it a day, to get out of Dodge, and, most importantly, to pull the plug on a future with Eddie. He was a great guy, but with a family from hell.

She had come to three very important conclusions. One, Eddie was a Spinozza. And the Spinozzas—with the possible exceptions of Teresa, Frankie, and Eddie, maybe, probably— were a family of sociopathic, greedy, thieving, backstabbing, rude, and vicious lowlifes. Therefore, Eddie was a latent creep waiting to emerge from the slime of these Albany sickos. Two, Eddie couldn't have grown up without knowing what his family was like and be aware of the criminal activities going on around him. No matter how much Connie shielded him, he would have to be dumber than a handball, have an IQ lower than a rutabaga, to not see his family for what they were. Three, Eddie hadn't exactly been supportive of her the last couple of days and would most likely choose, if he hadn't already, his family over her. Choosing her would mean leaving his family. Conclusion: Head for the club-house; the round was mercifully over.

"Good morning again," she said to the receptionist at the front desk. "Just for the fun of it, I thought I'd stop and have you tell me Detective Keibler wasn't in."

The woman looked up from her work, and Tess flushed with embarrassment. "I'm so sorry, that sounded very rude and sarcastic, and you aren't the same person who I've talked to the last couple of days. Please forgive me. I don't know what's gotten into me."

"Bad day, huh? The snow will do that to you. Actually, Detective Keibler is in." Her name badge read Mary. She was a diminutive, pleasant-looking woman with a warm smile and soothing voice. Mary picked up the phone, dialed an extension, and told Keibler that a woman was at the front desk.

It took several minutes before the detective emerged from the secured doors of the station. His facial expressions would make a poker player proud: Nothing could be gleaned. "Huh, Miss Kincaid, I was just thinking of you. Funny you should show up here."

Tess arched her eyebrows. Civility? Mild interest? A break in Teresa's case?

"Follow me, please."

Tess sat in the same metal chair that she'd been in before and waited for him to move a doughnut lying on top of a napkin from his pile of folders. Without looking up from the pile of folders, he said, "Yeah, yeah, yeah, I'm having a doughnut this morning. Have a chuckle, but I usually don't eat anything sweet. Diabetic, you know."

"Sorry to hear that. I wouldn't mind one myself. And a cup of coffee."

He nodded. "No problem. Cream and sugar?"

"Just cream."

"Jelly or glazed?"

"Glazed." Tess hadn't eaten a donut in months. But it sounded comforting, considering she was about to be discharged from the investigation, or discharge herself, and about to bail out of her relationship with Eddie. Scotch would have been better, but this would work.

Keibler returned with a Styrofoam cup and a doughnut on a napkin.

"Thank-you," she said.

"Well, I see here you had a visitor a couple of hours ago. A ski mask? Who wears a ski mask to a shakedown? Guys wear ski masks when they rob a convenience store. This was an amateur."

"Funny you should mention that. He didn't scare me as much as he just ticked me off. He had nice shoes and a nice jacket, so I think he was just a messenger more than a mugger. But you know what, I got the message. I'm taking his advice and leaving town. I've had enough. My language is going down the toilet, I'm becoming sarcastic and rude, and I'm really sick of this place. No offense."

"None taken. We New Yorkers roll that way. So, we really haven't made any headway in the abduction case. No leads and no witnesses, except you."

"What about Frankie and the shooting?"

"Same."

"The bomb at the cement plant?"

"The bomb? Who told you it was a bomb? We haven't released that information to the public."

"Well, ah, I just assumed it was a bomb."

He pointed at her. "You were there! We have an eyewitness who swore a car took off from just down the street seconds after the explosion. That was you, wasn't it? Don't lie to me. I'm the police."

Tess stared at her half-eaten doughnut. She looked up at him and said, "Yes."

"I knew it. It was just a hunch when you showed up today, but I knew you had more to tell me. You're too damned honest to hide it from the police. You're like, ah … ah … wholesome honest." He slapped the desktop. "I knew it. Lady, you just got yourself another couple of days added to your sentence here in the beautiful confines of Albany. What did you see?"

"Too honest compared to whom? The dirtbags you're supposedly investigating or the average person?"

"What'd you see and who were you with? The witness said there were two people sitting in a car that sped off. I'm going to need a statement in writing, but let's talk it through first."

"What happens if I don't want to talk?"

"You won't have to rent a hotel room. We'll be providing you with a room, bed, and three squares a day. It's called obstruction of justice."

"And the hits just keep on coming."

Dazed, exhausted, and without clear recourse, Tess recounted the events leading up to the explosion, the chase, and the name of the perpetrator who Eddie had followed. She also gave up Eddie.

Tess left the station in a complete funk and checked into the Hyatt six blocks away. She hadn't thought it was possible for things to get worse, but they had. Now, the police would bring Eddie in for questioning, and questioning would probably end up in charges because they needed a lead, and the best way to get a real lead was to get some leverage on who they knew was the real culprit. She didn't know which family it was—both were probably guilty of breaking a hundred laws.

Eddie had said the most important thing in his family, and to him as well, was loyalty, and she had just offered him up like a sacrificial lamb. She hadn't meant to do it, but fatigue, a strange environment, stress, lack of sleep, and the damned doughnut had all added up to a mistake, a really big one. She had inadvertently blabbed. Eddie would never speak to her again. His father would probably assert that he had warned Eddie about her. His mother would gloat. Thoroughly deflated, she lay down on the bed, put her hands behind her head, and eventually drifted off to sleep.

She awakened refreshed. It was time to do something. The good Spinozzas were dropping like flies—shot, kidnapped, and now questioned, maybe arrested. She pulled her homemade map of Albany out of her tote bag and spread it on the table. She started strategizing. The police would arrest the bomber, Otto Vitello, because Eddie wouldn't take the rap for someone like that or a crime like that, and Vitello would implicate the Spinozzas. Which ones? She didn't care. If it was the old man, it was about time he got his due, but they'd never prove it. The shooting in the nightclub was the Cuchinellis, but without a weapon or a witness, there'd be no case. Even if they had both a weapon and a witness, the shooter would never give up old man Cuchinelli.

So, as far as she was concerned, they could shoot each other and blow each other's businesses and homes up until kingdom come. The two families, the police, and the people they owned in the City of Albany government weren't going to change. In the end, maybe somebody else would start picking up trash or mixing cement or running prostitutes or selling drugs or doing whatever they did. The only dog she had left in this fight was Teresa. Tess felt compelled to do something. Perhaps it was because she didn't have a sister, and Teresa was as close to one as she had at the moment. And even though Tess had just sung like a canary to the police, she *was* loyal, she *was* honest, she *was* a good person. Eddie had to know that. She loved Eddie for a number of reasons, but none more important than the belief that he was truly a good person. He had a good heart, he was honest, he was smart, he was funny. He was probably gone now. She laid back down and cried into her pillow.

🍸🍸🍸

Within the hour, her resolve resurfaced, and she studied the map and her alternatives. Yes, she could sit in the hotel room for a couple of days, until the police sorted out the cement plant bombing, and then leave town quietly, never again to hear from Eddie or Teresa. She could go back to her life in Florida and forget this whole mess. She could let it wash away, like a good spring rain washes away winter grime. But as she'd heard her father say many times without elaboration, "It just wouldn't be right."

She'd argue, "What does that mean? That doesn't mean anything." And he'd say, "Tess, some things can't be explained, don't need to be. There's right and there's wrong. You know it or you don't. And *you* know what's right and wrong."

He never did explain himself precisely, and now she knew what he meant. Certain behaviors, regardless of the circumstances, required certain responses. Don't let bullies prevail, don't let liars get away with lies, don't let thieves steal when you can stop it, and don't let cheats get away with their cheating. Don't let the strong take advantage of the weak. Don't brag or bring attention to yourself. Always treat the military with respect. Be loyal to your friends. And family always comes first. That last one was exactly why she'd lose Eddie. He would be devastated by her disloyalty and retreat to his family. It was water under the bridge now, but she could *do* something. And that something would be to help the police find Teresa and probably simultaneously extricate Eddie from suspicion. How the two would coincide, she wasn't sure at the moment.

The Cuchinellis were holding Teresa somewhere, and it was quite simple. If the police really wanted to find Teresa, they could just stake out wherever the Cuchinelli brain trust operated. Wendy the librarian, with the help of just the phone book, had found their business locations and the homes of the old man and his sons. It was incredibly simple. The mobsters weren't stupid, though. The real dirty details of the business, the money transfers, the orders to kidnap and shoot people were given in less obvious places.

Wendy had said that the Spinozzas spent a lot of time eating and drinking at an Italian restaurant called Mauro's, on the southwest side of Albany near Delmar. The Cuchinellis spent their time at Gino's, on the north side of Albany not far from where she sat at the moment; they owned a pool hall and a bowling alley as well, but these were all too public to be field headquarters. So, she could find the second or even third level of the Cuchinelli family hanging out at Gino's. The big boys would never frequent the place. It might even be wiretapped. Okay, now that sounded like a television show. But wouldn't the actual low-level soldiers in the Cuchinelli army have to talk to someone, get cash, report in without calling on the phone? What if they dropped into Gino's? She could follow them back to Teresa.

It wasn't rocket science. She had time, and it was the least she could do for Teresa and for Eddie before riding out of town into the sunset. No contact, no confrontation, just do the grunt work the police were being paid to, apparently, not do.

The more she thought about it, the more she was certain that the Cuchinellis didn't know who she was. She was also certain that the Cuchinellis had little interest in Eddie and wouldn't have tailed him. So they couldn't have known that she was staying at The Morgan. Only the Spinozzas and the police knew that. The man who had pushed his way into her room hours earlier had expensive shoes and a fashionable coat. He spoke without a harsh New York accent. That was troubling. She got in her car and drove to Gino's.

21

TESS PARKED ON BROADWAY where she could see the front and back entrances to Gino's—a lucky break considering how many spaces had been lost to piles of snow. Six cars were parked in the restaurant-lounge's plowed lot, so she figured the Cuchinellis must have gotten restless, having been cooped up inside for two or three days, and hit their local watering hole for a little refreshment and bonding. Except for a small, beat-up foreign car probably owned by the cook, the vehicles were all full-size Cadillacs and Lincolns, iconic symbols for tough guys.

The self-anointed junior private eye on a stakeout had a couple of minor problems that might turn into critical ones shortly. The cold wasn't one of them. Tess had plenty of gas in the car, and the heater worked just fine. She was dressed well enough to live in the Arctic. Sooner or later, however, she'd have to leave to go to the bathroom. That would mean walking two blocks to a Burger King because no other businesses were open on this block and she didn't want to lose her parking space. The other dilemma was deciding who to follow when cars started exiting. She had no idea who inside was a Cuchinelli or just a local patron. On the other hand, what was the likelihood that some Joe Schmo would be driving a big Cadillac and be at Gino's right now? In addition, the odds of success were long and a little depressing because she could end up following people for days without any results.

She decided to wait, watch, and take a chance on someone. She was due for some good luck. As she stared at the red neon light flashing "Gino's" on the front window, her thoughts drifted back to a magical night with Eddie six months earlier at an iconic hotel in Denver. The lavish food, the romantic piano bar, the memorable next morning … She started thinking about the specific details when she saw an approaching vehicle. Good thing, because reminiscing would only make her cry, and that wouldn't be a good thing at this moment.

The car was the standard-issue large black vehicle that they all drove. It pulled into the lot and parked away from the other cars. A short, heavyset man got out and went into the front entrance. She didn't recognize him from The Dirty Martini, but she would have difficulty recognizing anyone from the nightclub. The Cuchinellis had been on the other side of the room, and the club had been as smoky as a forest fire. She recalled that they'd looked a little alike—most were thin, wiry, dark, and shrunken like raisins, but not this guy, who was more like a full-bodied grape.

Five minutes later, another car of similar make pulled in. It was covered by at least a foot of snow, so this guy didn't have the luxury of a garage and was apparently too lazy to clear the snow off of more than the front and back windshield.

And then she waited. After thirty minutes, she was beginning to feel anxious about the futility of this mission. Worse, she was beginning to feel the need to go to the bathroom.

She put the car in reverse, preparing to leave her parking place, and glanced at the rear windshield and saw another car coming up the street behind her, moving slowly with its turn signal blinking. She put the car back in park and slid down in the seat to hide. After the car turned into Gino's, she grabbed her field glasses and popped up to get a better view. The car parked facing toward the restaurant and sat idling for several minutes. It was a new, smaller car, which didn't fit the pattern. The driver's side door opened, and Tess gasped. "Holy shit!" It was the younger cousin—Joey, Vinnie, whoever—from the big get-together at the Spinozza compound.

What did this mean? Was he the Spinozza emissary? Were they making a deal to release Teresa? Were they negotiating terms for some realignment of their businesses? Were they calling a truce? Maybe this was over? Not likely—too many bad things had happened in three days.

A required bathroom break was becoming urgent, and she decided it would be better to go now and hopefully get back before anyone left the place. She decided to drive to the Burger King, to make it quick, and in ten minutes, she was back. She found her same parking spot, with a large Coke, burger, and fries in hand. To hell with eating healthy. The hot, greasy, salty food tasted heavenly.

The same cars were parked, meaning, probably, that no one had left. It must be a sign of some serious negotiating. She decided to just wait and see, but she would still have the difficult decision of who to follow, although following the Spinozza cousin was unnecessary. He wasn't going anywhere near Teresa and probably wouldn't leave here with knowledge of her whereabouts. She needed to stay focused with one singular purpose: discover Teresa's location and give the police the lead they seemed not to want. The junior varsity member of the Cuchinelli team would be the first out the door while the other fat one would eat dinner before leaving. That settled it. She'd follow the first Cuchinelli.

She listened to the radio and periodically turned on the ignition to warm herself. As the afternoon light began to fade, she yanked on her coat sleeve to see her watch. It was ten minutes before four. It would be much easier to follow someone and remember where she'd been if it was daylight. Come on! How much could there be to talk about with your arch enemy? They weren't catching up on old acquaintances, reminiscing about old times, asking about friends and family. Get on with it!

The front door finally opened, and the Spinozza cousin stepped out and looked in both directions, as if he was crossing a busy street. She slid down in the seat so her vantage was between the dash and the steering wheel. What was his name? And what was it with all the first names ending in "ie"? Eddie, Frankie, Vinnie. The unnamed Spinozza pulled his hat down on his head and walked to his car. One down.

Within minutes, a junior Cuchinelli came out the back door with a bag in his hands and quickly walked to his car. Not very smart to not even glance up and down the street or look over his shoulder, but this guy didn't have the job he had because he was brilliant. None of these guys seemed that smart. This was the guy to follow, she had decided. When she saw white exhaust belch out of his tailpipe, she started her car. He pulled out and turned right on Broadway.

This was it, do or die. She'd follow him with about a half block distance between them. Her only experience in this "tailing" business had been the previous night and what she'd seen on television shows. Not much training. Fortunately, he had only cleared a small part of his rear windshield, and while there were virtually no cars on the road, with bad visibility he wouldn't be thinking about someone following him. It would be easy to keep him in view.

She followed for a mile or so before Broadway turned into Highway 32. It had been plowed cleanly, and they picked up speed to almost forty miles an hour. She let him have several hundred yards' lead since they were basically the only cars on the road and the sun wouldn't set for another few minutes, giving her reasonable visibility. At a sign indicating that a town called Troy was two miles ahead, he put his left turn signal on and slowed. She followed the car, pulled off the highway, and came to an intersection where she read the road sign, Cemetery Avenue. That was a bad omen. The road angled, and she momentarily lost visual contact. When he came back in view, she saw a sign that was worse than the last one: Dead-end.

Her heart was pounding, and she had to force herself to stop breathing in short shallow breaths. *Relax. This is like the first tee box. Those who control their nerves hit it in the fairway.* He made a sharp right and continued on the dead-end road to the cemetery. She pulled over and waited several seconds before continuing slowly down the road, which she now realized ran adjacent to the cemetery. She could only see the very tops of some grandiose gravestones that were visible over the stone wall. She watched his brake lights come on several hundred yards ahead. She stopped the car, got out, and walked along a head-high snowbank toward a dimly lit two-story, red-brick building that the driver was now walking toward. He entered the front door without hesitation, which meant it was unlocked. That wouldn't help find Teresa, but it did indicate that if this was the kidnapper, then he was very confident that his location was secure and isolated. As she got within fifty yards of the building, she could make out that it seemed like an old abandoned commercial structure in the shape of an L.

She was studying the building when the front door opened. She froze and backed hard into the snowbank to conceal herself, but the plowed snow was as hard as packed dirt and it felt like backing into a wall. It jarred her a bit. The light inside the building backlit him, and if he had looked up the road, there's no way he would have missed her. But he walked to the car with his head down and retrieved the bag that he had carried from the restaurant and then returned to the building. He'd forgotten the dinner he'd brought back for his sidekick or maybe Teresa? Maybe there are two of them guarding Teresa? Hopefully, that's all they were doing, just guarding her. She imagined all kinds of bad things they could be doing to her. *Too many movies.*

She walked within ten yards of the structure and saw that there was no path cleared to the back of the building. The snow had drifted up against the windowless walls, forming an unassailable blockade around the structure. Anyone coming or going had to go through the front entrance. Behind the building and to the north were open fields. Approaching the building from either of those directions meant there was no cover of forest, just open expanses of deep snow. On the west side of the building was the cemetery. She couldn't tell what was behind the building on the east side, but the structure was situated like a little fortress, inaccessible and guarded for now by snow. No wonder the guy was so comfortable coming and going. This place seemed impenetrable.

There was nothing more she could do, so she returned to her car and backed up until she had room to turn around.

She decided to check one more thing. She drove back to Highway 32, but turned north and headed to the city limits of Troy. She kept her eye on the direction of the cemetery and saw nothing but open fields between it and the highway. *If police were to send in a SWAT team*, she thought, *there would be plenty of space for approaching the hideout.* She turned around and headed back to Albany, envisioning flashing red lights and sirens blazing down Cemetery Road. No escaping for the Cuchinellis. "See, this wasn't so hard," she said proudly and naively to herself.

🍸🍸🍸

She pulled into the police station a little after 6:00 p.m. and found there had been a shift change. The receptionist whom she'd been so curt with had been replaced by Jean Marie, a perky, friendly-looking woman in her early fifties.

"Hi, can I help you?"

"Yes, please. I need to see Detective Keibler, urgently. I have some very important information for him."

"You do," she answered. "Well, let's see if we can find him. I just got here, and I haven't been back to the lunchroom, but let me see what I can do." She dialed the extension. "Hi, Bud, I have someone here looking for Keibler." She listened to the response. "Okay. Thanks."

She smiled at Tess. "He's walking out the door for the day. Can someone else help you?"

"I don't know. Ah ... I guess anyone working on the Spinozza abduction case."

"Oh, that. Well, that would be a detective. Let me see." She scrolled down a list on the desk and stopped her finger mid-page. "Let's check with John Morris." She dialed his extension. "John, can you help a young lady with some information for Keibler about the Spinozza case." She nodded at Tess. "Thanks."

"He'll be right up."

Morris came through the door a minute later. He looked like he was in his midtwenties, red hair, and seemed entirely pleasant. "Hi. I'm John Morris. Can I help you?" he said with a level of eagerness Tess hadn't seen in any other cop.

"I have ascertained some important information, at least I think it's important, regarding Teresa Spinozza."

"You have! Holy cow, come on back to my desk." He held the door for Tess.

Tess followed Morris to a desk in the back of the pit at the opposite end from Keibler's desk. He settled himself and pulled out a notepad. "Okay then, what are we talking about?"

"I may know where she's at."

"Who?"

"Teresa Spinozza."

"Alrighty, let's take a look at this case. Can you spell that last name, Sp … what?"

"You don't know a thing about this case, do you?"

"We have a lot of cases we're handling."

"You're new, aren't you?"

He sat up straight. "I've been a detective for three of my six years that I've been in police work. True, I've only been in Albany a couple of weeks, but I take offense to your inference."

"I'm sorry, really I am. I guess I thought a lot of people would be working around the clock to solve a kidnapping."

"Kidnapping!"

"Yes."

"Oh, the case from Thursday morning. Yes. Yes. Well, that's being handled by Keibler and another detective. Let me take the information, and I'll get it to him pronto."

Tess relayed all she'd discovered following the Cuchinelli operative to Cemetery Road. "Very impressive. Keibler won't be in until Monday morning, but I'll call him tonight and hopefully catch him before he leaves."

"Leaves! Where's he going at a time like this?"

"I think his daughter is giving birth to his first grandchild over in Montpelier. It's a pretty big deal to him and his wife."

"*This* is a big deal!" Tess raised her voice, which caught no one's attention.

Tess rubbed her face realizing, once and for all, that she was attempting to buck a system so deeply entrenched that she might as well stand on the shore of the Atlantic Ocean and command the waves to cease. She inhaled and slowly exhaled, then biting her lower lip said, "Alright, why don't you give Detective Keibler the information. I'm sure you're right. A case like this could get messy if there were a lot of hands stirring the pot."

"I think you just mixed up your metaphor."

"Right. Okay. Let him know. I'll check in with him Monday morning.

CHAPTER

22

BACK IN HER ROOM at the Hyatt, she watched television, picked at the Chinese food she had picked up, and assessed her options. She could call her parents and lie to them about the events of the last seventy-two hours. She could call the Spinozza residence and try to get past the gatekeeper and talk to Eddie ... but tell him what? That she'd made a big mistake and talked to the police and she was sorry? That might be the truth, but it would be purposeless, and he probably wouldn't believe her. She could check out of the hotel and drive south, dump the rental car in Philly, and fly home to Florida. That would be the easiest course of action but the hardest to live with in the long run. If she visited Frankie and Tiziana at the hospital, it would create the opportunity for someone to follow her back to the Hyatt. As far as she could tell, no one knew where she was staying or if she had left town. That was an advantage. Now what?

She thought about what Wendy had said, to just do the right thing. It was the same advice her mother and father would give her. The challenge was that the right thing can be elusive, relative, and sometimes only right for half the people involved. So she decided to think the situation over in the bar downstairs, which was never a bad idea when she needed perspective.

Two gin and tonics later, she began to formulate a plan for what she needed to do and what she hoped someone would do for her if she was ever imprisoned in a cemetery building. Weren't we all supposed to do unto others as you would have them do unto you? The Golden Rule from Matthew in Bible studies. That wasn't exactly what the verse said, but two gin and tonics can make Bible verses a little fuzzy. She paid her bill and called it a night.

Riding the elevator up to the fourth floor, she recalled two years earlier when she and Eddie were trapped in the wrecked Cessna plane deep in the backwoods of Pennsylvania. If it hadn't been for the efforts of a Search and Rescue guy named Stone and his team, she would have probably died of exposure. Eddie almost died anyway. She recalled that Stone had hardly acknowledged her gratitude. That's the kind of guy he was, he is: the strong, silent, heroic type. She needed to repay the universe with a selfless act and help Teresa. She would *do* something. Teresa might not be in that old brick building. She might be fine if Keibler rode out there on Monday morning with the cavalry and rescued her. Maybe, maybe not? There were a lot of things left up to chance. There was nothing she could do until morning, but she had a plan, perhaps lacking in practicality and defying reality, but it was a start.

She awoke before dawn feeling rested and energized. The sun had broken the horizon, and the sky was clear of clouds, a positive start for the day. She pulled on her arctic garb, hopefully for the last time. She checked out of the hotel and loaded her luggage in the trunk of her car. First stop was a gas station on her way to the hospital. She hadn't used much gas, but she planned on using a whole lot in the next day.

The next stop was the hospital. She wanted to say good-bye to Tiziana and Frankie and wish them luck on what she knew would be a difficult journey: breaking away from the Spinozza family. She breezed quickly through the lobby and took the stairs to the surgical ward. There were no nurses at the central desk, so she walked quickly to Frankie's room. The door was closed, so she cracked it open and peeked in. He appeared to be sound asleep. There was no sense in waking him. She walked to the patient lounge and found Tiziana asleep on a couch. Tess touched her shoulder, and Tiziana awakened with a start. "What's wrong?"

"Nothing," Tess said softly. "I just wanted to say goodbye and wish you the best of luck."

"Oh Tess, thank-you. You're leaving?"

"I think it's best, under the circumstances, especially after yesterday."

"What happened yesterday?"

"You know with the police and Eddie and the bomb thing."

"No, I don't know anything about that. I've been here, and no one has told me anything."

She doesn't know. "Well, it doesn't matter. I just think it's best for me and everyone else if I head for home."

"We're going to leave too, as soon as Frankie can help pack and travel. We're leaving this place and getting away from here. I told Frankie everything that's been going on. We're more convinced than ever that if we don't leave now, we'll live our whole lives in the dark shadows of his family."

"I understand. I just wanted to say if there's anything I can do to help you, let me know."

"There is."

"There is?"

"You know Frankie's uncle lives in Chicago, and he's been the black sheep of the family for twenty years. But they leave him alone. That's probably why Connie sent Eddie to live with him. We want to go there to start over, and I know your family lives somewhere in Illinois. I can't remember the town."

"Champaign."

"Uh-huh, Champaign. The favor I'm asking is this," she hesitated and took a deep breath. "Frankie is a CPA. Can you open any doors for him?"

"Maybe. I'll see what I can do."

"Frankie doesn't know anything. He hasn't done anything. He's an outsider in his own family. I told you, it's his father's generation that pulls all the strings and Frankie's grandfather, of course. The family has long tentacles, but if they've left Tony alone all these years, then we'll be okay."

"Hopefully."

"So how does Eddie feel about you leaving so suddenly? I was waiting for the big engagement, the ring, the wedding plans."

"Well, that's not going to happen, Tiziana. There are too many complications, too many things that are so fundamentally different, and too much other *stuff* for me to handle."

"It's the damned Spinozzas. You have to rethink this, Tess. Eddie's the best, and he's crazy about you. Don't let his father ruin it. He specializes in ruining things. He loves and thrives on destruction. His life is about vendettas and revenge—that is, when he's not working on greed."

"That's most of the seven deadly sins."

"That bastard is the *deadly* sin. I hate him."

"Yeah, me too, but it won't change a thing," said Tess. "Move your family away from all of this."

Tiziana's eyes began to water. Tess leaned over and hugged her. "Tell Frankie goodbye for me, and you take care. I'm going to head out now."

"What should I say to Teresa for you when I see her? And I will."

"Tell her to keep practicing the harmonica," Tess said. "She's got potential. And also tell her not to do anything I wouldn't do." *Maybe I'll tell her myself.*

Tess smiled and left the lounge. She turned to her right and walked into the lady's room. She studied herself in the mirror for a while and forged a tight smile, confident in her resolve. She exited and turned back to the left just as Connie and Eddie were entering Frankie's room. *Oh God, should I go in there? What should I say? I wonder if the police have questioned him yet about the explosion. I wonder if he would believe me if I told him it was a mistake. I think the answer is clear. He's here with his mother. The family trumps girlfriends, especially ones who sell out family members to the police.* She walked past the room and the elevator to the stairs. Better not to see anyone.

She descended the stairs to the first floor and saw the sign for the cafeteria on the next level down. She was starving, it was Sunday morning, and more than likely nobody she knew would be in there, at least for a few minutes. She could slip in and fill up a Styrofoam container with all kinds of bad stuff to eat, like bacon and sausage, eggs, toast, and about four of those little containers of jelly. A giant coffee with lots of cream would be perfect. She went down another level, salivating.

She opened the door and walked down the hallway to the cafeteria and glanced through the glass before walking inside. She stopped in her tracks and backed up a couple of feet, taking herself out of sight of the customers. Standing in the line was Eddie's father and the Spinozza emissary cousin she'd seen the day before. It hit her like a door slamming in her face: The cousin was being directed by Eddie's father. Whatever negotiations were going on, it was his father who was pulling the strings. The cousin was the go-to guy, the heir-apparent, the new generation leader being groomed. She watched them get coffee and sit at a table across the dining room. They talked for less than a minute before she watched in astonishment as Eddie's father pulled an envelope from his coat pocket and surreptitiously slid it across the table. Cousin Spinozza slipped it quickly into his pocket.

It was now clear who was paying whom, but paying someone to do what? Was he paying a ransom for Teresa's release? Why would he be working through a low-level family member to do that? And why would Cousin Spinozza be meeting with a counterpart last night? If they were negotiating an end to a turf war, then the heads of the two families and their lawyer guys—whatever that Italian word for them was— would be meeting. Everybody knew that if they watched *The Godfather*. No, this was something diabolical.

A few minutes later, she was in her car going back to the Army Navy surplus store, hoping it was open on a Sunday morning.

CHAPTER

23

THE ONLY CAR in the Capital Army Navy's parking lot was a Jeep with a roof rack, and as she pulled in, she saw Ari unlocking the store's front door. She quickly got out and said, "Hey you."

"You again! Come on in."

She smiled and gathered herself, and made her way to the entrance. He held the door open for her. "So, you can't possibly be cold. Did you miss me?"

"Oh, I'm not cold. The jacket, the hat, gloves, and boots are perfect. And yes I did. Miss you, that is. Can we talk for a minute?"

The man built like a walking refrigerator furrowed his brow, and his bushy black eyebrows almost became one brow. "I'm all yours. What's the problem?"

"Well, I need some help, and I don't know who can help me but you."

"Me?" He raised his hands, palms open, shrugging his shoulders.

"Yes, I hope so."

"Well, let's not stand out here. Come on in."

They entered the store, and after he turned off the alarm, turned on the lights, and unlocked the cash register, they sat

in wooden chairs in the footwear department. Tess summa-
rized the events of the past three days. She finished by saying,
"I think they're holding her in that big building near the
cemetery."

Disapprovingly he said, "You think. You think. Come on."

"I can rescue her."

Ari bellowed, "Rescue her! Geez, lady. What are you
talking about? That's what the police are for. You're talking
about traversing across a half mile of terrain covered by three
to four feet of snow, in the dark, with a bunch of gear. On
top of that, you have no idea what shape the woman is in, if
she is even in that building, and whether she would have the
energy to cover the distance back out. And, let me add,
somebody in that old, haunted place could be waiting for you
with a gun. You're not thinking straight. This is crazy. Why
would you do something so dangerous? What have you got,
some kind of hero complex?" He shook his sizable head in a
disgusted way.

"I know you've done great things before," Tess said. "I
know you care about helping someone in a bad spot."

"Well, that might be a real big stretch, but I do root for
the underdog. But you're crossing a line with these gangsters."

"I know that too."

"So, what is it you want me to do?"

"I need you to sell me the same gear I bought, only for a
midget of a woman, maybe five feet two inches tall and size six
shoe, I'd guess. I need you to sell me a bunch of other gear, and
I need you to advise me on how to do what I'm planning."

He turned his head and squinted his eyes. "I'm both puzzled and troubled. I don't think you realize the risks."

"I know she's there. Oh, there's one more thing. I need
your help tonight."

He put his hands up. "Whoa, you might be jumping off a cliff tonight, but I gotta live here."

"You won't be directly involved."

"I'm directly involved now."

"Oh come on! A big tough guy like you isn't afraid of a bunch of skinny little weasels."

"I am when they have guns."

"They won't shoot anyone, unless of course you're at The Dirty Martini Club. Besides, my plan doesn't put you in danger. That much danger, anyway." She arched her eyebrows.

"Uh-huh." He stared at Tess for a couple of seconds and smiled. "You know, if you weren't so damned cute, I'd say forget it. But ..."

Tess rushed him and kissed him on the cheek and hugged him. She thought it was like wrapping her arms around an oversize dresser.

"Alright, let's start with the clothing."

Thirty minutes later, Tess's car was chock-full of gear, and she and Ari went back into the store to settle the bill. "You must really like this woman to spend this kind of money on a harebrained scheme. You're in for at least five hundred bucks."

"One of life's blessings is that I make a lot of money from multiple income streams. It gives me the opportunity to do things for people that might really change their lives."

"In this case, like saving a woman's life," he said.

"Suppose so."

He walked around the counter and began ringing into the cash register all the items Tess had purchased. When he finished, he sighed and said, "Okay, it's six hundred and twelve dollars and thirteen cents."

She pulled out her American Express card. Ari took it and looked at both sides of it. "Figures. I get maybe two or three Amex cards a year in this place. Not exactly the kind of place for exclusive cards."

"I'd give you a tip if I could." They both smiled.

He completed the transaction and handed her the receipt. "Okay, I guess I can't back out now," he said.

"I'll see you tonight. You won't let me down, will you?"

"I'd rather take a bullet."

God I hope it doesn't come down to that. Tess nodded and left the store.

24

TESS SPENT THE REMAINDER of the morning driving up and down the section of Highway 32 and Cemetery Road. She parked at several plowed open spaces and walked along the road. She stopped at Burger King for a late morning lunch break and walked to the back of the building. The lot had been cleared, and the plow had circled back behind the building, clearing a path to a cedar-fenced area with an open gate that housed a dumpster. The plow had continued behind the dumpster, clearing the snow to the back of the property line's six-foot fence. Snow in the parts of the field on the other side had drifted as high as the fence. *If I never see snow again, I'll be just fine.* She stepped off the distance from the dumpster to the property line fence, and estimated there was room to park her car and open the doors on both sides and be out of sight of Burger King's patrons and employees.

Since no one was going into Burger King now, and there would be only a slight chance that an employee would be dumping trash in the next few minutes, she decided to get a head start on the evening's work. She returned to her car and opened her trunk. She pulled out a compact, folded, aluminum snow shovel and extended the arm. It was featherlight and might not be useful to clear much more than a small area, but it was perfect for what she had in mind. Ari said it was designed to be packed into remote areas and dig out snow caves for overnight camping. The thought of being anywhere at night, in snow deep enough to be able to dig a cave, in temperatures that were severely cold, for *any* reason made her shudder. Ari said that some people love winter camping. How idiotic was that? It'd be like camping in the Arctic or the North Pole. Why anyone would do that was beyond her.

When she reached the snowbank behind the dumpster, she raised her leg to a ninety-degree angle and dug the shovel into the bank to mark the spot. She measured that distance with the shovel and made two more marks the same space up the side of the daunting glacier of snow. She methodically dug three shelves in the three locations, each about two feet deep and three feet long. She pounded down the relatively heavy, wet, and packed snow on the shelves. She stepped back and admired her work.

Satisfied, she headed back into town to visit Wendy at the library.

🍸 🍸 🍸

She breezed into the library, her snow pants swishing away. Wendy was at the main information desk, her head buried in returned books that filled a rolling cart.

"Hey Wendy. How are you?"

"Well, you're still here," she said. "I'm glad to see you. I'm guessing you haven't resolved your dilemma, or you have and you're here to say goodbye."

"I haven't resolved or solved anything, but I'm committed convicted to a course of action that should give me and someone else closure."

"The Spinozza boy?"

"No, Wendy. I really can't talk about it, but I'd love your help if you've got a few minutes."

"For you, you little celebrity, of course. What are we researching? Research is my middle name." She adjusted her glasses on the bridge of her nose.

"I need to study a topographical map of an area near here."

Wendy studied her for a moment. "Tess, I'm not sure if I should assist you or try to talk you out of whatever you're planning. First, your trust in me is unwarranted and unearned. And secondly, I believe you are reacting to this situation with an abundance of fatigue and misplaced emotion. Why don't you think through this some more?"

Tess pursed her lips and said firmly, "I have, and I just need a little direction in the library, nothing more."

"Okey dokey. Well, I tried. Follow me." Wendy led Tess from the main body of the library to a small room with a sign above it that read Map Room. The room contained one long wooden table in the center and had low-hanging fluorescent lights above it.

"As you might imagine, we keep our maps in here," she chuckled.

Tess pulled off her outerwear, laid it on a chair, and shook out her hair.

"The maps are extremely detailed and cover fairly small areas. We have them cataloged, so I can pull out the map you need if you'll tell me the coordinates of your search area."

"Coordinates? I don't have a clue what they are."

"Okay, why don't you just tell me what area you'd like to study."

"A mile in any direction of the Saint Agnes Cemetery."

Wendy's face turned curious. "Dear, that's only a couple of miles from here, and there's nothing there but the cemetery and an old building that used to be a warehouse for a local mill. It's been abandoned for years."

"That's it. That's the place."

Wendy rubbed her forehead. "Okay, you're in luck. Our inventory was donated to us by the US Army Corp of Engineers, and for this locality, they're in one-mile sections. Give me a minute."

She disappeared into the labyrinth of map racks and returned with four maps that covered a four-square-mile area, with all four maps encompassing a corner of the cemetery. "This should help you. What are you looking for?"

"Creeks, changes in elevation, and outbuildings."

"For what purpose?"

"I really can't say. I don't want you to know just so you don't know."

"I think that's called a syllogism, but I'm not even sure of that. In other words, it's better for me not to know if someone ever asks me."

"Right. A sillygism."

Wendy began to correct her and realized Tess was teasing. "Okay, I'll leave you to your maps and your secret mission. Tess, be careful."

"Wendy, thank-you. I will be."

"They're no good for at least three generations and probably more. They're like rabid dogs, and I'm talking about both families."

"Not all of them."

"No, not all of them, just the ones you're dealing with." She touched Tess's forearm and left the room.

YYY

Tess put the maps together adjoining the sides. The maps pre-
dated the construction of the Burger King, but that was an easy
spot to locate. She marked the distance from the turnoff to the
cemetery, which she'd noted with the car's odometer. The brick
building at the end of Cemetery Road stuck out like a sore
thumb on the map. The dark gray roof of the main building
loomed above the rest of the terrain in any direction as if it had
been built as a fortress. It was L-shaped as she'd guessed, and
there were two outbuildings within yards of the main one. She
hadn't even seen them on her reconnaissance mission, but the
snow covered a lot of things. One outbuilding appeared to be
a garage and the other perhaps a storage area. Tess had seen
light in the main building the night before, so she assumed it
had power. How would a building, probably constructed in the
late nineteenth century, be heated? Would there have been a
coal- or oil-burning furnace? She concluded there was a decent
probability that there was no central heat and that the source
of heat was probably an electric space heater. It would be real
chilly in there now. She closed her eyes and thought of Teresa
stuck in a locked room with a small little heater to keep her
warm. *Bastards!*

She made a scale to measure the distance between where
the Burger King should be on the map and the warehouse. It
was very close to a thousand yards. She could normally walk
a thousand yards in less than ten minutes, but traversing it
in deep snow might take ten times longer. Getting far enough
away from the building before the kidnappers discovered
Teresa was gone was crucial. If the kidnappers had handguns
or shotguns, she knew they'd have a vantage point from the
second-story windows and a range with their weapons of at
least a hundred yards. She needed to make her getaway with
enough time to be out of that range.

If her calculations were correct, within around 125 yards east of the building, the terrain of the land dropped one of the contour lines of elevation shown on the map—she thought that was five feet, but couldn't be sure and didn't want to ask. If all went according to plan, and she extracted Teresa from the building without being detected, they would disappear from ground level at that point but not from the second-story windows. How long it would take to reach that point was unknown and unknowable until it happened. If it happened. The lay of the land was basically flat from that point all the way back to the highway.

The last calculation she made was the direction she'd need to traverse and then retrace in the cemetery field. Ari had provided her with a compass, and she'd need to follow it and correct course, if necessary, on the fly. It was east to northeast away from the building. Coming back, if she didn't get lost, she could follow her own tracks like Hansel and Gretel in snow. The thugs in the warehouse could figure out her egress point from the field at the Burger King, but they'd have to know where she started. She had to get back and get out, before they discovered Teresa was gone and which way they'd left from the warehouse. There was no possibility of changing direction. It was a scary-tight perimeter of time and distance, with so many variables that Tess felt a little queasy thinking about it. So much could go wrong.

And was Teresa even in that building? If so, where in the building? What if they had her in an interior room so she couldn't see Tess from outside? Could she get Teresa out? What if she was bound? What if she was incapacitated? What if one of the thugs was in the room with her?

So many possibilities for disaster. This was not like figuring out the wind and slope for a golf shot; it was more like figuring out a golf shot from Earth to the moon.

25

TESS SPENT THE REST OF THE DAY driving around, killing time. Late in the afternoon, she sat in Denny's drinking coffee, trying to quell butterflies of anticipation and anxiety about the evening ahead of her. It seemed to her that everyone involved in this case—the organized crime thugs, the police, and even those barely connected to it—was content to just let things play out. It was business as usual, except, of course, for Teresa, who was a pawn in this life-size chess game. She'd spent nearly three days in captivity. Tess thought about how frantic and panic-stricken her own parents would be if she had been the one abducted. She imagined the Champaign police would canvass neighborhoods, the local media would run articles, and the community would respond. Albany might as well have been Mars in comparison.

The sun was dropping toward the horizon, and the sky began to glow red and orange in the west. It was time. She paid her bill, went to the bathroom, and left the restaurant, heading toward Highway 32 and the Burger King.

When she pulled into the BK, there were two cars parked in the back lot. She saw no customers inside, and the clerk at the front counter was staring at a newspaper. She assumed the other employee must be in the kitchen doing something similar. They were obviously expecting a slow night, and she watched the clerk in front as she drove past the windows on the side of the store. He never looked up. The coast was clear.

She pulled in behind the fenced dumpster and moved quickly and methodically, having thought through exactly what she was going to do and in what order. She bundled up her collar and pulled the drawstring on her hat tight. She opened both back doors of the car and angled out the small wooden toboggan that she and Ari had wedged into it earlier in the day. It was about four feet long and two feet wide, made of wood that had been shellacked numerous times to create a highly polished, slick surface. The front of it was horn-shaped and acted as a small snowplow, but it had to be pulled or go downhill using gravity to move forward. Tess would supply the force required to move it.

She placed square pieces of plywood, from a packing box at the surplus store, on the shelves she had dug earlier in the day and stepped on them to make sure she didn't sink. They were solid and supported her weight. She hoisted the toboggan up the steps and set it on the snowbank. She went back to the car and unlocked the trunk, pulling out her prepacked backpack and two sets of varnished wooden and leather snowshoes. They were light, which made it easy to carry them up her handcrafted steps. The damned snowshoes were expensive and looked like ancient pieces of art, but if they worked, somebody was going to get them as a wonderful gift when this was over. She never again wanted to see snow deep enough to use them. She returned to the car, locked it, put the keys in her snow pants, and zipped the pocket.

She climbed back up the snowbank and kneeled on the edge, putting one set of snowshoes on the toboggan and the backpack on top of it. She strapped it tight with the canvas straps equipped with premade hooks at the ends. She placed the other set of snowshoes next to the toboggan. She wrapped her miner's light around her head and turned it on. It shone brightly ten to fifteen feet in front of her. All according to plan and done in less than three minutes.

The first step off the edge of the snowbank into the snow sent her down several feet. It was like quicksand and the more she struggled to get solid footing, the more she burrowed into the snow. Finally, she grabbed her snowshoes and rolled off the ledge and back down the face of the snowbank. She strapped the snowshoes on and sidestepped like a skier up the steps and onto the snow. Her first step gave her pause, as she sank about a foot into the snow. She pulled the shoe up and tried the other. Again, down a foot. If each step was down a foot and ahead two feet, she'd be lucky to reach the warehouse a half mile away by morning, assuming she didn't collapse from exhaustion or freeze to death. What had she been thinking? This seemed impossible. She realized the difficulty of her challenge. It was now real.

She stopped moving, collected her thoughts, and regained her sense of purpose. She high-stepped to the front of the toboggan and connected the straps to the belt she'd wrapped and connected to her waist. The load was light, so that wasn't going to be a factor, but Ari had instructed her to walk on top of the snow. On top! She was dropping down at least a foot with each step. Ditching the sled and carrying the pack would only make it worse as she'd be heavier and be carrying another twenty-five pounds of dead weight. She'd never make it.

She trudged ahead, putting one foot in front of the other for a dozen steps and stopped short, suddenly panicked with a bigger problem than the difficulty of moving forward. It was pitch-black, with no light in front of her to use as a guide; for 180 degrees, it was a black hole, and the moon was only a sliver. She turned quickly and looked back at the lights from the restaurant. They'd be gone in a few hundred paces, but there was a streetlight just to the right. She pulled the compass from her pocket and shown her headlamp on it. The needle pointed east-southeast, which was as she'd planned. With any luck, she'd be able to keep her bearings straight from the compass, the streetlight, and the moon. She decided not to abort her mission just because she might get lost or end up falling down into an unseen ditch or creek. No, no, no. This was on. She pulled back her sleeve and looked at her watch: thirty-five minutes past five o'clock.

She gauged the distance by counting her steps, which seemed at most a foot and a half long; so every two steps would be about a yard. It was important to keep track: If she needed to correct her course, she'd at least have a general idea of how far she'd gone.

Two hundred strides in, she stopped and loosened the string on her hood. The trek was strenuous enough to make her feel warm. She caught her breath and looked at the sky. Clouds had just hidden the moon. She could still clearly see the streetlight, however, and felt the wave of panic recede. She glanced at the compass and felt relieved. She was going in the right direction, but blackness has a way of unnerving even the calmest people and she wasn't in that category to begin with. Another three hundred strides, and she rested again. This time, she flipped off her hood and loosened her coat. She was sweating profusely and breathing hard. It wasn't frigid, maybe thirty degrees, but in her arctic cocoon, it felt like Florida in the summer. She put her hands on her knees and breathed deeply.

A few yards later, she veered downward. It was the railroad tracks she'd seen on the map. She knew she was two-
thirds of the way to the warehouse. She felt the toboggan hit
her in the back of the legs on the gentle slope down, and
then felt its weight increase as she climbed out of the small
valley. She pressed forward, the streetlight now faded from
view, looking for anything that could serve as a beacon. She
saw nothing.

She covered another hundred yards with no idea where
the building was. She was in trouble. Maybe she'd just stum-
ble into it. Maybe there were no lights in the back of it.
Maybe she was way off target. She kept going because what
else could she do.

Ten minutes and two hundred yards more, she was
breathing as rapidly as if she'd been sprinting. Worst of all,
she was now afraid. How could she have been so stupid? How
could she have thought she could pull this off? Why am I the
only one out here. Doesn't anybody else care? She was
quickly falling into a scenario of disaster. She stopped and
studied the horizon. It was dark but for her little circle of
light from the miner's lamp perched on her head. Which
way?

Then she heard a sound to her left. What was that, a car
door? She rotated forty-five degrees to the left and continued. She stopped counting strides, instead listening for any
sound every ten strides. There was nothing more, so she
turned off the miner's lamp and moved very slowly and cau-
tiously.

Suddenly her thigh hit something solid. She was afraid
to turn the light on, so she felt her way along the surface.
She guessed it was the roof line of a small building, which
poked up just a couple of feet above the snow line. She

worked her way along the structure to the corner and turned, pulling the toboggan at an angle. Another five strides and she was at the corner, almost certain that it was the small building near the warehouse. She'd missed the warehouse by a couple hundred yards, and considering the distance she'd traveled and the energy she'd exerted, that was a lot. She looked to her left and saw a small glimmer of light probably shining from the front of the main building.

Thirty more strides and she could see an outline of the larger structure. She continued to veer left toward the back of the building. When she was close enough to actually see a wall, she realized the size of it. The building had to be a hundred feet in length and fifty feet wide. Most importantly, there were no windows and that meant no way to get someone out besides the front door. She reached a corner of the building and stopped to gasp for air.

She studied its daunting length. The side of the building that connected perpendicularly to the long section was at the opposite end from where she stood. She continued to move away from the front and rotate around to the west side of what must have been a mill at some time in the past. She guessed that the front of the building must be offices. She found a double door the size of a garage door at another corner. There'd be no opening these. It would take half the night to shovel the snow away. She had bolt cutters in the backpack, but they'd be no use here. Too bad, they were heavy.

As she turned the corner and moved along the wall, she calculated that the snow was at least two and in some places three feet higher against the wall than the other side. Drifting. She came to a window, one that she hadn't seen earlier because of snow drifts. It was three feet wide and extended from the snow line up at least four feet. Did that mean there were two, three, or even four feet of window beneath the snow? There was no way of telling without digging out the window. She stopped and calculated. She must be a good ninety feet from where the offices and the warehouse connected. If she stopped now and got an idea about the window size, then the time spent at the window where Teresa might be would be well spent. It sounded like a plan. She unhitched her belt, unstrapped the backpack, and pulled out the shovel.

After five minutes of digging, she discovered the windows were about eight feet high and three feet wide. She also knew if she found Teresa, it would take five minutes to dig out the window to get access. That was the good and bad news. Five minutes was an eternity. Would Teresa be able to open the window from the inside? Tess had bolt cutters, a glass cutter and suction cup, and assorted other small tools akin to a burglar's tools, which was a good part of the weight she'd hauled this far. Now how to find Teresa ...

She pulled out the flashlight and shone it in a downward direction, but enough into the window to see the interior. It was an open space, high ceilings, maybe twelve feet, and boxes stacked on one side of the room. She was confident no one was inside. The building may at one time have been an open room, but at least this part had been partitioned off into rooms with doors. The door leading to this room was closed. She flipped off the light and stared at the door. No light was coming from under the door. Maybe there was a hallway with a bunch of rooms. She put her gear back together, leaving the flashlight inside the outer strapping and moved on.

Window number two, same scenario except no boxes. Window number three, bigger room and more boxes. Window number four, small room and shelves with even smaller boxes. Somebody was warehousing something in this building in a very organized fashion. She guessed there were four more windows, after which all bets were off; she'd be at the corner of the two wings. If they had her in the front office area, it would be pure dumb luck to get her alone and out of the building. She moved to window number five and continued.

She came to the last window on the side of the building, her despair deepening at having gone to such lengths to find and extract Teresa, only to find an empty building. She stopped and was about to turn on the flashlight when she saw a faint red glow coming from inside the last room. She studied it, then realized it might be emanating from an electric heater. She'd been right! But what if she flashed her light into the room and it wasn't Teresa? What if it was one of her guards? Her energy was nearly spent, she had no weapon, and couldn't even get away fast enough to avoid being captured and God knows what else. On the other hand, she was certain to fail if she didn't take a chance and throw some light into the room. Maybe the guy inside the room would be asleep and not see the light, but it was too early in the evening for sleeping. It was do-or-die time.

She turned on her flashlight and looked into the room. It was empty except for a small card table, two simple chairs, a bed without bedposts, and a bag or sack on the floor. And … two boots with heels! She saw a lump on the bed covered by a blanket. It had to be Teresa! Her heart jumped into her throat and before thinking, she shone the light at the bed. Nothing moved. She tapped gently on the window with the flashlight. Nothing. She tapped a little louder and longer. Movement. A head came up and rotated to the window. A moment later, Tess felt like she'd just sunk a putt to win the US Open, which in fact she'd done two years before.

It was Teresa! She wanted to yell, to scream with jubilance, to throw her hands up and celebrate, but Teresa wasn't moving. She had put her hand over her eyes as if she was staring into the sun. *The light is blinding her.* She must have been asleep. Tess yanked off the hood and turned the light on her own face, holding it there for several seconds. When she flashed it back into the room, Teresa had gotten out of the bed and moved toward the window, looking unsure of what she was seeing.

Tess waved frantically, euphoric that she'd accomplished what the police hadn't been able to do. A female golfer who'd never searched for anything but a lost golf ball in the rough or the perfect pair of boots or the right set of earrings had become an investigator, a detective. She'd found her! Teresa now stood in front of the window, slowly realizing who this was. Tess put her finger to her mouth and signaled silence. Teresa put her hands on her head and dropped to her knees. Tess thought she might be crying, but that had to stop. They were on the clock, and time was flying.

26

TESS TAPPED ON THE WINDOW lightly and motioned with her hands for Teresa to open the window. Teresa waved her hands laterally and turned her head side to side, mouthing "No, it doesn't open."

Tess mouthed the words "Are they in the other room?" and pointed toward the door.

Teresa nodded her head up and down and mouthed "yes."

"How many?" Tess asked silently.

Teresa stuck up two fingers.

"Guns?" Tess mimicked a gun with her hand.

Again, Teresa affirmed a silent "yes."

That's when Tess noticed that Teresa had a blackened eye, what looked like a split lip, and a bruise the size of a golf ball on the side of her swollen face. Tess had to pause to control her emotions. She had learned the lesson so many times: When emotions go up, intelligence goes down.

Tess mouthed slowly, "When did they last check on you?"

Teresa held up both hands to indicate ten minutes and then silently expressed, "They will be back again in twenty or thirty minutes."

"I'm going to cut the glass," Tess mouthed while making the motion.

Teresa stood there dumbfounded, as Tess opened her pack and pulled out the snow shovel. She positioned the flashlight on the pack, shining it on the window, and began digging. Five minutes later, she had removed the snow to the bottom of the window, which appeared to be the height of Teresa's waist. She returned to her pack and pulled out a suction cup the size of a small teacup and a glass cutter that looked like a toothbrush. She affixed the suction cup to the center of the lower half of the pane, which was three feet wide and four feet high. She dug the cutting edge of the cutter into the glass and held onto the pane with the suction cup. She cut along the bottom edge, the sides, and across about three feet up, making a square.

She traced over the initial cut five times before she heard a cracking sound. The noise seemed magnified by a thousand times and sent a jolt of panic through Tess. The glass began to break. She couldn't let it fall or it would make an alarming sound and all hell could break loose. She had to cut and hold and hope. Finally one side broke free, and she retraced her cuts until the section cracked free. She held the glass in her hand and slowly rotated and laid it up on the snow. They hadn't heard. Tess blinked and took a deep breath in relief.

"Oh my God, Tess, I can't believe you're here. Thank-you. Thank-you." Teresa extended her hands out through the window. Tess touched and held them for a moment.

"It's okay, now. It's okay. I'm going to get you out of here. Careful, you'll cut yourself." Tess turned back to the pack and handed Teresa a bundle containing socks, boots, pants, coat, hat, and gloves. "Put this stuff on quickly. Take your other boots and clothes and put them under the blanket. Maybe that old trick will give us another couple of minutes, but I doubt it. Hurry."

Teresa took the gear, walked to one of the metal chairs, and dressed while Tess dug two shelves for Teresa to climb up to the top of the bank. She had two more pieces of plywood to secure footing and laid those in place. She also put a hotel towel on the bottom edge of the cut glass. Minutes later, Tess helped Teresa navigate through the window without catching herself on the cut windowpane, and they stood together in the snow dugout.

They hugged briefly. "Tess, I'll never forget this."

"You'll forget pretty fast if they come through that door shooting. Come on, let's get the hell out here. Are you okay?"

"Weak."

"Up we go." Tess helped her to the top and had her sit on the pack on the toboggan, while she affixed the snow-shoes on Teresa's boots. It was probably the only time that Tess had witnessed silence from Teresa, who seemed to be in shock. "Okay, one foot in front of the other. Like this. Okay, good? We have to move. Let's go."

Tess held Teresa's hand as they retraced her steps to the back of the building and away from it, toward the shed. Tess thought if anything, going in this direction would throw them off. Within a couple of minutes, they reached the shed. Teresa was gasping.

"Tess, I'm so tired, I can't go on. I just can't."

"Teresa!" Tess said quietly but sharply. "You have to, and you will. Now let's go. Count the steps. We'll take ten and rest. Ten and rest."

They took ten steps and heard breaking glass. Their escape had been discovered, and they were not more than a hundred and fifty yards from the warehouse. Tess flicked off her miner's light. "Come on Teresa! Time's up."

Lights on the second floor of the building came on. Then glass shattered in an upstairs window, and a large beam of light shown on the yard next to the building and on the shed. The light followed their trail, but the beam of light didn't reach their location. She saw a flash and heard a gunshot at the same time. They were shooting in the direction of the trail they'd left. The first bullets fired at where they would have been if they hadn't turned already, correcting their course. They kept firing round after round, covering the escape route methodically. They were getting closer, and Tess heard the unmistakable zing of a bullet close by.

"Drop! Now!"

Tess jerked the toboggan onto its side, creating a shield of sorts, which would have actually done nothing to stop a bullet, and pulled Teresa behind it. Teresa seemed almost unresponsive, and Tess strong-armed her behind the sled. A bullet struck the backpack, and both women cried out, giving the shooters a better idea of their location. More bullets were fired, and a round sailed over them. Several more struck the snow a few feet on either side of the toboggan. Tess felt so helpless—all this planning and execution only to be gunned down like sitting ducks. Tess wrapped her arms around Teresa, who was shaking violently, and whispered, "It's okay. They can't see us."

A bullet struck the front of the toboggan. "Shit!" Tess seethed.

There were more shots, all striking within a few feet. Then silence.

"They've run out of ammo."

"Not for long," Teresa said.

"They've got to go back downstairs. Let's go. It's now or never."

"Tess, no. It's the oldest trick in the book. Stop shooting and wait for movement. They're going to kill us. They have to."

"That may be, but we don't have a choice. Let's go."

Tess pushed the toboggan over and stood up on her snowshoes. She pulled Teresa to her feet. No shots.

"We're lucky," Tess said. "We've got a minute or two. Let's go. No stops."

They slogged forward without counting for several minutes before the shooting resumed, but it was behind them and off line. And without snowshoes, they'd only be able to plow through the snow far enough to get a beam of flashlight on the area that the two of them had already traversed. Tess felt that if she was lucky, they would miscalculate which direction they were heading and go back to Cemetery Road and head north. They'd probably call in reinforcements to look for them to come out somewhere on First Avenue.

Tess stopped to rest and could hardly catch her breath. She realized that she'd made a critical error. She was parched, and she had exerted so much energy that she was soaked inside her coat all the way through her sweatshirt. How could she, someone who worked out every day in heat, forget something so essential as water? Especially when the workout was so much harder than a normal one and fueled by adrenaline, fear, anger, and desperation. The cold weather had fooled her again, tricking her into leaving out a lifesaving component for survival. She unzipped her jacket, threw back her hood, and wiped the sweat from her face. Teresa had fallen to the side of the toboggan and lay motionless. She knew Teresa smoked, drank, didn't exercise, and probably had a pitiful diet, not to mention having been in captivity for three days, but Tess hadn't expected her to collapse within ten minutes of escaping. Tess knelt down beside her.

"Teresa, we have to move on. We can't stay here. They will figure out something and come after us, whether it's on snowmobiles or by scouring the streets where we might come out. We've come this far. You've got to help me. Come on, let's get up."

"Tess," her voice was hoarse and weak. "I can't."

"What do you mean, you can't? You have to."

"Leave me. You've done enough. You need to go. What you've done already was heroic and I'll never forget it, but I can't. I blacked out when we stopped. I can't go any further."

Tess didn't respond. She pulled Teresa's sleeve up and took her pulse. It was racing. Her forehead was clammy and cool. Teresa was shutting down. They must have denied her nutrition, water, sleep … and probably physically or psychologically abused her. She hadn't expected or planned for this contingency either. Her stupid gaffs in planning were mounting up and beginning to look like an enormous failure. Now what? She was sweating, thirsty, and as she knelt next to Teresa she felt a slight tightening of her hamstring muscles. Cramps would kill them both.

She looked to the east and saw only darkness except for the arc of her miner's light. Checking her compass, she knew they were moving in the right direction. She figured they must be at least eight hundred yards from the car. She could leave Teresa and get help, but by the time she returned, Teresa would be in bad shape, maybe dead. She could wait for help, but that would be disaster because the only person who knew what she'd planned was Ari, and she'd made him swear that under no circumstance was he to follow. He might call the police, but that would probably not have any positive outcome either.

Tess stopped thinking about all the negative outcomes and thought about the time she'd had to get out of a crashed

plane. She'd kicked out the side of the plane, lowered Eddie
with a rope, and climbed down a tree trunk. It was all in
darkness, and now here she was with another Spinozza, another pitch-black crisis, and no alternatives, except ... well
... except a real bad outcome. She knew what she had to do.
She grabbed a handful of snow and gulped it down, and then
another. It helped.

She zipped her coat, pulled her hood over her head, and
tied the string. She unstrapped the pack from the toboggan
and dropped it a couple of feet away. She removed Teresa's
snowshoes and left them with the pack. *Nice find for someone
in the spring.* She picked Teresa up by the torso and laid her
on the toboggan, then lifted her legs on and jerked her as far
forward as she could. The toboggan was five feet in length
with a curved front end, which meant the sled portion was
maybe four and a half feet. Teresa's boots hung over the toboggan, which would create even more drag. Tess strapped
her in, and stepped to the front of the toboggan and attached
her harness. She filled her mouth with snow again and took
her first step. She couldn't move. She tried again but was literally dead in her tracks. Teresa probably didn't weigh a hundred and twenty pounds, but it felt like five hundred. It
couldn't be this hard.

She tried several more times, then let out a growling
sound out of anger and desperation. Then she remembered
the scene from *Call of the Wild* when Buck couldn't move the
sled because the tracks of the sled had frozen. She unstrapped
her harness and grabbed the front of the toboggan and
jerked. It didn't feel frozen in place, so she connected her
harness and drove forward with every ounce of strength inside her, growling again with effort. The toboggan moved a
foot. Tess didn't sink in any deeper, but her stride was only a

foot, which meant the final stretch was going to take fifty percent more strides. She had to keep the momentum of the toboggan going; starting again after stopping might prove impossible. Each stride was brutal. Her thighs burned. Her butt burned. Stopping was not an option because she feared she might not be able to get moving again, but her throat was so dry that her grunts and growling became silent, ricocheting around the inside of her head.

As she slogged forward, she knew there'd be no stopping to check on Teresa, no breaks for rests, and if the straps or clips gave way, it would be over. Ten minutes later, she spotted a decline ahead and knew she was approaching the railroad tracks. Going down would give her a momentary break, but if she didn't push even harder once she reached the flat area at the bottom, she'd never make it up the other side. She heard herself scream as she descended, and when she started up the incline, she put all the effort of deep knee squats into the next ten strides. She leveled off on the other side and tried to find enough spittle to swallow. She had stopped breathing through her nose and sucked in gasps of air through her mouth, making her throat burn even more. Her legs ached so intensely that she was woozy.

But she couldn't stop now. She put her head down on her chest, closed her eyes, and drove forward like a plow horse working itself to death. The feeling that she wasn't going to make it began as a soft voice in her head and intensified to banging like rock music. As the decibel level grew louder and louder, Tess slowed and lifted her face to the sky. "It's over. I'm done."

And then she opened her eyes and caught the faint twinkle of a streetlight in the distance. If she could have yelled or cried or fallen to her knees in relief, she would have, but it would've meant failing within site of the finish because she'd never be able to get up and get the sled moving again. She put all other thoughts aside except for her mother's face. She could hear her mother saying over and over, "Tess, I believe in you. Tess, I believe in you."

She was within twenty yards of the end when a head popped up from the edge of the snowbank.

27

A WAVE OF FEAR HIT HER as if she'd just confronted a burglar. She slowed her pace. Her eyes watered. She couldn't catch her breath, her legs were cramping, her nose was running, her throat burned … now what?

"Tess?"

It was Ari.

"Come on, just a few more steps. Come on, Tess."

Relief beyond description. Heaven. She blasted into the harness, and twenty strides later collapsed into Ari's powerful arms.

"You made it!"

Tess didn't speak, and Ari, an experienced outdoors and ex-military man, immediately assessed her condition and the situation, and took action. He laid Tess aside, unstrapped her snowshoes, disconnected her harness, and pulled the toboggan to him. He unstrapped Teresa and returned to Tess.

"Tess. The keys?"

"My pocket," she whispered.

He tried one pocket and then found them in the other. He quickly went to the car, got the back door open, and returned to the women. He lifted Teresa like a doll and laid her down in the back seat. He quickly moved to his car and pulled out a green woolen blanket and covered her. He returned to Tess and helped her to her feet. Her legs wobbled, and she was faint and slightly disoriented. He walked her to the driver's seat and started the car.

"I'll be right back. Don't move," he said, and Tess watched him disappear.

A few minutes later, he returned with two large white Burger King bags. He opened the passenger door and set them on the seat. He peeled the paper liner off the straw, jammed it into a large drink, and handed it to Tess. She took a long draw and felt the liquid hit her throat like lava.

"Easy. Slow," Ari said. He took another drink to Teresa and made her sit up and drink. "She's pretty unresponsive," he said to Tess.

As the two of them drank, Tess watched Ari pull the toboggan down and load it onto the roof rack of his car. He returned to Tess and opened the wrapper for the Whopper.

"Eat."

"No," she said.

He pulled a Hershey bar from his pocket and repeated the process. Tess took a bite. He did the same routine with Teresa, and then he was gone again, loading the snowshoes into the back of his car.

By the time he finished and sat back in the passenger's seat, Tess was beginning to stabilize. She'd finished most of the sugary drink and had eaten the candy bar. She now ate bites of burger in between gulps. Ari opened the second bag and pulled out another burger. He looked into the back seat and saw Teresa sitting up. "Are you doing a little better?"

Teresa nodded yes. He put the food back in the bag. "She's not going to eat anything right now."

He returned his attention to Tess. "You've got to get out of here, just like we planned. The cops and a bunch of big black cars have been going up and down the street for the last thirty minutes. When you feel up to it, which is about *now*, you've got to drive out of here. Remember, you turn right and follow Highway 32 to Highway 7, then turn south onto Interstate 87. Don't stop driving for at least an hour or two. I'm turning left, and with this toboggan on top of my car, I'm sure I won't get very far. But I'll delay and distract them long enough for you to get out of town. You good?"

In a low, cracked voice, Tess answered, "Yes. Ari … thank-you. Thank-you."

"Of course. Now go!"

Tess watched him get in his car, back out, and make a U-turn toward the street. She managed in a low, hoarse voice, "Teresa, you're going to have to lay down under the blanket for a few minutes until I can get to the interstate. Okay?"

Teresa disappeared without saying a word.

She put the car in gear and wiped her eyes. She inhaled deeply and forced herself to focus on getting out of the parking lot. At the exit of Burger King, she looked both ways and, not seeing another car, pulled into the street. She turned right and within a block saw a police car, lights flashing, heading in the opposite direction. Her hands tensed on the steering wheel. Would they stop Ari? What would they charge him with, carrying a concealed set of snowshoes? Harboring a known fugitive toboggan? Within minutes, she was on Interstate 87 heading south. They drove for an hour without talking before she pulled into a rest area. She got out and leaned against the car, willing her legs to hold her upright. She pushed off the car and opened the back door. Teresa lifted her head and said, "I'm okay Tess. I'm okay."

Tess felt Teresa's face, checked her pulse, and looked at the size of her pupils. Everything seemed normal or as normal as things could be. "You have to sit up and drink and eat before we get back on the road."

Teresa followed directions and ate some of her food and drank her soda. Tess knew she wanted to talk, but they needed to move, to get as far away as they could from Albany and the reach of both the Cuchinelli and Spinozza families. She felt rejuvenated by the food and the quart of soda she'd gulped down.

"I don't suppose you need to use the bathroom?" she asked.

Teresa didn't answer. She was already sound asleep. When Tess was back on the highway, it dawned on her that she really hadn't planned on any destination after leaving Albany. If she was honest with herself, she hadn't expected to successfully rescue Teresa. She had thought of numerous scenarios in which she'd be stopped at some point, even up to the point where she'd get on the interstate. But nothing had stopped them, even as they barreled down the road a hundred miles from Albany.

Now it all came cascading down, the reality of their situation. They were driving south at seventy miles an hour, out of the grips of that wretched place and those wretched people, and Tess really hadn't planned where to go. Interstate 87 would take them west of New York City and toward Philadelphia. That was as good as any place. She'd drive another hour or two and begin to look for a hotel off the highway where they could get some rest and figure out what to do with the rest of their lives.

CHAPTER

28

TESS WAS DEEPLY FATIGUED when she checked into a hotel near Poughkeepsie. She grabbed her overnight bag and pulled Teresa from the car. Teresa draped her arms around Tess's neck, and they slogged to the door of their room. Tess leaned her against the wall while she opened the door and then hoisted her onto one of two queen-size beds, moving gingerly as she felt a charley horse ready to seize control of her leg. She bent over and stretched before pulling Teresa's boots off, then straightened her on the bed and gently covered her with the blanket. She sat on the edge of her own bed and removed her boots. She pulled Ari's phone number from her coat pocket and dialed the number. He picked up on the second ring.

"Hi, Ari, this is Tess."

"Are you okay? Where are you?"

"Yes, we're fine, just tired. We made it to outside Poughkeepsie. Are you okay? What happened?"

"Nothing. They must not have known you used a toboggan. I drove home with it on top of my car, but no one took notice."

"Oh, I'm so glad."

"Get some sleep."

"Thank-you. I can't thank-you enough."

"I'd do again in a heartbeat."

They bid each other goodbye, and Tess flopped back more exhausted than anytime she could remember. She closed her eyes and within minutes fell into a deep slumber. They slept until midmorning.

Tess rolled out of bed and awakened Teresa just to make sure she was all right, or at least, under the circumstances, reasonably okay. Tess dropped to the floor and stretched. Leg cramps in the night hadn't turned into spasms, but it had been close. Her body was sore and fatigued to its core. Lifting her arms hurt. Her legs revolted with every movement. Bruises on her wrists and neck from tugging and pulling the toboggan were already turning black. Her stomach muscles screamed when she straightened and stood up.

Knowing she would have to help Teresa get cleaned up and possibly get medical attention, Tess decided to attend to herself first. She walked into the bathroom and drank two full glasses of water to try and soothe the pain in her throat that felt like a dozen cold sores. She took a hot shower and shampooed her hair, happy to see a second tiny plastic container of lavender-scented shampoo on the counter for Teresa. She brushed her teeth, used the hair dryer, and splashed her signature perfume on her discolored wrists and behind her ears. She had no clean clothes, so she pulled on her jeans from the day before and a T-shirt and sweater she'd worn the day she arrived in Albany. She stored the smelly, sweat-soaked clothes from the rescue in the plastic bag the hotel provided.

Teresa continued sleeping as if comatose. Tess decided she could sleep in the car and woke her up to assess her condition. She helped Teresa remove her clothing, and Tess studied the bruises on her shoulders, arms, and legs and square contusions the size of playing cards on her back. Her lip had crusted blood where it had been split, her cheek was bruised, and her left eye was swollen half-closed. Tess remained calm, almost clinical, in the face of what looked like a vicious beating; perhaps the sleep and hot shower had helped in that way.

She walked Teresa into the shower and held her standing for the first minute. Teresa began to come around, and once she was talking Tess decided to let her continue on her own while she waited in the bathroom. Teresa showered, shampooed, and rinsed for what seemed like thirty minutes. Tess didn't rush her. Once she was finished, Teresa was more alert and able to dry herself and her hair. Tess gave her a toothbrush and a small bottle of mouthwash. Without any other clothing, Teresa was forced to wear what Tess had given her the night before.

Once they were both sitting down in the room, Tess asked her hoarsely, "Teresa, I saw the bruises and abrasions and scrapes. They beat you up pretty good, but those don't require medical attention as far as I can tell. I'm sorry to ask this, but"—she hesitated, staring into Teresa's eyes—"did they molest you?"

"No."

"Do you think we need to go to the emergency room for anything?"

"No."

"Under normal circumstances, I would take you to the emergency room to be checked out, but this isn't normal and I don't want to leave any footprint for anyone to follow. We'll go downstairs, eat, gas up the car, and drive south. You can sleep, and I'll drive us the hell out of here. Are you good with that plan?"

"Yes. I'm starving."

Tess packed the remainder of her belongings in her compact bag, which now felt so much heavier. As they walked to the elevator, Tess's fatigued legs feeling each step as if walking out of wet cement, she locked arms with Teresa, who was wobbling. Once in the dining room, without a word of conversation, they ate eggs, sausage, bacon, biscuits, and hash browns, and drank orange juice and coffee, after which Tess paid the bill in cash and left a large tip.

When they got to the car, Tess opened the door for Teresa and saw the blanket Ari had covered her with the previous night. It was a standard-issue Army blanket, most likely from his magical surplus store. She smiled and was gratified that Ari had made it home and wouldn't be involved any further. She pulled into a gas station next to the hotel, filled the tank, and bought some extra supplies before getting on the interstate and heading south. Once on the road, Teresa was asleep almost immediately.

Tess drove on without thinking, following a truck and only occasionally glancing at road signs. She drank a large Coke and sucked on throat lozenges, trying to soothe her throat pain. The interstate didn't have tolls, the road wasn't crowded, the weather was clear and sunny, and most importantly, very little snow had fallen in this part of the state. They were two hundred miles south of Albany, and there were maybe four to six inches of snow. Albany just wasn't right for her in so many ways.

Her thoughts frequently returned to Eddie. What was he doing now? Was his family engaged in another round of revenge bombings, shootings, or kidnappings, or was there some other vendetta they could exact on the Cuchinellis? What would the Cuchinellis do now? They'd lost a bargaining chip, but probably could find many new and inventive ways to continue the grudge match. All of it was so mean, so ugly, so diabolical, and she couldn't understand how it could continue. But Tiziana had told her this kind of thing had gone on for centuries in Sicily. Whole villages had been depopulated of young men, killed in mob-related violence. She was resigned to the fact that her relationship with Eddie was finished, and she cried as she drove. Even if he had been the world's best liar about his knowledge of the Spinozza family business, he'd been her lover, her friend, her companion, and her future. Now, it was done. He would stay in Albany and support his family for however long these wars lasted, and maybe longer if he was drawn in. His family would be his undoing. It made her sick to think about it.

It occurred to her that at some point during the day, Teresa should call her mother and let her know that she was safe. Would she return? Why hadn't her father or grandfather expedited her release? Would Frankie and Tiziana be trapped, or could they escape the family? It also occurred to her that in the next several hours, she'd have to decide where she and Teresa were going. She turned onto Interstate 287 and continued south. She also needed to call her own mother and at least keep up the charade that things were weird but tolerable in Albany.

She drove and contemplated her situation, until nature called. It was nearly noon. She turned off at a large rest stop at the intersection of Interstates 287 and 78, and awakened Teresa. They used the bathroom, then Tess bought them a sub sandwich, which they split and spread out on two napkins. Tess's throat had begun to feel better, and her voice was almost normal pitch and volume.

"Teresa, do you want to call your parents? There's a bank of pay phones right over there," she said, pointing.

"Why should I? They clearly don't care. But ... maybe if I do, they won't look for us."

"Good thinking, and yes, you should."

"I'm not going back. I can't take any more of this. The whole business is just so disgusting. Can I come with you, wherever you're going?"

"Teresa, I'm going home to Florida. You can come with me, but what will you do in Florida?"

"Anything. I'll be a waitress, drive a bus, or work for you."

"Let's take one thing at a time. Why don't you call your parents. But don't tell them I had anything to do with your ... your release. If you do, they'll know where you're going, and they'll come for you. They'll also find out where I live. Right now, they think I just left town, and that's the way I want it to stay. Can you do that?"

"Yes. What if Eddie asks about you?"

"He won't, and don't tell him anything. Not a word. This is like ripping off a bandage, a really big bandage, and it's got to be fast and clean. I ripped it off two days ago."

Tess gave Teresa change for the phone and watched her walk to a row of at least a dozen metallic phones, most of them occupied. On the wall next to the phones was a giant map of New York, New Jersey, and Pennsylvania. Tess saw the red dot showing their current location and looked at the options of routes they could take. She could drive all the way to Florida, but that would be a crazy amount of time and energy that she wasn't willing to expend right now. She followed Interstate 78 west from the rest stop until it turned into Interstate 81 and ran into Harrisburg.

Harrisburg was the place she and Eddie had departed in a small plane almost two years before. The plane went down an hour later. She stopped herself from rehashing that memory, but something did flash into her mind. Stone. Gregory Stone, but everyone just called him Stone. The rugged, handsome search and rescue guy who had found the crash site and saved her and Eddie. Stone was the humble guy, built like a football player, who wouldn't take credit for having discovered and identifying the crazy psychopath who had been stalking her. After getting to know him, she learned he had demons bouncing around in his head from a time when he failed to save a little girl from a horrible death in the woods years earlier. If she remembered correctly, he also had a drinking problem, and his marriage was shaky.

"They're crazy mad."

Tess snapped out of her thoughts and looked up at Teresa. "At you?"

"No, he's furious with the Cuchinellis, not me. That's the weird part. At first, my father sounded like it wasn't that big a deal. He was glad I was found and wanted to send someone for me right away."

"That isn't surprising, considering—"

"No, but when I told him about them hitting me and tying me up and toying with me. He lost it."

"Toying?"

"Yeah, like tying me up and pulling my sweater and bra off and pulling my skirt up and panties down and then not doing anything."

"Teresa, you told me they didn't do anything like that! That's not toying! That's the same as rape!"

"I told you they didn't rape me, but they had their way with me. But they didn't do anything more than terrify me. When they untied me, I kicked one of them in the balls and hit the other with a lamp. That's when one of them punched and slapped me in the face, and the other hit me with something, maybe the butt of his gun in the back. That was it. Then they left me alone. But I'm sure if it had gone one more night, I would've been in big trouble. The Cuchinelli men are mean drunks. And they were drinking when you got there."

Tess said, "The Cuchinelli men are a lot more than mean drunks. They're sociopathic criminals."

"So how did the conversation with your father end? Did you tell them who got you out?"

"I told them I got out on my own, and I was fine. That I just needed to be away from everything for a while."

"That's it? What did your father say?"

"He asked if I needed money."

Tess was so astonished she couldn't find words to respond. "You really are on your own at this moment."

"I'm beginning to think I was on my own the whole last four days. I have no money, no clothes, and no place to go. I don't want any money from my father. Money is control." Her face showed anger and defiance.

"Okay, let's go."

"Where?"

"Harrisburg."

"Harrisburg! I don't even know what state that's in."

"It's only a couple hundred miles or less from here, and it's in Pennsylvania. We'll be there early this afternoon."

"Why there?"

"I know someone there who specializes in rescuing people."

"I don't need to be rescued. You did that. I need to hide and start my life over."

"I understand and, in a way, I need to do the same. Well, not hide but start over."

CHAPTER

29

Monday, Four days after Thanksgiving; Albany

IT WAS 11 A.M., and the Spinozza Deli and Bakery was busy
with the usual lunch business. Many of the people who
worked in the surrounding buildings housing the bureaucracy
of New York State were regular customers, as were profes-
sionals from financial and insurance firms and the employees
of dozens of legal firms; consequently, the Spinozzas had a
thriving lunch trade. The delicatessen in the back of the
shop specialized in Italian meats, cheeses, and fresh fish, and
made sandwiches to-go. There were also a half dozen two-
top tables for a few lucky customers with good timing and
patience.

The front of the store had a large glass display case that
ran perpendicular to the front door and contained pastries
and Italian desserts like cannoli, slices of cheesecake, and
tiramisu. Several customers waited in turn for a clerk to pull
their selections, bag them, and hand them to another clerk,
who stood at the cash register and rang up their purchases.
Lining the walls between the two parts of the store were rows
of shelves stocked with imported Italian olive oils, tomato

products, pasta, canned fish, and other specialty goods and ingredients. Spinozza's was a center for the local Italian American population.

This was Detective Keibler's favorite lunch spot, because he could not only get his favorite pastrami sandwich, a Jewish specialty that the deli had started serving years earlier due to demand, but also fill his sweet tooth. It didn't hurt that he didn't have to pay, as his bill always went on his "tab." Keibler was adept at working both crime families to his utmost advantage, and this was one of the perks. Today he'd eaten his lunch in the back deli area and was waiting to order a pastry to go.

Salivating over his choices, he didn't see the black Lincoln roll to a slow stop in front of the plate glass windows that ran from one side of the storefront to the other, nor did he see the windows on the passenger side slowly roll down. No one did. Shotgun barrels were held just inside the windows, a tactic used to keep ejected shells with any evidence of fingerprints in the car. And then the barrage of bullets began.

The pellets from the 12-gauge pump shotgun blasts shattered the plate glass with explosive force, throwing shards like a furious hailstorm into the line of customers and creating chaos. People screamed and instantly scattered behind counters or dove to the floor, into the blanket of glass and scattered debris. The first volley had traveled over the heads of the patrons and clerks and caused no injuries.

Everyone buried their faces with their hands and arms, except for one. In an extraordinary moment, perhaps not bravery or valor, but from years of training, Keibler pulled his .38 revolver from its holster with rather astonishing speed, assumed the standard police firing position—bent legs, arms extended, two hands on the gun—and sent two shots through the shattered windows at the shooters. Instantly, fourteen more rounds, the combined capacity of both shotguns, were fired. It was a devastating, scorched-earth assault that left the bakery area almost completely destroyed. Each blast cleared an area half the size of a pool table by the time the pellets hit the back wall. Shelves and signage and glass cases disintegrated. Keibler was struck multiple times in the throat and upper body, and was dead before he hit the floor, his blood quickly forming a slick, red pool of death that seemed to soak up broken glass. Ten seconds later, with smoke puffing from the ends of the gun barrels like a smoldering campfire, the windows rolled up and the vehicle sped off. For a moment, an eerie silence descended on the scene as the victims lay dead or paralyzed with fear.

The police arrived minutes later as the station was only a few blocks away. The first officer came through the door with gun drawn swinging it from side to side screaming for everyone to get down, even though everyone was already prone on the floor or had been shot. The second officer came in behind him, gun drawn, with his head swinging back and forth attempting to assess who were the shooters and neutralize them. He stepped over several prone customers and kept bellowing for everyone to get down. No one moved. Sirens screamed in the background and a third officer from a second car that had pulled up onto the sidewalk called for an ambulance.

30

AN HOUR LATER, Vinnie Spinozza hung up the phone in his study and told his assistant to call a meeting, and within minutes the room filled with his brothers, several nephews, the consigliere, and several heavily armed lieutenants, all of whom were in the house. Connie, Eddie, and his grandfather were noticeably absent.

"We've been attacked," Vinnie began, as if making an announcement on the evening news. "About an hour ago, criminals shot up our flagship store, killing a policeman and wounding several employees and maybe a customer or two."

"Then we hit them back," someone said.

"That's exactly what they want us to do and exactly what we're not going to do."

"Why? We will look weak."

Vinnie looked around the room and studied several faces. He walked around and sat in the desk chair, putting his elbows on the desk and tenting his fingers in a display of his control over his realm. "The time has come to hunker down. I've been informed that the mayor has called the governor, and an action plan has been formulated. The FBI and the special organized crime unit have begun operations using the RICO Act—"

"What's that?" someone asked.

In a professorial tone that sounded as though he was reading from an encyclopedia, he said, "The Racketeer Influenced and Corrupt Organizations Act. It's been around for almost a decade but never implemented outside the major families until now. It's intended to break us by offering informants new identities and hiding them somewhere else in the country. I've also been told that our phone system has been tapped by the FBI. We all know already that we are under twenty-four-hour surveillance from the streets in front of our homes and businesses. We are under siege. This is war, but that doesn't always mean we should be on the offensive."

The consigliere asked, "What do you want to do now, boss?"

"I want to lock down and let this pass. We're legitimate businesspeople, and we've done nothing illegal. We have nothing to hide. We sit and we wait for the FBI to make a move." There was a buzz of disagreement and murmuring, but no one challenged the head of the family directly. His authority was absolute. "No one leaves the grounds," he announced. "No one uses the phone. No one communicates with anyone until I say so. No newspapers and no news on the television. It will only mislead people."

As the men left the room, Connie entered and was given a brief, watered-down version of what had happened and what was going to transpire over the next couple of weeks. She simply nodded, accepting the situation as if it were an interruption in deliveries by the milkman. She walked into the den and found Eddie watching television. She put her hands on the arms of a large leather chair and took a long drag from the cigarette she was smoking.

Eddie looked up at her. "What? What's going on?"

She blew smoke from the side of her mouth. "Well, there's been a shooting. The FBI is now involved, and your sister called."

Eddie sat up at attention. "She called? Where is she? Is she okay? When did she call? Why is the FBI involved? What have you heard about Tess?" He fired the questions in rapid fashion.

Connie's tone was filled with disgust. "She's in Pennsylvania. Apparently, she was able to escape the Cuchinelli thugs yesterday and then got a ride from someone to Pennsylvania. It all seems curious to me and rather suspicious. I don't know a thing about your little girlfriend."

"My little girlfriend," he growled. "You know, Mom, you're a real piece of work. Where is Teresa exactly?"

"I don't know and don't know why she ran away like that. What's in Pennsylvania?"

"Did they hurt her? What else do you know?"

"Nothing. I think she's a fool to run."

Eddie considered arguing with his mother momentarily and then thought better of it. "Where's Dad?"

"In the study, but he's busy with a meeting."

"Why didn't they ask me to come to the meeting?"

"I don't know. Ask him yourself," she tutted.

Eddie got up from the couch and brushed past his mother. He stormed down the hall and pushed open the door to the study with more force than was required, causing it to bang against the wall. His father, the consigliere, and an armed aid of the family looked up at the disruption. Eddie couldn't help noticing the sheer size of the guard—six four or five, maybe two hundred sixty pounds, and bulging arms that were half the size of Eddie's waist. Didn't matter. Eddie was infuriated.

"What the hell is going on? I want to know, and I want to know everything right now!" he hollered.

"Sit down," his father said. "You don't need to be concerned. Your sister is safe, and we're handling the situation here with the attack."

Eddie lost all self-control and lunged at his father, taking a swing at him. Only the consigliere stepping between them and absorbing a glancing blow to the cheek saved what would have been a knockout. Eddie yelled "To hell I don't!" and charged his father again, throwing another punch. Only the speedy reaction of the guard catching Eddie's fist in a cupped hand stopped an assault. Eddie instantly felt an intense pain as his fist was crushed in a vice grip, and he relaxed his hand. The guard held his hand as he twisted his arm behind Eddie's back and jerked it up to an attention-getting position. Eddie struggled as he was restrained.

"I know more than you think!" Eddie seethed, particles of spittle landing on his father's desk. "I know you had Vitello blow up the cement plant. I saw him. I know what you're doing and what you've done. I—"

"Shut up! You're nothing but trouble. You've been a mama's boy since the day you were born. You're not even part of this family, but you're at the center of my headaches right now. You have no place here. Get him out of here and have Panda sit on him twenty-four hours a day until we can figure out where to send him."

Eddie struggled to free himself but couldn't break the guard's lock on his arms. As he was being pushed to the door, he saw his mother leaning against the wall. "Mom, say something!"

She looked at Eddie and glanced at her husband. "What do you want me to say? Huh? He's right. You aren't a part of this family, and that's what I always wanted."

"What? What are you talking about?"

"I never wanted you to be a part of this ..." She waved her arm as if she was sweeping the crumbs off a table. "That was our deal. I stayed with him because of you and the agreement I made with him." She cast her eyes in her husband's direction for a moment.

Vinnie bellowed, "Enough! I said get him out of here!"

As Eddie was strong-armed out of the room, he yelled over his shoulder, "This isn't over, Dad!"

In the hallway, he jerked his arms away from the guard and pushed him in the chest. The guard smirked and said, "Really. You gonna go there?"

Eddie held up his hands in surrender. "I'm sorry. I apologize. I'm really sorry." He went down to the basement and, as he did in high school when things were not going well, and lifted weights at a frenetic pace. A few minutes later, Panda joined him, sitting on a metal chair, and watched Eddie work out. In between sets of curls, Eddie said, "I gotta get out of here before I hurt someone. Panda, I have to use the phone."

"No can do, man. They got wiretaps."

"You have to be kidding. Who does?"

"FBI."

"This can't be real."

Panda nodded. "Oh, it's real, man."

"So, what are we supposed to do and for how long? I just want to call Tess."

"No can do. The FBI will hear it and go after her too. Just stay put and don't call or go anywhere. I don't know how long."

"Well, what do you know?" Eddie barked.

"Hey, Eddie, you know I'm just the hired help. I just work for a paycheck."

"I'm sorry, Panda. I'm sorry."

31

TESS STAYED ON INTERSTATE 81 and passed Harrisburg. Thirty minutes later, they pulled into Carlisle and drove past the county courthouse, Dickinson College, a number of beautiful nineteenth-century homes, shopping areas on the outskirts of town, and into downtown.

"This place seems so peaceful, so relaxed," said Teresa, now sitting in the passenger seat. "It looks like a place where people are settled and happy. It looks like 'a small-town, all-America.'"

Tess saw the city's firehouse and pulled into the parking lot adjacent to it.

"Let me understand this, Tess," said Teresa. "This is the guy who pulled you and Eddie from the plane, right? And he's a fireman?"

"Yes, to the fireman part. And 'not exactly' to the first question. We were on the ground, but he bushwhacked through the woods for miles, at night, to find the plane and get us out of there."

"Sounds like movie material."

"No, it wasn't like that, but the guy is really quiet and"— she hesitated— "solid."

They walked into the firehouse and met a fireman whose protective suit was folded down at the waist as he swept the floor. He looked up when they walked in. "Hey, ladies, good morning," he said cheerfully. He was a young man, maybe mid-twenties, Tess thought. He was handsome, fit, and wore a smile as big as his face. He laid the broom against the wall and wiped his hands on his pants. "What can I do for you?"

Tess glanced at Teresa, who appeared awestruck. She elbowed her lightly. "Good morning. We were just in town, and I wanted to say hello to a friend of mine, if he's in. Stone. Greg Stone."

"Oh. No, this is not his shift. He was on for three and now he's off. Can I help you? Sorry, my name is Clete."

"Nice to meet you. Clete, like in baseball cleats?"

"Spelled differently, but yeah. It's of Greek origin, meaning 'called forth,' but I'm named after Clete Boyer, the Yankee baseball player."

"Well, I haven't heard of him being a Chicago Cubs fan myself, but I'm a friend of Stone, well, not a friend. He helped me two years ago when the plane I was in crashed."

"You're the woman! The golfer. You landed in a tree and then there was the stalker and all that. You're her!"

"Yes."

"Well, I've heard a lot about you. It's really cool to meet you. I should say everybody around except Stone has talked about that. He doesn't talk much about anything, especially now."

Tess tilted her head, hoping to get more information, and extended an open hand gesturing for more information.

"He got divorced last year, and he's been a little quieter than usual."

"Oh boy, that's not good. Do you know where he lives? Maybe we could just drop by and say hello, and I could thank him again for all he did." Tess nodded at Teresa for agreement and got no response as Teresa continued to stare like a dumbstruck puppy.

"He moved to a new place after the divorce. She got the house and kid. He lives way out off of Ritner Highway in the woods."

"That doesn't surprise me. He would probably live in the woods in a cave if he didn't have to have a phone. Would it be okay if I got his phone number and called him?"

"Sure, you bet. Come on, follow me."

He led them into the office and scrolled down a list taped next to the phone on the wall. He found the number and showed it to Tess. "Go ahead and call from here. Just make it quick. Not that anyone has ever had a long conversation with Stone. I'll go back to my cleaning."

Teresa sat and Tess called the number. There was no answer. "Figures. He's probably out hunting or fishing or walking around in the woods. If I remember, he's that kind of guy."

"I've never been in the woods. Are all firemen this good-looking?" Teresa asked.

"I have no idea. I know you and Stone would be like oil and water, as much as you talk and as quiet as he is."

"Let's go to his house, Tess. We don't have any agenda, nowhere to be, and maybe he's outside doing whatever outdoor guys do."

"We can't just drive up to his house out of the blue."

"Sure, we can. Why not?"

"No, we can't. It's not right."

"Actually, you can," said Clete, who had walked back into the office. "It's a ways out but not hard to find. I'll make you a map. He could use a visitor or two."

YYY

Twenty minutes later, they turned on a dirt road and found a mailbox with black, stenciled stick-on letters that spelled out "Stone," sitting on top of a pile of granite rocks.

"This is it. Now listen, Teresa, let's just take this very slow, and I'll do the talking. Fair enough?"

"Sure."

They followed the meandering driveway to a clearing in the woods with a small house at the far end. An old, wooden rocker sat next to an aluminum pail on the expansive front porch where Tess imagined Stone settled in the evenings, smoking cigarettes or chewing a wad of tobacco. An empty beer bottle nearby probably collected the waste products of both habits.

They walked to the porch, and Tess knocked on the screen door, then knocked again. "Well, looks like he's off hunting or something."

"I hear a dog barking," Teresa said.

They walked to the side of the house and saw a man walking their way from the woods. When he got within a few yards, he stopped and studied them for a moment. "Tess Kincaid?"

"It's me. And I got here without crashing into the trees!"

Stone walked to Tess, and they embraced. She inhaled the smell of sweat, musty dirt, and manliness.

"Well, well, well. What can I say?" he said. "What are you doing way the hell out here, and why do sound like you've been chewing on gravel?"

"I'd like to say I'm developing a raspy voice to make sexy commercials. But in reality, I lost my voice, and it is a long story. I was just passing through and couldn't resist stopping and seeing you."

"You are not just passing through! You don't pass through anywhere. Who's this?" he asked, stepping back and looking at Teresa.

"This is Teresa Spinozza."

He didn't reach to shake hands but smiled broadly. "Are you a pilot too?"

Teresa was speechless, which was extraordinary and forced Tess to speak for her. "Nope, she's Eddie's sister, and we're on a little adventure."

"Your whole life is an adventure. Is anybody chasing you, following you, or photographing you this time? Have you hit anyone with a bat, a golf club, or weapon of any kind in the last day or two?"

"Well, Mr. Stone, funny you should ask. You have any beer, coffee, wine, or Scotch in this place? You better be nice, or I will hit someone soon."

"I've got rye."

Tess made a face. "Who drinks rye? We might as well drink Drano. Let's have a drink anyway, and we'll tell you everything."

They sat at the table in Stone's sparsely furnished kitchen. There was a commercial-grade salt and pepper shaker on the table, a toaster on the otherwise bare counter, and a dish towel hanging from a nail. Stone pulled three red plastic glasses out of a cabinet and a bottle of rye from another. As she watched him pour shots of the near poisonous stuff, Tess noticed he seemed to have lost weight. His jeans fit a little loosely, and he had cinched his belt two notches from where it appeared to normally be hooked. But his plaid shirt was snug on his shoulders and chest. He was still, as they say, chiseled, which Teresa had clearly noticed.

"So, you're Eddie's sister?"

Tess had to kick Teresa under the table to get her to respond.

"Uh-huh."

"How's he doing?"

Neither of the women answered.

Stone turned his head slightly. "Okay, then. Now we're getting somewhere. Who's going to tell the story? By the way, Tess, you look great."

"Thank-you. You look like you've lost weight."

"Lost more than that."

"We heard, and I'm sorry."

"So, what's going on?" He pulled a chair up to the table and handed them their cups. "Cheers."

"Cheers," the women answered.

Thirty minutes and another shot of rye later, Tess finished a two-year overview of her life and an intensive recap of the past week. Stone put his muscular arm on the table and rested his chin on his hand. He pursed his lips and scratched his neck. "Never heard one like that before. I usually find people who are lost in the woods, not people lost in their lives. I'm afraid I don't know what I can do to help."

"Stone, we're not here for help, just a rest. Can we stay here for a day or two? I need to buy some clothes for Teresa and other things and just figure out what to do."

"Do I have to cook for you?" he asked with a smile.

"Well, you don't want me to cook!" Tess answered.

"I can cook! I'm a great cook!" Teresa burst out, her first full sentences since arriving. Tess and Stone stared at her.

"I wasn't sure if you could even talk," Stone said.

"Believe me, this is the quietest she's been since birth," Tess said.

"Do you like Italian food?" Teresa asked.

"Who doesn't?" Stone answered easily.

Teresa stood up and said, "Then it's settled. We need to go to the grocery store, then I need to buy some clothes and some makeup. We need music too. You got an 8-track or a stereo?"

"Whoa. You go from first to fourth in a hurry. There's nothing in the cabinets but saltines and booze. I got two beds but sheets for one of them, and no television or stereo. I don't have or need curtains, and I don't lock my doors or my car. I got a lot of guns and a good dog. And you're not staying that long."

Teresa was unphased. "Let's start with dinner and some sheets. Tess, you have plenty of room on that American Express?"

Tess nodded, knowing she had basically unlimited credit and had probably made thousands of dollars in the last week just on her perfume sales. Being wealthy had many advantages. This was one of them.

Two hours later, Tess and Teresa returned with a small stereo and recordings by the Temptations, the Four Tops, the Supremes, the Beatles, the Rolling Stones, and Frank Sinatra, but *no* Dean Martin. They carried in bags with sheets, towels, a small set of pots and pans, and a variety of cleaning products. Stone carried in eight paper sacks of groceries and two boxes of assorted wines and spirits. Teresa took full command. She had Tess—who couldn't boil water—peeling, cutting, slicing, and frying. She had Stone hanging racks, putting away dishes, and making beds.

Before the sun set, they'd polished off a bottle of wine, and before they'd finished a dinner of chicken piccata, Caesar salad, French bread, and carrot cake, they'd burned through another bottle of wine. And a lot of music.

Tess pushed back from the table and said, "I'm sure it must be getting cold outside, but why don't you two bundle up and go a have a smoke and some Scotch. I'll knock off these dishes."

"I can't beat that offer," Stone said. "Let me grab another chair. Teresa, you can sit in the rocker. I've got a lawn chair. Blanket?"

"Oh yes."

"Scotch?"

Teresa nodded.

"Stone, may I use your phone?" Tess asked.

"Considering what you've spent on me today, talk all night."

Tess busied herself with dish duty, until Stone and Teresa were settled on the front porch, and she could hear them chatting. She pulled a small spiral notebook from her purse and dialed the Spinozza family home number. It rang once before someone with a gravelly voice answered, "Yo."

"May I speak with Eddie please? Eddie Spinozza."

"He's gone. Not here." Click.

She thought that whoever answered was likely carefully instructed on how to respond to any call regarding Eddie. She dialed the hospital and asked for Frankie's room, but was told he'd been released. She resigned herself that Eddie probably wouldn't want to speak to her and that his family would be delighted if he never saw her again. Maybe he'd been arrested. She busied herself with the dishes. She called her mom and spent twenty minutes whitewashing what had been happening, but when she hung up she was convinced that her mother hadn't bought the story.

She walked to the front door. Teresa was covered from head to toe in a gigantic comforter, and Stone had on a hat and heavy down coat. "Aren't you guys freezing?"

"No, not at all," Teresa said. "Get a drink and join us."

Tess was tired and depressed, and her throat still ached. "You two enjoy yourselves and don't catch pneumonia. I think I'll turn in."

She turned down the new sheets and blanket for herself and did the same for Teresa's bed, and slipped into a Colorado State University sweatshirt and pajama bottoms. She thought about reading, but there was no nightstand and only a single light fixture overhead. The room had no other furniture other than a small chest of draws, and there was just one heat register. *It's going to be freezing in here by morning,* she thought.

She got up, turned off the light, and laid down. It wasn't long until her thoughts turned dark. Eddie must despise me. I despise *his* family. He must have known about his family's business and he had to know that his father was the embodiment of a hard-core criminal. I'll never go there again. I'll never see them again. How can I like his sister, his sister-in-law, and his Uncle Tony in Chicago so much? How can I like … how can I love him so much? She continued to argue and question herself until she began to cry. The harder she cried, the deeper her thoughts sank, and she cried even harder. She had wanted it to work out with his family at least to a degree that they were compatible. Now it was a train wreck. She buried her head in the pillow. Sleep came agonizingly slowly, but she eventually succumbed.

YYY

The sun was already showing through the curtainless windows when Tess heard laughter in the kitchen. She glanced at the other side of the bed and saw the pillow had been folded in two and the blankets had been pulled and tugged out of place. Teresa must have had a turbulent night of sleep too. Funny, for as poorly as she'd slept, she hadn't heard Teresa come in or get up. When she sat up and stretched, she shivered. *God, it's freezing in here.*

She got up and put on her sweatpants and the heavy woolen socks she'd bought from Ari. She inhaled, sighed, and fought another wave of depression. *I'll call Eddie again this morning just to see if he's okay.* She slipped into the hall bathroom and brushed her teeth and her hair. Now she felt better physically anyway.

When she walked into the kitchen, Sinatra was singing softly in the background and Stone was sitting at the table drinking coffee and laughing. He wore a button-down, collared, deep blue shirt and jeans with an actual crease. His hair was still wet from the shower. His dog was asleep in his bed in the corner of the room, and Teresa was at the stove in shorts, a T-shirt, and white crew socks.

"Good morning," Stone said.

"Same to you. Teresa, aren't you freezing?"

"No, not at all, but I'm in front of this stone-age stove."

"That room is a little chilly on these fall nights. Sorry about that, but I never use it," Stone apologized.

"I wasn't cold," Teresa said. She seemed to have recovered from her initial bout of speechlessness. "Your voice is better, Tess. Coffee?"

"Oh, yeah."

"Cream is in the fridge."

"You have cream?"

"I picked up half-and-half, knowing you are high maintenance," Stone said, smiling.

"I am not! Okay, I am when it comes to my coffee. What smells so good?" she asked.

"We had a choice, French toast with the leftover bread or eggs. I decided to make eggs." She turned from the stove and put a plate on the table in front of Stone. There were two eggs in the middle of two slices of browned French bread that had the centers cut out, and several strips of bright red peppers were draped over the eggs. Next to them were three pieces of bacon.

"Wow!" Stone said.

"I cooked them in olive oil, Italian style. Tess, you ready?"

"Oh God no. I need to wake up, warm up, and get into my coffee." She eyed a package of Oreo cookies on the counter and grabbed one. Stone noticed and smiled.

"So what are you two up to today?" Stone asked.

"I don't have plans," Teresa answered before Tess could even contemplate a response.

"I was thinking that maybe you'd like to take a little hike in the woods around the place," he said. "There's no snow on the ground yet, the snakes are in hibernation, and we might just see a few deer."

"I love walking in the woods!" Teresa said.

Tess inhaled a gulp of air and coffee simultaneously and coughed. Teresa hadn't been in the woods in her entire life. She wanted to say that the closest Teresa had ever been to the woods was standing next to a real Christmas tree—but she didn't. "If you two don't mind, I think I'll stay here and make some phone calls and review some business stuff that I need to do."

"Great!" Stone exclaimed.

"Great!" Teresa parroted.

An hour later, carrying a snack that could hold them for days, the two of them and the dog walked into the woods, giggling and laughing like a couple of high school kids. *Who would have seen that coming?* Tess thought.

Tess relaxed with her coffee and warmed up. She changed into her jeans and boots and sat down at the kitchen table, pulling the receiver from the wall-mounted phone. She had her standard legal pad with a list of names on it. She cross-referenced the names with another list of phone numbers and went to work. She had another conversation with her parents and called her grandparents, avoiding any real discussion of the previous week. She talked with her coach, her trainer, her business partner in the cosmetics company, her partner in the eyeglass company, the foundation accountant, her accountant, and her house sitter in Florida. She dialed information and got the number for Delta Airlines in Philadelphia and booked a flight for the following day to Miami. Just for the heck of it, she tried the Spinozza number and got the same result: "He's gone." It was just after 11:00 a.m.

She left a note on the kitchen table and drove into town, looking for lunch. In the central business district, she stopped at Ida's Diner after seeing enough cars parked on either side of the block to convince her that this where the locals ate. After a chef's salad and two glasses of iced tea, she realized her throat didn't hurt, her legs didn't ache, and her bruises were fading. Now, if her damaged heart would only heal as quickly.

As she walked to her car, she passed a hair and nail salon. Why not? She got a pedicure and manicure from a petite young woman, tipped her well, and looked at the clock; it was 2:00 p.m. Would they be back? How far can you walk in the woods before something scratches or bites you or you get wet, tired, or sick of the woods? Tess realized that she was a little jealous. She thought Stone was a handsome guy, but there was no longer any attraction between them. Why would he and Teresa snap together like two magnets? There's no explanation, but she did feel a little bit alone, a little left out, and depressed. She drove back to the house.

$$\Upsilon\Upsilon\Upsilon$$

Stone was sitting on the front porch drinking coffee when she drove up and parked.

"How was your walk?"

"Real nice."

She sat in the lawn chair. "So where's Teresa?"

"She went in for a nap. I don't think she's used to hiking around for hours."

"No, I can guarantee you she's not."

"She loved it though."

"I think she likes *you*."

"Maybe."

"Where are your daughter and your ex-wife living now?"

"They're here in town, so I see my daughter every other day and have her on alternate weekends."

"That's good." Tess had been brought up not to pry into people's personal business, so she just sat silently, staring out into the yard. Stone didn't elaborate. After several minutes, Tess said, "You know, a little nap sounds good."

"Okay. Teresa and I thought we might all go out for a steak this evening. Sound good?"

"Sounds great."

That evening, after dinner and several beers at the steak-house, Tess told them about her plans to fly to Miami the next day. She told Teresa that she would wire money for her when she got home to help get on her feet. Neither of them offered the slightest resistance, which surprised Tess.

When they got back to Stone's place, Teresa and Stone went out to the front porch while Tess sat in the living room and read. After an hour, she decided to turn in, knowing she was going to have a big day tomorrow. She thought briefly about calling Eddie again, but decided, *What's the point?* Sleep didn't come any easier than the night before, but eventually she dropped off. She awakened later to the unmistakable sounds, coming from Stone's bedroom, of two people engaging in sex. She soon concluded that it was the sounds of two people who hadn't had sex in a while. She covered her head with Teresa's pillow and fell asleep again.

32

TESS AWAKENED early in the morning and wasn't surprised that the blankets on the other bed had not been disturbed. She dressed in her usual garb, padded downstairs, and made coffee, enjoying the half-and-half. She found cereal in a small cabinet and had a quick breakfast. She returned to her room to pack her bag and carried it downstairs. She stood in the kitchen, wondering about saying goodbye. She decided to sit down and have another cup of coffee, and was relieved to see Teresa make her way into the kitchen. Her hair looked like she had just survived a tornado, her T-shirt was on inside out and backward, and she yawned before saying a word.

"Good morning. Tess, I'm so sorry. You must think I'm—"

"Oh stop it. For God's sake, this is 1978. I'm delighted for both of you. I think of you as a sister, and I wouldn't dare judge you."

"Well, I hardly know him."

"You know him a lot better than you did!"

They both laughed. "Teresa, I love Stone as a friend," Tess said in a serious tone. "He's a really good man. He has immeasurable integrity, great work ethic, is solid as a rock, and apparently is a really good lover." They both smiled. "But he has a lot of baggage. It would be wrong of me not to say something about it. He's had some issues, not that he can't overcome them or change. We all do. I just wanted to say that. That's all."

"I know what you're saying, and let's face it, Tess, I've got more baggage than your average Delta airliner. I'm just hiding right now and deciding what to do. This is nothing serious or permanent."

"I understand."

"If I talk to Eddie sooner or later, what do you want me to say?" Teresa asked as she pulled a cup from the cabinet.

"Nothing. I guess that ship has sailed."

"You underestimate him. I'm telling you, he was never a part of anything. He didn't know anything. My mother made sure of that, and you *know* my mother."

"I'm sure things have changed, so let's just move on."

"What time is your flight?"

"Four o'clock."

"How do I pay you back for everything? I mean you've done so much, spent so much, and helped me get away."

Tess sighed and tears formed in the corner of her eyes. "Teresa, I've been rescued several times in my life, and I can tell you one thing for sure. There is no paying back. You pay going forward. You owe me nothing except an occasional phone call!"

They hugged until Tess nudged her away. "So, what do you want to do?"

"I shouldn't stay here, so I guess go with you to Florida."

"I agree with you that it might be a bit, shall we say premature, to stay here, but it's not a good idea to come to Florida either. They'll be able to find you easily if they want to. I'm not saying they will, but that might be one of the first places they look. Do you think you can start over in Chicago with your uncle? They have left him alone for years, as I understand it."

"Maybe. I guess so. I really don't have anywhere else to go, and I could stay with him for now. Could you front me the money for a plane ticket?"

"Of course. Get your stuff together."

An hour later, Tess and Teresa loaded their bags into the car as Stone stood on the front porch. Tess closed the trunk and walked back to him. "Well, Stone, here I go again, and all I can say is thank-you. Thank-you so much. You are a good friend." She began to turn around when Stone grabbed her wrist.

"I believe this calls for a hug, all things considered."

Tess wrapped her arms around him and found herself patting him on the back, thinking of one of her father's farewells. "Let's stay in touch," she said, turning and glancing at Teresa.

Teresa barreled into Stone with such force that he had to take a step back. "You are the best, Stone, and I won't forget you or last night." She kissed him and whispered in his ear, "I think that was what we both needed."

Stone pulled her in for another hug and said, "Anytime you're in the neighborhood, stop by and cook for me." He laughed. "You two call me if you need anything."

Teresa answered him, "I will, Stone, I will."

🍸🍸🍸

With plenty of time to get to the airport in Philly, the women were able to unwind during the drive. Teresa sang along with radio and reflected on her brief time with Stone and how relieved the experience made her feel.

"Teresa, you and perhaps Eddie will be in a better place now, and I can get on with my life too," said Tess. "It seems hard now, but I think it's for the best."

At the airport, Tess bought Teresa's ticket and walked her to her gate. With few possessions and having only the cash Tess had given her, no responsibilities, only one contact, and almost no plans, Teresa was suddenly morose.

Tess said, "I'll call you tomorrow. I'll help you get on your feet. There is light at the end of the tunnel."

"Really? Because it doesn't feel like it."

"I know this transition is hard. It's so hard. You will find something, someone, and a whole new life."

"Tess, thank-you. From the bottom of my heart, thank-you."

They hugged, and Tess smiled as she backed away. She finally turned and walked to her gate. Tess caught her flight and was in Miami as the sun set.

33

TESS FELT A SENSE OF COMFORT when she found her car in the airport parking lot. It was a fast, sporty, red BMW 320i, and it was exhilarating to drive. She zoomed up Interstate 95 to Boca Raton and was home in less than an hour. It felt so good to walk into her house and see her grapefruit, orange, and lemon trees in the backyard and feel the warm, humid air of south Florida. She had only been gone a week, but the weight of all that had happened made it seem so much longer.

Once she was settled, she made calls to her parents, grandparents, and her manager, assuring them all that she was home, safe, and ready to get back into her regular routines the next day. Routines and regimens gave her life order and control—or at least she had convinced herself that was the case. She relaxed in the screened-in Florida room in the back of the house, listening to a newly installed water feature that sounded like a small waterfall. She poured herself a glass of Pinot Grigio and had some sliced Gruyere cheese and crackers.

She decided that a call to the Spinozza residence was going to be her last attempt to reach Eddie. It was becoming clear that she was butting her head against a wall. The last thing she wanted was to appear desperate, because she wasn't. She just wanted some closure, which sounded like advice from an article in one of those popular magazines in the racks at grocery stores. The advice was always something like, when you chase someone, their inclination is to run away. She didn't want to be "that girl." Tomorrow was a new day, and she'd simply start a new chapter in her life. Sounded simple and relatively pain-free now, but she knew it wouldn't be. And she wouldn't buy any magazine offering advice on how to deal with a breakup.

No one picked up her call to the Spinozza house, and she had no other contact numbers. That was that. Done.

She flipped on the television after the sun set and turned to *The Mike Douglas Show*. Bob Hope was the guest, and Tess watched with mild amusement as a kid named Tiger Woods, who was two years old, putted a golf ball and then drove a ball off a tee. The audience loved it. She wondered how a child with that kind of talent would do in life with all the attention that would surely follow.

She'd been lucky. She hadn't played until she was a young girl and never did play competitively until high school. It was on a boys' team, and that had garnered her some attention, but she'd steadfastly attempted to avoid the limelight. She had flown under the radar—or, more accurately, the camera's lens—until she won the US Open in 1976. It was then that someone with an unhealthy psyche began taking photos of her. This led to full-blown stalking and near-fatal results for Eddie and probably herself, if not for a small miracle. So, she wished the kid named Tiger, the boy wonder, good luck with his fame and future and went to bed knowing full well the odds were against him living a normal life.

The following day, Thursday, she awoke at her regular time, 6:00 a.m., like she hadn't missed a beat. *My God, was Thanksgiving only a week ago?* she thought. She pulled on her running shorts, a T-shirt, and white athletic socks and padded into the kitchen. She had picked several oranges the night before and now squeezed fresh juice. She put on a small pot of coffee and walked out the front door to retrieve the newspaper. It was sultry, the humidity hanging in the air like a steam bath. *God it felt good.* As she picked up the paper, she heard her next-door neighbor, Mr. Shapiro, ask, "Hey, Tess, how was the trip?"

"Eh. You know. Good morning to you, and thanks for picking up the newspapers the last week." Mr. Shapiro had retired a decade before and moved from New York City, where he had owned a very large bakery. He hadn't been quite the same since his wife of fifty-five years passed away last year, but Tess couldn't have asked for a better neighbor.

"I've got your mail too. The maintenance people were here Friday for your yard and that fountain thing in the backyard. They got everything pretty well cleaned up. The guys at the clubhouse were wondering when you'd be back for another shellacking in shuffleboard."

Tess laughed. "Thanks for everything. You tell the boys I'll be there this evening, and they better bring their A game. I guarantee somebody will be buying me a gin and tonic before sunset."

He waved, pulled his pajama pants up over his waist, and walked to his front porch where he sat down, unfolded the paper, and slid on his reading glasses like he did every morning. Tess went inside, sat at the kitchen table, and drank her juice and coffee while reading the paper. And as was her usual routine, she made a list of things she wanted to get done. She never finished everything on her to-do list, but that wasn't the point; the point was making the list and prioritizing. She tried to at least get the most important things done.

First things first, however. She laced up her running shoes and set out for three miles of road work. Running wasn't on her list; it was a daily activity if she wasn't playing in a tournament. She took the same premeasured route she always ran, and felt strong. The week away, despite the tortuous night of pulling the toboggan, had given her a mental and physical break, and she powered through the run with long determined strides. It felt cathartic. She sprinted the last hundred yards.

After showering and drying her hair, she ate a grapefruit and scrambled eggs for breakfast. An hour later, she was at the golf course working on her first bucket of balls. This, she remembered, was her job. Life could be a hell of a lot worse. She started with her pitching wedge and moved up through her irons, pulling out odd-numbered ones: first the nine, then seven, then five. She set new targets, went back to her sand wedge, and then pulled out the even-numbered irons.

The third bucket of balls was for her driver and the three and five woods. Afterward, she hit a fourth bucket of balls with her five and seven irons in low-trajectory shots, as if she was hitting from under a tree or through branches. Then she walked to the putting green and started in on five hundred putts, working in concentric circles, beginning at a distance of three feet and moving out at three-foot intervals until she reached thirty feet. Finally, for her last one hundred putts, she positioned herself ten feet from the hole and completed her practice. That, she considered, was her kill shot: the dreaded ten-foot birdie, or maybe par-saving putt, for the win.

From there, she drove to the gym and lifted weights for an hour before heading home and cleaning up. She ate a salad for lunch and left again, this time for a business meeting at her agent's office.

Tess sat on a plush leather couch across from Dave Steckleberg, her agent for her merchandizing business; his assistant, Mary; and Beau, the marketing director for her company. Dave was in his late sixties—bald and weathered by the Florida sun—and managed the careers of a dozen athletes who had become celebrities. Mary was in her fifties and attractive, with just enough gray in her hair to make her look distinguished. She seemed to be charged with turning most of the campaigns that Dave put together in his head into a reality; in other words, she got things done. Beau was the junior member of the team and did the legwork. He had blond curly hair and an athletic build, and looked like a surfer. They made a good team. After polite conversation, the business part of the meeting began.

"Tess, we've been over the numbers, and sales of perfume are terrific," Dave began. "We, well, you should be happy. We netted just under $175,000 last month on sales just over one point one mill. The margins are phenomenal. We've dug into Chanel and Charlie's share in most major markets, but especially in the South. We've added two more high-end retailers to the distribution chain, and we've got full retail exposure with sunglasses, fragrances, and clothing lines."

"That sounds great," said Tess, looking around at all the faces that she now noticed were so serious. "But why does everyone look glum?"

Mary chimed in. "Miss Kincaid."

"Tess."

"Yes, I'm sorry. Tess. We think that with Christmas less than a month away, we should take the next step. We went to great lengths ahead of time to prepare for this meeting. We purchased the studio time, lined up the ad company, and bought airtime. We have everything tied up and put together with retailers. We're ready."

"Still great. So, what's the problem?"

"There really isn't, except for one thing."

Tess nodded her head and opened her hands. "Uh-huh."

"We want you to film a couple of television spots."

There was dead silence. Tess sighed deeply and sat back. Then she got up and walked to the window. She stared at incredible specimens of tall coconut palm trees in the greenbelt next to the building. "You guys know I hate this stuff. I've been pretty clear, right? The magazine photos were about as much as I can do. I did those commercials last year and said I'd never do anything like that again."

Beau took a run at it. "Tess, with a TV spot we could double sales. It's all about exposure. You and your name mean something."

"What?"

"They mean classy, cool, and yet girl-next-door sexy."

"I'm not doing it."

Mary chimed in, "We've got it all planned out. There will be just shots of you with sunglasses and a golf club in your hands, dressed in our signature shorts and golf shirts. Classy."

"Sorry, that's more than I can do. Still no."

"Tess, we could drive sales over two mill for the holiday season," Dave said. "Let me ask you this. Could the foundation use a new wing? Hell, a new building?"

"Come on, Dave!"

"It's true though, right?" Dave said. Tess flopped back down on the couch. "The kids," he added.

Tess held up her hand. "Stop! I don't want your sales pitch. Do you know what this means in terms of privacy? Do you know what it's like to go places and have people always bothering you? It's miserable. And silly. All I do is hit golf balls. I don't save lives. I don't take care of sick people or provide anything real. I'm just an entertainer."

"Actually, Tess," Mary said in a calm, soothing tone, "you do all of those things with the foundation and the charitable contributions you make. You really do change lives."

Tess inhaled and closed her eyes, thinking about Kincaid House back in Champaign. It expanded every year in its capacity and the range of services it offered to abused women and children. The foundation had ambitious plans to continue growing. She vigorously rubbed her forehead.

"Alright, alright. When do I do this?"

"You leave tomorrow morning, Friday," Beau answered.

"Tomorrow! Where am I going?"

"Hollywood, of course."

Tess nodded agreement. "How long will it take?"

"Probably two days."

"You guys have been planning this ambush for some time, haven't you?"

In unison they all said, "No, no, no."

On Friday morning, the following day, Tess was on a plane to California. The next few days were grueling twelve-hour marathons of shooting the same scene over and over in different light, different backgrounds, with different outfits. It wasn't even the tiniest bit glamorous or exciting. It was some of the hardest work she'd ever done. She kept going because it distracted her from thinking about her time in New York and Eddie. She also knew that the results would be worth it. Making money, a lot of money, would enable her to do things she'd never thought possible and would provide opportunities for so many people in need.

34

The Spinozza house; Albany

EARLY THAT SAME FRIDAY MORNING, in the downstairs back room of the house—before most of his father's soldiers and family had awakened—Eddie and Panda studied each other's faces in the middle of a hotly contested chess game. The room was adjacent to a small kitchen and next to the sitting room with a door leading to a driveway behind the house. There was a big, open storeroom off to the right where Eddie had set up his weights, and the remainder of the room was used for storage.

Panda studied his move and looked up. "Hey man, I'm starving. You want some toast or something?"

"Sure," said Eddie. "Can I get peanut butter and jelly on that and scrambled eggs?"

Panda blew out his breath and said sarcastically, "How about if I make eggs Benedict while I'm at it?"

"Sure, and snap it up, will you?"

Panda walked into the kitchen as Eddie heard the trash truck coming down the driveway and knew this was his chance. He'd been planning and thinking through several scenarios to escape, and decided this was his best and maybe only opportunity. He got up, turned on the fan in the small bathroom, and closed the door without entering. He quickly walked to the storeroom and grabbed someone's jacket, gloves, and hat. He stood by the back door, looking over his shoulder for Panda and watching the trashman stop his truck and begin loading several cans stuffed to the brims. The trashman finally finished and walked back to the driver's side door. Eddie could hear Panda in the kitchen, and he quickly and quietly slipped out the back door.

The driver climbed into the cab, and Eddie walked around to the opposite side of the truck before the driver could see him. Eddie was going to latch onto the side of the truck when he saw six steel rungs forming a ladder attached to the side of the truck for access to the top of it. Small miracle. As the truck began to move, he climbed the rungs to the top of the truck and laid flat across the cab, holding on to the built-in handles. The truck inched away from the house. Eddie saw two men sitting in the front seat of a black sedan parked across the street. He could see them move their heads to look at the guard and then the driver, but not up at him. *So there's the FBI surveillance,* Eddie thought.

Panda sat down at the table and said in a loud voice, "Your toast and eggs are ready, your lordship, and it's your move." He heard the bathroom fan buzzing and studied the chess board. "Geeze, are you dying in there?"

The trash truck moved slowly down the drive. Eddie raised his head slightly and saw a man exit the guardhouse to meet the truck. The truck came to a stop.

"You want to check the back for bodies or something?" the trashman asked.

"Actually, I'd better," said the guard.

Eddie held his breath. The guard walked around and peered into the back of the truck, then stooped down looking underneath it. He glanced along the side as well, but since the rungs of the ladder Eddie had climbed protruded only a couple of inches, he didn't notice them. He grew more nervous, wondering how long it would be before Panda got suspicious and knocked on the bathroom door. With no lock on that door, Panda would be able to walk right in and discover Eddie's subterfuge. He would probably rush upstairs and call the guardhouse.

Eddie knew that he had maybe three to four minutes before his disappearance would be discovered. That time was half gone.

"Got to go, man," the trashman said.

"See you next week," the guard responded.

Please turn right and go next door, Eddie thought. *Please. I can't hold on if he goes more than a couple of miles an hour, and I'll freeze. Please.* The truck stopped at the end of the driveway. What was the driver doing? Did he hear something? Did the guard see me? Had Panda raised the alarm? Eddie raised his head just enough to see the driver through his side mirror and saw that he had stopped to eat what appeared to be a cookie. Seconds later, he turned right. *Oh thank God,* Eddie thought. *Please stop at the next driveway.*

The truck slowed in a hundred yards and turned into the neighbor's driveway. As the attendant in that guardhouse came out to meet the truck, Eddie climbed down the ladder and walked down the street. The truck blocked the line of sight from the surveillance team, and by the time the gate opened and the truck drove into the driveway, Eddie had covered close to a hundred yards of the curving street and continued unnoticed.

He walked several blocks on back streets to a gas station and called a cab. Having planned for this, he was flush with cash and paid for a ride to the airport. Once there, he paid for a flight to Philadelphia. He called Tess and after letting it ring ten times, hung up. He landed in Philadelphia and caught a bus to Pittsburgh, where he purchased a flight to Buffalo, again in cash. He called Tess again, with the same result. His company had a plane in Buffalo heading for St. Louis, and Eddie jumped on board. In St. Louis, he caught a bus to Chicago and called his uncle to pick him up.

CHAPTER

35

AFTER RETURNING TO FLORIDA, Tess began her Christmas shopping in advance of her upcoming holiday trip to Illinois. She wanted to get the big items done first, then fill in with last-minute smaller gifts. For her grandfather, she ordered a sixteen-foot aluminum Tracker Grizzly fishing boat and motor mounted on a trailer. The dealer in Champaign knew her grandfather and told Tess this would be his dream boat—and that it would be in his driveway on Christmas morning. For her grandmother, she ordered the biggest color television she could find at Sears, knowing that she and her grandfather would have it tuned into *Wheel of Fortune* every night. Delivery was set for two weeks, and she arranged for setup as well.

After looking at Steinway baby grand pianos in a showroom in Miami, she ordered one from a store in Chicago for her parents; it would double as a housewarming gift. The piano was black, sleek, and beautiful and would be delivered to her parents' new home, which was still under construction, when the time was appropriate. Her mother had played piano as a child and had talked about resuming ever since Tess could remember. She also bought her father a McDermott pool cue with its own carrying case, which would give him plenty to brag about at Checkers Tavern.

She thanked God for the small miracle of being able to get the big presents taken care of in a timely manner. The small gifts would be easy to find in Boca Raton.

Tess knew full well that the lavish gifts were over the top, but she lived a thousand miles away and saw her family a couple of times a year. Her experience in New York had, if nothing else, taught her how much they meant to her. Her grandparents were getting old, and Tess felt intense guilt about not being around them more often than just the holidays and a midsummer break that lasted a couple of days. She'd left Champaign after high school to build a career and had missed so much of their lives in the past decade. Her family meant everything to her, and if she splurged, then it came from a good place. And she could afford it.

The gift-giving helped distract her and occupy her time, but didn't relieve her of the gnawing emptiness of her failed relationship with Eddie. They had been undone by events that had spun out of control. He had made it worse by staying with his family in Albany, making her question whether he had ever been a part of the family business. She made it worse by exposing him to a police investigation. He hadn't called or made any attempt to reach her, and she couldn't reach him. It was over. She knew it. And it felt like she was mourning a death.

A week before Christmas, with all her plans for the holidays in place, she only had to clean up some final details around the house before leaving for Illinois. She had just returned from her morning run when the phone rang. She picked up the receiver and poured herself a glass of orange juice at the same time.

"Hello, this is Tess."

"Hi, Tess, this is Tiziana. Merry Christmas!"

"Oh my gosh! Merry Christmas to you too. How are you? Where are you? How's Frankie?"

"We're in Chicago. We just up and left in the middle of the night a week ago. We loaded everything we could fit into a small rental truck and left."

"Wow! Frankie is okay, I mean able to get around and everything?"

"Yes. You'd be surprised how quickly someone can recover from a gunshot wound when the bullet misses vital organs."

"I am surprised. So, what did he say to his parents?"

"Nothing. They've been locked up in the house for weeks, and we took that as a sign and an opportunity. We just left without telling them. Frankie decided he was done with them, and I guess they just let him go. The women in the family are not rolling over anymore. This is not 1930. They want their children to get out and live normal lives. We're at Uncle Tony's here in Chicago, and the rest is up in the air."

"How is Tony?"

"Bald, overweight, bowls all the time, watches too much sports, drinks too much beer, and loves life." Tiziana and Tess both laughed.

"Tony is great. I loved him. The best." Tess was overcome with sadness. It hurt so much to think of Tony and Eddie and how they reduced her to silliness, something no one else had ever done. "I'm sorry, Tiziana. I just—"

"It's okay. I wanted to thank you. I'm not sure we would have made it if you hadn't encouraged me."

"I did virtually zero. This was all you and Frankie. So where are you going to live?"

"Here, in Chicago. Frankie is looking for a job, and we rented an apartment for now."

"Good. That sounds like a plan."

"If you wouldn't mind, we'd like to come and see you and meet your family over the Christmas holiday."

There was a long pause as Tess thought about opening a fresh wound and starting again with the Spinozzas. She clenched her fists and relaxed them. "Tiziana, I don't think that would be for the best right now. Why don't we plan on something this spring when I'm back at my parents' house. Would that be okay?"

"Yes, Tess. That would be great. Really, I just wanted to say thank-you more than anything else."

"I didn't do anything, so don't think about it."

"One more thing."

"Uh-huh."

"Teresa will be giving you a call as well to say the same thing, I'm sure."

"Okay. She's doing well? I haven't heard from her."

"Yes she is." Tiziana paused for several seconds. "She's been really busy, you know, working through things."

They talked for a little while longer about life and how it had moved so unexpectedly in the last month. Tess didn't ask about Eddie, and Tiziana didn't mention him. Tess hung up and decided she'd best keep busy, so she did some mundane chores around the house and tried to stay positive. She lost that battle and by noon was banging golf balls on the range to stave off another bout of regret and depression.

The next day, she was on a plane for Chicago.

CHAPTER

36

THE GRAY SKY AND CHILLY AIR on Christmas morning didn't dampen the traditional morning routines at Tess's grandparents' home. The driveway and street held a half dozen relatives' cars, and the house was full. It was ten o'clock, long past breakfast, and Tess's grandmother was preparing a ham for that afternoon's meal. Sue, Tess's aunt, mixed dough for dinner rolls in a large bowl. At one end of the kitchen counter, Betsy was working on a cake for dessert, while her sister, Jesse, visiting from Chicago, was at the other, snapping the ends off green beans for a casserole. They all wore stained aprons and laughed and chided one another and argued good-naturedly about who was better-looking, Tom Selleck or Paul Newman.

Even with all the extra hands, there was no question as to who was in charge. If General Patton ran a kitchen, he'd have nothing on Tess's grandmother. She had the menu, the schedule, and the personality to run the show. Tess knew her place as third tier and stayed out of the way of the seasoned pros, instead circling the house and pouring coffee in every empty cup she could find. By the time she'd made her rounds, a new pot of coffee would be brewed. The dining room table was already filling up with food, dishes, and silverware. Tess didn't think twice about the fact that one meal seemed to run into the next, and her grandmother never lost control of the operation.

Meanwhile, Franklin and Tom, Betsy's brother visiting from southern Illinois, were cleaning up a small mountain of paper wrapping, ribbons, and bows from what had been a wildly unrestrained morning of unwrapping presents. The living room was still in shambles. Franklin didn't bother with hauling wrapping paper to the trash; instead, he burned everything, stoking the fire in the fireplace until the room was hotter than a sauna. Tom circled around picking up pieces of tape and gift boxes, and burned those as well. The two men were planning a card tournament that would start as soon as order was restored in the living room.

Tess served her grandfather a refill on the back porch where he brazenly smoked a cigar, knowing his wife of fifty-three years might notice. He hugged Tess, and she noticed a tear in his eye.

"Honey, I don't know what to say about that boat," he said. "You shouldn't have done it. It's too pretty to put in the lake."

"Well, that's why I'll be there to help you. Catching that catfish this summer was as good as any birdie putt I've ever made. I want another shot at it."

"We'll do that, honey. We'll do that."

Tess swallowed hard, knowing that time was short. She'd feel blessed for another day on the lake. Just one more day.

She turned away and walked inside to reload the coffee pot. As she pulled the old filter out of the drip pot, she heard a knock at the front door. She stopped and looked across the room. Everyone—aunts, uncles, parents, grandparents—had also stopped and were staring in the direction of the front door. No one moved. It was Christmas morning, and no one else was expected. No one spoke. Her grandmother began a deliberate walk to the door. Tess set the coffee pot on the counter and watched her grandmother with everyone else.

Her grandmother opened the door and stood still for several seconds, staring at the guest. She rubbed her hands on her apron and said, "Well, come on in before you catch your death of a cold. Well, come on, now."

Eddie slowly walked into the small area near the front door that served as a foyer. He wore a brown leather aviator jacket, a Cubs baseball hat, jeans, and white Converse sneakers. Tess's heart skipped a beat. She couldn't move, paralyzed with emotion. She also saw all the eyes in the house turned back to her. Eddie stood frozen as a statue. She watched everyone turn their heads back to him and then back to her again. No one spoke or moved. It was like an old Western gunfight, a standoff. Then the back door creaked open, and Tess watched the thin, stooped figure of her grandfather. He looked at Eddie and squinted. "Well, glad to see you, son. Come on in and have some coffee." The ice was broken.

Eddie walked to the center of the living room and hesitated. Tess walked into the room and gathered herself. The two stared at each other for several seconds.

"What's going on?" Tess asked.

"I wanted to talk to you."

"Now?"

"Yes, now. Is there somewhere we can talk privately?"

"Eddie, I think my family should be here and hear this. I've told them pretty much everything anyway."

Eddie looked around the room and then back at Tess. "Okay."

"Go ahead," she said warily but with a tone of defiance.

"Tess, I've never been a part of my family's business."

Tess nodded slightly, encouraging him to continue.

"I would never have asked you to come to New York if I knew how this was going to turn out."

"Why didn't you answer my calls?" Tess asked.

"No one could use the phone. And then my father had me put under lock and key. And then I escaped from the house."

"When?"

"It was maybe a week or ten days after you left. I didn't know until much later that you got Teresa and left Albany."

"So, you really were gone. Why didn't you call me after you left?"

"I did, several times a day, every day. I figured you didn't want to talk to me. But I did call, many times."

"I guess that's when I was in California, but I kept waiting for you to call. Where did you go when you left your parents' house?"

"I came to Chicago by way of a number of other places."

"I'm sorry I told the police about the explosion at the concrete plant," Tess said apologetically.

"You told the police?"

"They didn't bring you in and ask you questions?"

"No. Who did you tell?"

"Detective Keibler."

"He was the policeman who was killed at the bakery. Your confession must have died with him."

"There was a shooting?"

Before Eddie could answer, Tess's grandmother said, "Okay, you two, you don't need an audience for this. It's not our business. It's time you finish the conversation privately.

Tess, get some coffee and a couple of those biscuits from breakfast and take this up on the back porch. The rest of you go back to whatever you were doing. Show's over. Betsy, let's get back to Christmas." Her command was definitive, authoritative, and obeyed.

Eddie walked to the porch, while Tess filled two cups with coffee and cream, put biscuits with honey on a plate, and then joined him. He sat on the rocker and she on the swinging chair. Her mother stepped out on the porch and handed her a coat.

"Eddie, before we start, why haven't I heard from Teresa?"

"Tess, to be honest, Teresa talks like a window fan buzzes, and there was just no way for me to keep her quiet and let me handle this on my own terms. She'll call immediately when I tell her it's okay."

"Okay, tell me everything."

37

AS SHE STARED AT EDDIE, Tess realized her hands were trembling and her lips were quivering. "I can't believe I'm looking at you," she said. "Eddie, I don't know what to say. I'd given up on you, not only because I had told the detective about the cement plant, which might have made you a suspect. But I genuinely thought you were compromised by your family. And then I didn't hear from you for weeks."

Eddie raised the Cub's cap on his head, and his unruly black hair fell out in a disarray of curls. He had dark circles under his eyes, and she could tell he'd lost weight. He took a deep breath, dropping his head to his chest. He looked up and began, "My whole life has been a delusion. I won't call it a lie, it just wasn't real. My mother knew that my father, his brothers, and my grandfather were part of organized crime."

"Eddie, that's all history and I know that, but this isn't about other people. This is about Eddie Spinozza. It's about you—your character and what's in your heart."

"But I need to explain. My grandfather was a small-time offshoot, so-to-speak, of one of the five families in New York and only took control of the trash business from a special contract negotiated by some people from New York City. And he ran gambling too. No prostitutes, no drugs, no loan sharking. I'm not saying that's admirable or noble, but it doesn't seem as bad. The Cuchinellis started later, and they got the concrete business. There was a kind of peace for a long time. My father and his brothers joined the business after they all came back from the war in the forties, and the Cuchinelli family grew too."

Tess inhaled a deep breath and exhaled slowly. Eddie didn't make eye contact with Tess and continued.

"Taking a couple of percentage points off the top of every building project, the protection money from the other family and criminals in general, the loan sharking, the gambling, the women, and especially the drugs continued until the construction of those gigantic city and county buildings were finished in the late sixties. For many reasons, the Cuchinelli family income was drying up, and they started calling for meetings and concessions from the Spinozzas."

"So what? Eddie, I don't need a history lesson here. I need you to tell me what happened to you."

"I'm getting to that, Tess," he said curtly. "The Spinozzas saw no reason to give up their territory, and both sides called in the big guys from New York."

Tess shook her head from side to side, growing irritated. "And so what? I mean, *really*, so what?"

"Let me explain! I learned that my father actually paid a ransom for Teresa. Well, actually not a ransom, just a payout to ensure that Teresa wouldn't be touched, just held as a hostage."

"Well, I think I witnessed that, and I might add that your father's ransom or payment was for nothing. Now it makes sense. So that's why he was mad when Teresa called home when we were on the road. The Cuchinellis didn't fulfill their part of the 'deal.' You realize how absurd, how sick, how twisted your father is? Huh?" Her anger and disgust from the past month rose to the surface, making her voice grow louder. "*Really*, who pays a ransom thinking that it's just to keep the victim, his own daughter, from being 'touched'? He's evil. Speaking of evil, and I'm sorry that I sound so angry, but I could slap the crap out of you right now." She hesitated, trying to decide where this conversation should go. "So, how does your mother really fit in because I can't tell."

"I think she was aware of who she married and what business my father was in. Had to be, back then. I'm guessing, but I don't think there were any illusions from either side. As we grew up, my mother watched my brothers join my father in the legit part of the business. They weren't involved in all the illegal stuff because by the sixties the mob was in many legitimate businesses, like the import business to launder the money they were getting from all the other stuff. You know my brothers are accountants, salespeople, and that kind of stuff.

"But when I was about five years old, my parents had a huge fight, my uncle Tony told me. It bordered on divorce, but that was never going to happen because they're so Catholic. My mother saw her sons becoming my father. She couldn't allow that to happen to me, so they went to battle, and for the only time in the forty years they've been married, my mother won. From there on out, I went to private schools, went across town to high school, and I never had to or was allowed to work at the deli, bakery, or store. And the day I graduated from high school, I was told I had to leave the next day. So like Uncle Tony did, I went to Chicago."

"Eddie, how could you not have seen or talked about it with your brothers when you were growing up?"

"My brothers are eight to thirteen years older than me. They were gone from the house or in high school and dating and all that, so I'm not that close to them. I think my mother also put the fear of God in them if they involved me."

"So how did you find all this out and from whom?"

"The day after you left, I demanded to talk to my father. It was a bad situation, but he was there and so was his lawyer and his bodyguard. I told them that I saw Otto Vitello blow up the Cuchinellis' cement plant, and I started yelling at my father. I was so angry I actually tried to punch him. He said I was a mama's boy and never really part of the family. He told me to get out, and that's when I went at him again. I got hauled off by his bodyguard and held in a kind of house arrest for more than a week. I couldn't go anywhere but the bathroom and bedroom without being escorted. I tried using the phone, but it was probably tapped, so I guess I'm thankful I never did reach you or that you didn't get through to me, because then the FBI would have been listening."

"Imagine what that would have done to my career," she said with a note of sarcasm.

"My father can't stand the sight of me. He stared at me with a level of disgust you would have for a dog that just relieved itself in the house. I knew then that Vitello was sent there to retaliate for Frankie's shooting. I knew then that everything I've said is true. I knew it all. As I was being dragged out of the room, I saw my mother's face, and I knew then that she hated him too."

Tess covered her eyes. "This is all so awful. I almost can't stand to hear about it."

"I also learned from Panda—"

"The driver with the hairy neck?"

"Yes. Apparently, it all started to go wrong at The Dirty Martini Club, when their guy shot my brother. I'm not sure that they planned on taking it to the next level with a hit like that, but it escalated the warfare. It was intentional, and maybe they thought the Spinozzas would roll over rather than strike back. Revenge and saving face were part of it. Had to happen."

"So, let me get this straight," said Tess. "The whole drama is over who gets to strong-arm the concrete and trash businesses from the unions and the city. The shooting was actually unnecessary, and the bombing got out of hand. Do I have it right?"

"That's what Panda said."

"So what about the kidnapping of Teresa and the beating she took, to say nothing of almost being raped?"

"That's the really bad part."

"What do you mean 'the really bad part'? How can it be worse?"

Eddie sighed deeply and shook his head before answering. "I think my grandfather knew about it in advance. At least that's what I'm guessing after hearing some stuff since I got out of there. They knew where she was and so on."

"You mean they could have stopped all of it?"

"It was a game. They were going to let the Cuchinellis hold her for a day or two, and then the heads of the five families were going to meet in New York, where the big guys would settle it."

"Not only can't I believe it, I can't understand the kind of people they are."

"They've lived so long like this that even their children become dispensable parts of a real-life chess game. When my father found out about how Teresa was treated, the kidnappers were both beaten so badly that they were hospitalized."

"So, what was the final result of all of this?" She closed her eyes and rubbed her face.

"The Cuchinellis got the trash business in the areas outside of Albany, and apparently everyone called it even. All of that violence for a trash contract. That's the bottom line, except for the fact that the feds are actively investigating, and some of my family members will be going to jail for tax evasion, racketeering, and more."

"Your father?"

"Likely."

Tess was quiet, trying to comprehend what she'd just heard. Watching stories like this at the movies or reading them in books was very different than experiencing them in person. "I don't know what to say," she finally said.

"When I heard all this, I was incredulous. I hate my father. I hate all of them. I left for Chicago and ended up at Tony's. And here I am now. I came here to tell you the truth. I needed to do that, and you deserved to hear it from me in person."

"What a nightmare, Eddie. I thought ... well, I thought all kinds of things."

"Probably not good things."

"You're right."

"I don't know, Tess. I figured once you heard the whole story, you'd say goodbye to me, and we'd be done."

She stared at Eddie's face and made the slightest nod of her head from side to side. "Eddie, this has been a terrible shock, a terrible month. It's a horrendous revelation, and I really don't know what to think or do. I am a cautious person by nature, and I can be skeptical with very little cause.

There's an awful lot to be skeptical about here. In fact, 'suspicious' would be a better word. I hear what you've said, and I want to believe you, but there's been so much. I can't go forward on a prayer and hope."

"I understand, Tess, and I accept the consequences."

"I'm not saying you were at fault for what happened. I realize you were caught in the middle. But, Eddie, I need time to decide if this can work for me, for us. There's no escaping who you are and where you come from and what made you the person you are."

"That sounds like a goodbye."

"I'm not saying that. I believe in redemption. I believe people can overcome. I know people can change and be better than the sum of their parents, upbringing, and events that happen to them. I started a foundation to give people a second chance. I just need to think and let this all settle in. Eddie, I want you to know one thing, even though I'm saying maybe." She hesitated and smiled slightly. "I love you. I love you too much." She choked with emotion. "I'm remembering two years ago when I got on that stupid little plane of yours and we crashed into the trees."

"That wasn't my fault!"

"I know it wasn't."

"It was bad luck," he said.

"In a way. But it was also good luck. Here we are and still standing."

She looked at him. "I think it would be best if you leave now, and maybe we'll talk in the future."

"Okay. That would be a start."

"Let's walk around the side of the house rather than go back inside."

They walked to where his Uncle Tony's '66 Chevy Impala was parked. Tess smiled. "Nice car."

Eddie nodded and looked at Tess. "I'm so sorry."

"I know you are."

"I love you more than anything, Tess. I'll do whatever it takes to gain your trust back. We can go as slow or as fast as you like, but don't give up on me."

Tess swallowed hard and fought tears. Her mind raced desperately for the right words but failed her. She nodded. He waved goodbye and slowly drove down the street.

ACKNOWLEDGMENTS

I WANT TO ACKNOWLEDGE the enormous and invaluable contribution of my wife Deb Hibdon in the writing of this novel. We worked together, tirelessly for months writing and rewriting the story. The dialogue and events were as much the product of her imagination as mine. I'd like to thank Susan Hindman for her meticulous, detailed, and professional help in editing the book. Her efforts and research into the period are invaluable to the final product.

Bud Kiebler, Elizabeth Daly, Erak Hillman, and Susan Routzahn read and critiqued the manuscript and helped guide me in the story line and plausibility of the plot and the characters. Their effort and interest made the project what it is today. Cailean Goossens, always my trusted assistant. Thank you. Bob Schram's creative talents made the cover perfect.

ABOUT THE AUTHOR

JUDE RANDAZZO was born in New York and lives with his family in Colorado. His paternal grandfather was born in Sicily and emigrated to New York. He is the author of the Tess Kincaid series; *The Golden Cocoon, The Omen of the Crow, What You Don't Know Can Kill You,* and *The Gray Fedora.*

The Gray Fedora by Jude Randazzo
History, Heritage, and a "Hero"
TThis is the epic story of a young man who leaves Ireland for America in 1860 to escape years of famine, only to be shanghaied to Palermo, Sicily. It's the beginning of the Risorgimento, or revolution for Sicilian independence. This fast-moving, action-packed story includes, heroics, a love story, and a future with promise and foreboding.

The Omen of the Crow by Jude Randazzo
A Tess Kincaid Novel

Click . . . Click . . . CLICK!

The delicate sound of a camera shutter penetrates the silence with menace in a rugged, isolated, wooded area where a small plane has crashed. It's not possible that in this place, at this time, someone could be hidden from sight, photographing the scene. Or is it?

What You Don't Know Can Kill You
by Jude Randazzo
A Tess Kincaid Novel

What You Don't Know Can Kill You is like getting off a moving Ferris wheel. Once you get on it, you're on for the full ride. The eclectic cast of characters, lightning-paced action, and romance will keep you flipping pages and guessing.

The Golden Cocoon by Jude Randazzo
A TESS KINCAID NOVEL

Tess Kincaid strolls through the vineyards surrounding a beautiful villa in Tuscany, trying to understand what has happened. She's at a crossroads and is faced with the most daunting challenge of her life. She knows that if she doesn't win this battle, her future will be very uncertain. Can this restful place and a new-found, mysterious discovery give her the courage to face a conflict that has plagued her since childhood?

Made in the USA
Middletown, DE
28 May 2024